THE

HUSTLER'S

DON

BY

IKE CAPONE

Black Print Publishing Inc.
289 Livingston Street, 3rd Floor
Brooklyn, and NY11217

ISBN 0-9748051-4-9

This and many other titles Published by Black Print Publishing Inc. may be purchased for educational, business, sales or promotional use. For information please write: Marketing Department, Black Print Publishing Inc 289 Livingston Street, Brooklyn, NY11217

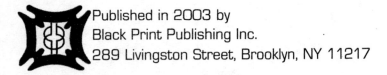Published in 2003 by
Black Print Publishing Inc.
289 Livingston Street, Brooklyn, NY 11217

Printed in Canada

INTRODUCTION

There used to be this gang around my way
Called the "Questions".
Straight thugging and mugging with aggression
Was their profession.
There was "Who"
The most ill, hardest to kill cat,
And "What"
No matter what, "What" always had "Who's back.
Then there was "When" and "Where"
Who stay creeping, hunting for some action.
While "Why" and "How"
Laid low in the cut, bubbling them Jacksons.

Who, What, When, Where, Why, and How
Were down for what ever.
Each man played his position
and they all ate together.
If a crime was committed,
Who, What, When, and Where did it.
Why and how wasn't even around
But they still benefited.

Everything was going sweet
Until they got into it with these thugs.
All over these chicks
"If", "And", "But" and "Because".
Who knew,
the main reason the Questions was stroking them.
Was so they'd set up this other click
That was also poking them.

This other click was rich
They were known as the statements.
You know the type Iced out Roleys
Matching pinky rings and bracelets.
The statements were Jamaican
There was "Explomation",
Comma", Period", "Simmecolon",
and the Twin "Quotations".

Now If, And, and But
Were down to set the Statements up.
Under the impression, that the Questions
Were goanna bless them with a cut.
But Because fell in love
With that thug, Semicolon.
Who bought her jewelry, clothing
And kept her pockets swollen.

She couldn't see herself
Flipping on that man.
She told her peops she wasn't with it
But they didn't understand.
They begged and pleaded with her
Tried to tell her it was a must do.
Not knowing she had already told Semicolon
What they were up to.

The Statements busted into their house
With their Taheaters out.
Those Momma's really felt the drama

Once Comma begin to shout.
What's the raz clog deal
With these Questions kids.
Me wanna know how many are they
And where do they live
As a matter fact forget that
Take me to their home.
Because big or small I'll give them all
Two to the dome.

The lady's were shook of these crooks
So they did what they were ordered to.
Their fear left them unaware
That they were about to be slaughtered too.
They took them to Why and How's crib
And they whole crew was there.
Watching set it off
Puffing trees, drinking beer.

They knocked in code
Entered as they were supposed
The Questions saw the Statements and all hell
begin to expload
The first shot went off
Then all you heard was basting G
Each thug left off slugs
Man it was a gatastrophy
Once the smoke cleared
There were nothing but dead thugs.
Laid out on the rug
In their own pools of blood.

CHAPTER 1

It all started back in June of 1989. Franklin Whitehead, 19, better known as Wyte Yak, a slim, 5' 9", light-skinned, black male with light-brown eyes, rocking a one-inch thick gold Gucci link chain, a gold nugget watch, and two big gold two-finger, ram-head rings on his left hand, had just finished high school and was overwhelmed with the fact that he had graduated and didn't have to attend school any longer. Although at the time he was only a petty hustler, he had planned on becoming a huge rap star along with his buddies, Deuce, an 18-year-old, 6' 1", brown-skinned black male with braces and, Trap, a 6' 2", 18-year-old, light-skinned, black male, with a huge gap in the center of his mouth.

Two days after graduation Wyte Yak, Deuce, and Trap stood rapping on Myrtle Avenue in front of Fort Greene Youth Patrol Center. Deuce was playing the beat with his mouth, while Wyte Yak and Trap took turns rapping. Trap had just finished rapping and passed the mike to Wyte Yak.

I be spitting with my lyrical intuition. Representing Fort Greene, Ingersoll, and Walt Whitman. Throw them rocks away this ain't no play land. The body counts a large amount because my niggas be spraying Me, I'm a thug with mad love for the gangsta's in my city. From Dizz Capone to Six Capone, to Frank and P-Nitty. It's all good, but please don't come to my 'hood stunting see. Because my niggas are miserable and misery loves company. So I suggest you go 'head before you get my niggas fed. The lead ain't piercing through your leg it's off with your fucking head, but since you tough, come die hard while your family cry hard, you'll be forever dreaming while your moms screaming, oh my God. Knowing that he who gat bust the loudest makes his owner the proudest, while he who lives the foulest lays flat while his soul arouses. These dudes in the Projects live for the wreck. So Wyte Yak packs a Mac 'cause it's more action than a Tec. Once Wyte Yak was finished rapping, Deuce and Trap slapped him five and gave him his props.

"That was phat, Wyte Yak," said Trap.

"Yeah, I'm feeling that. We gotta get in the studio," said Deuce.

"Funky Slice only want fifty dollars an hour. Let's put some money together and do this demo," said Wyte Yak. "I can put up fifty dollars when I get paid on Friday," said Trap.

"I can put up a buck on Friday," said Deuce.

"That's cool. I can put down two hundred right now to reserve us some studio time and probably another three by Friday," said Wyte Yak.

Just then a red Cherokee Jeep passed them and stopped thirty feet away at the light on Prince Street. Wyte Yak noticed that his girlfriend Tiesha was in the passenger seat. "This bitch must've lost her mind," he said. Then he ran over to the jeep and snatched the door open saying, "What the fuck you doing, bitch? Get the fuck out of this nigga truck.

"No, I'm going out to eat with Shakim," she said.

"You ain't going nowhere!" Wyte Yak yelled. Then he grabbed her arm and pulled her out of the jeep and over to the sidewalk. Shakim double-parked the jeep and hopped out.

"What the hell is wrong with you, Tiesha? How the fuck you gone try to play me like that?" Wyte Yak screamed.

Shakim walked over and approached Wyte Yak.

"Nigga, don't be snatching nobody out my truck!" Shakim warned. Wyte Yak held his hand up to Shakim's face and said, "This my shorty. Back the fuck up!"

Shakim smacked Wyte Yak's hand down, got all up in his face, and said, "She with me right now, so you back the fuck up!"

Wyte Yak pushed Shakim, and they started to scuffle. Shakim slammed Wyte Yak against the wall. Trap ran up behind Shakim and banged him upside his head with a forty-ounce, breaking the bottle and splashing beer all over Shakim as he fell to the pavement. Blood leaked from his head as Wyte Yak, Trap, and Deuce started stomping him. Out of nowhere Wyte Yak's brother, Pooh Berry, a six-foot, muscular, brown-skinned gorilla rushed over and pushed the group off of Shakim.

Yelling at the three of them, Pooh Berry asked, "What the fuck y'all niggas doing?"

"That nigga had Tiesha in his jeep. Then he gone step to me on some gangsta' shit," Wyte Yak explained.

"You out here fighting over a bitch, man? Fuck that bitch! If she wanna fuck with that nigga, let her. You don't need her, you bigger than that. Come on, let's get the fuck off the Avenue before the police roll up."

The four men left the Avenue and headed back into the Projects. Wyte Yak looked back at Tiesha and saw her helping Shakim up off the ground as he kept touching his head and looking at the blood on his hand.

"They got that," Shakim said, "but I'll be back. Believe you me, I'll definitely be back."

Shakim hopped back into his jeep and peeled off. Pooh Berry went upstairs while Wyte Yak, Trap, and Deuce went to cop a nickel bag of weed from Little Pillsbury and sat on the bench in front of 342 Hudon Walk, a building in the Projects. Trap took the plastic off the cigar and started to roll up the blunt. Rahtiek, a 17-year-old, 6' 1", slim, brown-skinned, black male walked over and slapped the three men five. He sat on the bench, pulled a blunt from behind his ear, and lit it. After taking a few puffs, he passed it to Wyte Yak.

As the four young men sat back smoking the two blunts, Shakim came running around the corner with a 9mm handgun in his hand.

"Look out, Sun. He's got a gun," Trap yelled.

Trap and Deuce ran off while Rahtiek ducked behind a tree and pulled a .357 Magnum from his waist. Wyte Yak stood face to face with Shakim and was shot twice in the stomach. Wyte Yak fell to the ground, and Shakim stood over him with his gun pointed at his head saying, "Now what, you bitch-ass nigga?"

Just as he was about to kill Wyte Yak, Rahtiek stepped out from behind the tree and emptied his .357 into Shakim's back, killing him instantly. His body fell on top of Wyte Yak's. Rahtiek then walked over to Wyte Yak with the smoking gun in his hand, pushed Shakim's body off Wyte Yak's, and asked, "You alright, Yak?"

"Nah, Sun! I'm shot. Call an ambulance," Wyte Yak pleaded.

"Somebody, call an ambulance! Say a fucking cop got shot!" Rahtiek yelled.

Wyte Yak looked up at Rahtiek and said, "Good looking out, Sun, but you gotta get the fuck out of here."

Rahtiek looked down at his injured friend. "Alright, Sun, be strong and hold on. The ambulance will be here in a minute."

Rahtiek walked away, and a crowd formed around Wyte Yak and Shakim. Trap and Deuce ran back over Wyte Yak's aid and talked to him to try to keep him from losing consciousness. A few minutes later the police arrived on the scene and started questioning the crowd. Then the ambulance came, and the attendants put Wyte Yak on a stretcher and rushed him to the hospital.

Moments later Pooh Berry arrived on the scene and was heatedly questioning Trap and Deuce, "What the fuck happen to my brother?"

Deuce started to explain, "That nigga, Shakim, came back through with a gun and shot Wyte Yak. He would've killed him if it wasn't for Rahtiek."

"Damn! All this shit over a fucking bitch!" Pooh Berry spat.

"I tried to warn Wyte Yak, but he didn't run," said Trap. "You know that nigga wasn't gone run from nobody. Fuck! I'm about to take a cab to the hospital."

"We coming with you," said Deuce.

The three men walked to Myrtle Avenue to catch a cab. Four cabs passed but didn't stop for them. Finally a cab driver who wasn't afraid stopped and took them to the hospital.

The next day Wyte Yak was lying in the hospital bed with an I.V. sticking out of his left arm. Pooh Berry was sitting in a chair next to Wyte Yak's bed and screwfacing Detectives Rogers and Lawson as they questioned his brother about the shooting.

"You expect me to believe that you don't know who killed Shakim?" asked Detective Lawson.

"I don't care what you believe. I'm telling you I didn't see him," Wyte Yak insisted."

"How could you not know who shot him? You just said his body fell on top of you," Detective Rogers reminded him.

"I was on the ground shot already. All I saw was that 9 pointed at my face," said Wyte Yak.

"If you did know who shot him, would you say?" asked Detective Rogers.

Wyte Yak laughed and shrugged his shoulders.

"Alright Rogers, we're not going to get anything out of this guy. Let's just hit the streets and see what we can find out," said Detective Lawson.

When the two detectives left the room, Pooh Berry said, "The police stupid as hell thinking you gone snitch on the nigga who saved your life. I don't know what the fuck is wrong with them."

"Like you said, they stupid. If they knew better they'd do better," said Wyte Yak. The two brothers laughed.

A few minutes later, Trap and Deuce walked into the room. They both slapped Wyte Yak five.

"You alright?" Trap asked.

"Word, Sun! You alright?" asked Deuce.

"Yeah, I'm good," Wyte Yak responded. "I got lucky. The slugs pierced right through me. They didn't hit nothing vital. I'll be home in a couple of days."

"Man, Yak, you crazy. Why didn't you run?" asked Deuce.

"I know you heard me say, 'he's got a gun,' " said Trap.

"I wasn't gone run so he can shoot me in my back," Wyte Yak explained. "Fuck around...and have me paralyzed."

Trap stared Wyte Yak in the eyes and said, "Nigga, he would've killed you if it wasn't for Rahtiek!"

"Yeah, I owe Sun big time."

"You don't owe him nothing," Trap argued. "That's your man. You would've done the same for him."

"You need to chill, brah. All the motherfuckers you done saved in the Projects, it's about time somebody stepped up for you," said Pooh Berry.

"True," said Deuce.

"So what up with Tiesha?" Trap asked. "Did she come to check you, or was she too busy making funeral arrangements for her new man?"

"She came up here earlier trying to apologize, and this nigga was about to fall for her sob story like a dickhead. But I barked on that bitch and threw her the fuck out," Pooh Berry fumed. "She's lucky I don't blast her fucking ass."

"Word," said Trap.

The room was silent for a few seconds then Pooh Berry said, "I'm about to take a trip down to Va., see what's up with our family and try to get some of that money down there. You with it?"

"Yeah, I'm with it," confirmed Wyte Yak.

"Alright, cool. We out the Saturday after next. You should be back to normal by then."

"Yeah, I should have my strength back by then," Wyte Yak said.

Pooh Berry, Trap, and Deuce hung out with Wyte Yak all day, reminiscing about all the drama they had and all the women they slept with. They laughed and talked so much, they didn't even realize how much time went by until the nurse came by to inform them that visiting hours were over. They said good-bye and let Wyte Yak know that they'd be back to see him the next day.

Back in the 'hood Rahtiek was sitting on the bench in front of 48 Fleet Walk rolling a blunt. He lit it and took a long, hard draw. As he exhaled Deuce and Trap walked up.

"Pass that," Deuce teased. "We smoke the weed all day, fucked up all in the game, so why play?"

Deuce and Trap slapped Rahtiek five and sat down on the bench. Rahtiek took another puff then passed the blunt to Deuce.

"We just came from checking Wyte Yak," Trap said.

"Word? How my nigga doing?" Rahtiek asked.

"He alright. He'll be home the day after tomorrow," said Trap.

Deuce inhaled then waited a few seconds before exhaling the smoke through his nose, saying, "That nigga tripping, Sun, talking 'bout he owe you big time."

"He don't owe me shit! He would've done the same for me!"

"That's what I told him. He acting all sentimental and shit, talking 'bout you saved his life and he don't know how he gone repay you," said Deuce, passing the blunt to Trap.

"Tell that nigga to bless me with a dime bag and a couple of Forty's and I'm good. That's my motherfucking man. I'd do it again if I had to," Rahtiek bragged.

Trap blew the smoke out of his mouth and said, "Wyte Yak and Pooh Berry heading out to Va. next week to set up shop."

"Word? That's what I'm talking 'bout," Rahtiek added. "Set up shop so they can bring a nigga like me down there to get some of that paper. I heard our nickel sells for twenty out there."

"Yeah, man, and niggas be making four to five G's a day," Deuce chimed in. "That shit is lovely. I can't even make a G a day out this bitch. Fuck that, take me out of town!"

Trap passed the blunt to Rahtiek and said, "Me, too," before they headed to the store to get something to munch on.

A week and a half later Wyte Yak was in his bedroom packing his bags when Pooh Berry entered the room, took a seat on the bed, and asked, "What up, bro? You ready to blow this joint?"

"Hell, yeah, I'm ready to go get this money."

"I feel you, but we not only going to get this money," Pooh Berry added.

"We not?" Wyte Yak asked with a puzzled look.

"Nah, brah, I want you to go to college."

Wyte Yak twisted his lips. "I'm done with school. Twelve years was enough for me."

"Come on, brah, you know I promised mommy I'd make sure you finished school and make something of your-self," Pooh Berry pleaded. Wyte Yak zipped his bag. "I need you to go to school, Yak, so when we make this money we know what to do with it. You know, open a business or some-thing. Go legit. I don't have a diploma. I couldn't fuck with school; but you smart, that shit's nothing to you. You've been a A student since the first grade."

"I don't know, Pooh. I wasn't planning on going to school, but I'll think about it."

"Fuck thinking about it. Be about it."

"Alright, Pooh Berry. I hear you."

"So you gone go?" Pooh Berry asked eagerly.

"Yeah, I'll go."

Pooh smiled, placed his arm around Wyte Yak's shoulder, and said, "Alright, baby bro, let's get out of here."

The two men walked out of the bedroom, walked through the living room, and opened the front door to leave. Just then they saw Tiesha standing in the hallway about to knock on the door. Pooh Berry started to go off on her, "What the fuck you want, bitch? My brother don't got shit to say to you."

"Chill. I got this," Wyte Yak said, holding up his hand to stop Pooh. Pooh Berry looked at his brother and, pointing at Tiesha, said, "Fuck this bitch!"

"I said, I got it."

"Alright, Yak. Don't let her make us miss the bus."

Pooh screwed his face at Tiesha and walked off shaking his head. After putting his bag down, Wyte Yak locked the door and turned around to face Tiesha. "What you want?"

Tears flowed down Tiesha's cheeks as she begged, "I'm sorry, Wyte Yak. I didn't mean for none of this crazy shit to happen. It's just that you never take me nowhere. You don't even spend no time with me."

"You don't ever have to worry about me spending time with you."

"Don't be like that, Wyte Yak. I love you, and I know you love me."

"I'm out."

Wyte Yak picked up his bag and was about to walk away, but Tiesha grabbed his arm and asked, "Where you going, Yak?"

"To Va."

"Yak, I know you going out there to hustle. Take me

with you. I know y'all riding dirty, but you know they don't really be messing with girls like that. Let me carry the drugs for you. Them buses are hot."

Wyte Yak looked Tiesha in the eyes and said to her, "Which part don't you understand? I'm not fucking with you! Find somebody else. I'm sure I will." Then he walked away.

Tiesha became really upset, saying to herself, "If I can't have you, nobody will," and stood there with a devious look on her face as Wyte Yak walked down the stairs.

CHAPTER 2

Wyte Yak and Pooh Berry were riding the A train to Port Authority. "You alright?" Pooh Berry asked Wyte Yak, who had his head down.

"Yeah, I'm good," Wyte Yak reassured him.

"Fuck that bitch! It's plenty of honeys in the south, and they all got fat asses."

"I not thinking about Tiesha; I'm thinking about getting this money."

"That's what I'm talking about. Let's get paid, my brother. Fuck a bitch!"

The train stopped on 42 Street, and the two brothers got off and walked through the train station to Port Authority.

Back in Brooklyn, Tiesha, still upset at being rejected, entered her apartment looking for the yellow pages. She set the phone book on the counter next to the telephone and thumbed through the pages until she found the number for Greyhound. She dialed and the phone rang twice before a voice came on with,   "Greyhound, Cynthia speaking. How may I be of assistance?"

"I'm just calling to give y'all a tip," Tiesha snitched. "Two black guys are getting on the bus to Virginia with drugs--one is light-skinned and the other is brown-skinned--and they both are carrying black duffle bags."

"Who is this?" the clerk asked.

Tiesha quickly hung up the phone and, with a devilish grin on her face, said, "Sorry, Wyte Yak, but if you're not fucking with me, you're not going to be fucking with nobody!"

The two brothers entered the Greyhound bus terminal. Wyte Yak stood outside the ticket station with the bags while Pooh Berry purchased the tickets.

"Can I have two one-way tickets to Norfolk, Virginia?" Pooh Berry asked the clerk.

"That'll be one hundred and thirty-nine dollars, sir," the clerk said.

Pooh Berry gave the clerk seven twenty-dollar bills, and she handed him the two tickets and a dollar change then said, "You board downstairs at gate 13. You gonna have to hurry if you wanna make the next bus."

As Pooh Berry walked away the clerk nodded to two undercover agents--a black agent in his late thirties with a thick mustache and a lit cigarette dangling from his lips and a clean-cut white agent in his late twenties puffing on a Marlboro-seated at a table across from the ticket counter.

Pooh Berry walked over to his brother, grabbed his bag, and said, "Come on, Yak. We gotta hurry up."

The two brothers rushed downstairs to gate 13 unaware they were being followed. They boarded the crowded bus and walked to the back to find two available seats before placing their bags in the overhead storage compartment. Meanwhile the two agents boarded the bus and took seats up front.

"Hello, my name is Larry," the bus driver announced as he closed the doors. "This is the express bus to Norfolk, Virginia. We will be arriving in Norfolk at approximately 5:55 a.m. The only stops we will be making will be Washington, DC and Richmond, Virginia. There is no smoking on this bus, and the rest room is in the rear. If you have any questions, I'll be happy to answer them. Enjoy

13

your trip, and thank you for riding Greyhound.

As the bus driver backed out of the parking space, Wyte Yak sensed that something was wrong. "Something don't feel right, Pooh Berry."

Pooh Berry, thinking his brother was just nervous, attempted to calm him, "Everything's cool, Baby bro. Just relax."

"I hope so," Wyte Yak said, looking around suspiciously.

Pooh Berry reclined his chair and relaxed while Wyte Yak gazed out of the window checking out the scenery for a while. Both brothers were asleep by the time the bus arrived at the DC bus terminal. Pooh Berry woke up when the driver released the brakes and turned on the lights.

The driver stood up and made another announcement: "This is Washington, DC. For those who will be remaining on the bus to Virginia, this is a twenty-minute rest stop. You may get something to eat, use the telephone and the rest rooms. We will be leaving the station at exactly 3:15 a.m." He then opened the door and exited the bus, followed by a little more than half of the passengers.

Pooh Berry nudged Wyte Yak to wake him up. "Wake up, Yak."

Wyte Yak squinted his eyes, not really wanting to be bothered. "What? Are we in Norfolk?"

"No, we in DC. I'm going to get something to eat. Do you want anything?"

"Yeah, I want you to leave me alone and let me sleep.

Pooh Berry laughed and was about to get up to leave the bus when he saw the two undercover agents approaching with their badges out. He nudged Wyte Yak again and when

Wyte Yak opened his eyes this time he saw the agents.

"Damn! I knew something wasn't right," Wyte Yak groaned.

The two agents approached the brothers. The white agent said, "We received an anonymous tip that two guys fitting your description were traveling with drugs."

The black agent pulled down both of their bags from the overhead compartment and asked, "Will you give us permission to search your bags?"

"No," Pooh Berry said, shaking his head.

"Well, we're going to have to search them anyway," said the white agent.

The agents searched through the bags, and the black agent found nine ounces of crack cocaine. "Bingo", he said, holding the drugs up for all the passengers to see.

"Damn! We're fucked," Wyte Yak said, lowering his head.

Pooh Berry screwed his face up at the police officers and asked, "Why didn't y'all search us at the Port Authority."

"It wouldn't have been a federal offense," the white agent smirked. The Agents arrested the two brothers and escorted them off the bus.

One month later the two brothers were in court standing in front of Judge Goldstein, an old, ugly, female judge who looked like she hadn't been properly fucked in years and got her rocks off by sending young black men to prison. She looked down at the two defendants over the rim of her thick, rectangular-shaped glasses.

"Mr. Whitehead, you are charged with trafficking nine ounces of crack cocaine with the intent to distribute. How do you plead?" Judge Goldstein asked.

"Guilty, Your Honor," Wyte Yak pleaded, taking the weight for the drugs. "The drugs were mine; my brother didn't know I had them with me."

"Don't listen to him, Your Honor. The drugs were mine," Pooh Berry interrupted. "They found them in my bag. He didn't know I had them with me."

The judge looked down at the two brothers. "You're both claiming the drugs. That's unusual. Usually the defendants try to blame each other," she remarked.

"May I speak, Your Honor?" Pooh Berry asked, attempting to persuade the judge.

"You may, Mr. Cortland."

Pooh Berry cleared his throat then said, "See, Your Honor, we're brothers. We have different last names because we have different fathers...neither one was ever around. Our mother passed a few years ago, and I promised her I'd watch after my brother and make sure he finished high school so he could make something out of himself."

He looked over at Wyte Yak, adding, "He did graduate but started to get in trouble back in Brooklyn, so I convinced him to enroll in college. I was bringing him to Virginia so he could go to Norfolk State, but he had no idea how I planned on paying his tuition. So, you see, Your Honor, this whole mess was my fault. I'm willing to accept any punishment you see fit, but I ask that you, please, allow my brother to go free so he can go to college and continue his education."

"Although that is a touching story, Mr. Cortland," the judge noted with a crooked smile on her face, "I do believe that Mr. Whitehead knew more than you're willing to admit. So I'm going to accept both of your guilty pleas. Only, I'm going to sentence you, Mr. Cortland, to ten years in a maximum security prison in Leavenworth, Kansas, and I'm going to sentence you, Mr. Whitehead, to five years with three suspended. You will be going to a minimum security prison in Fort Dix, New Jersey, where, if you like, you could take a few college courses."

Wyte Yak screwed his face at the judge, saying, "Send me with my brother!"

Pooh Berry, knowing that the judge could have very well given them both ten years since they both pleaded guilty, tried to calm his brother. "Chill, brah. I'll be alright," he said. Then he looked towards the judge. "Thank you, Your Honor."

The bailiff led the two brothers into the back. In two weeks they were both going to be shipped off to begin their sentences.

Pooh Berry was taking a long ride on the jail bus to Leavenworth Federal Prison. Next to him sat Nicky Latronica, a slim, 5'10" Italian, with dark, shoulder-length hair. Nicky seemed a little frightened--this was his first time going to prison--and claimed his father was a mobster. He was talking Pooh Berry's ear off, but Pooh didn't seem to mind.

Nicky was telling Pooh Berry the story about how he got arrested and Pooh Berry was all ears, "I didn't even know the police was following me until the unmarked car flashed its lights and told me to pull over. They opened the back of the truck and found two hundred and fifty ki's of the purest coke in America." Nicky lowered his head and continued, "I fucked up, man. I never shoulda drove. I shoulda waited until my driver was able to make the run. My dad is pissed. He didn't say anything, but I know he's pissed."

"You got caught with two hundred and fifty ki's!?" Pooh Berry exclaimed. "How much time did you get?" he asked, thinking Nicky must have received a life sentence.

"Ten years," said Nicky, dropping his head.

Pooh Berry's face tightened, annoyed by Nicky's sentence. "Ten years!?" he griped. "I got ten years and all I had was nine ounces,a fucking lousy quarter ki!"

"Who represented you?" Nicky asked.

"I had a bullshit, court-appointed lawyer."

"That's why, man," Nicky explained, "those bastards work for the courts. What do you think, they're there to help you? Nah, man they're there to fuck you. You shoulda known that."

"I know now," Pooh Berry said, nodding his head.

"That's a hell of a way to find out….Anyways I'm Nicky "Short Legs" Latronica. They nicknamed me Short Legs because I can't run for shit."

"I'm Harold Cortland, but everybody calls me Pooh Berry."

"Pooh Berry? You're not funny or anything, are you?"

"Never that!" Pooh Berry said, turning up his lip.

"I have to be honest with you, Pooh Berry," Nicky started to confess. "I never did any time before and, to tell you the truth, I'm a little nervous."

"I never done anytime neither," Pooh Berry said, looking at Nicky.

"Alright, then let's watch each other's back. Anything you need, just ask, and it's done. What's mine is yours."

"Cool. As long as you go for yours, I got your back," Pooh Berry promised. The two men gave each other dap to seal their friendship. Meanwhile there were two huge, mean-looking, black inmates on the back of the bus, Fred and Robbie, scheming on Nicky.

"Hey, Robbie, man, we're facing a lot of time," Fred said.

"Don't I know it," said Robbie, gritting his teeth.

"We gone need us some fish to relieve the tension," added Fred.

"I hear you."

Fred tapped Robbie and motioned his head towards the front of the bus, saying, "Do you see what I see?"

"Yeah, I see him, our pretty, little, Italian fruitcake."

"That's gone be our bitch for sure," Fred said, nodding his head.

For the next twenty-two hours Robbie and Fred fantasized about when and how they were going to rape Nicky.

Over at Fort Dix, Wyte Yak had been strip searched and given his prison gear and was being escorted down a long corridor to his cell. The correction officer stopped in front of an empty cell and yelled, "Open twenty-four!"

The gate to cell number twenty-four opened, and Wyte Yak walked in. The C.O. closed the gate behind him and walked off. Wyte Yak unrolled the mattress and started to make his bed. Just then, a brown-complexioned, gray-haired, seventy-year-old from the next cell called out to Wyte Yak. The broad-chested man had huge arms and, due to his long imprisonment and great physical shape, looked more like he was in his early fifties.

"Hey, young blood," he said.

"What's up?" said Wyte Yak, walking over to the front of his cell to see what the man wanted.

"What prison did you just get shipped from?"

"I didn't come from any prison. I just got sentenced," Wyte Yak said.

"You just got sentenced? You must of caught a light

bid."

"Yeah, I got five years, but the judge suspended three," Wyte Yak said.

"That's not shit," the old man said. "For the last thirty-two years I've done time in damn-near every federal prison in the country. This one here is the sweetest. This joint is pretty calm. Most of the people here are on their way out. Just mind your business and try to stay out of trouble and you'll be out of here in no time."

"I hear you," Wyte Yak said, nodding his head.

"What's your name?

"Franklin, but my peoples call me Wyte Yak."

"I'm Jeffrey Carter. My friends used to call me JC, but in here mostly everybody calls me Pops."

"Which do you prefer?"

"Either one. It doesn't matter much to me."

"Alright then, JC, I'll kick it with you later."

Wyte Yak finished fixing his bed and tried to relax.

It was only Pooh Berry's second day in Leavenworth, and already there was trouble. Pooh Berry was laid back on his bunk just relaxing when he saw Fred and Robbie scheming on Nicky, who was in the shower. Pooh watched Fred come from out of the shower area and whisper something to Robbie. Then they both rushed into the shower area. Pooh Berry knew that Nicky was the only one in the shower so he figured those two freaks were about to try him. Quickly he hopped out of bed and took his pillow out of the pillow case. Then he grabbed the lock off his locker and Nicky's, placing them in the pillow case, and headed to the shower.

Fred had Nicky yoked up while Robbie continuously punched him in the stomach saying, "You're our bitch.

Don't try to fight it!"

The blows were weakening Nicky, and he was scared shitless, thinking he was about to be raped. That was up until Pooh Berry rushed in and swung the pillowcase, connecting on the back of Robbie's head. He fell to the ground and was temporally knocked unconscious. Fred released Nicky, and he fell to the floor holding his stomach. Fred rushed towards Pooh Berry and Pooh Berry swung the pillow case again smacking the locks across Fred's jaw. You could hear the bone crack upon impact. Pooh Berry continued swinging as Fred fell to the floor connecting on different parts of his grill with every swing. By the time Pooh Berry stopped swinging Fred's face was swollen and covered in blood. His face was rearranged so badly, his own mother wouldn't have recognized him.

Pooh, noticing Robbie was trying to get up, jumped on him and beat him with the locks until his face looked almost identical to Fred's.

Once Pooh Berry felt that he had done enough damage, he helped his friend to his feet and asked, "Are you alright, Nicky?"

"Yeah, man. Thanks," Nicky said, nodding his head.

Pooh Berry handed him a towel, and Nicky wrapped it around his waist. The other inmates had rushed in to see the action and they all stood there astonished by the way Pooh Berry handled the two huge freaks, clearing the way as Pooh Berry walked through the crowd escorting Nicky back to his bunk.

Robbie and Fred were taken to the infirmary and treated for multiple fractures to the face and head. After that they were both transferred to another dorm and never bothered Nicky again. Whenever they saw Pooh Berry anywhere in the prison, they lowered heads to avoid eye contact.

CHAPTER 3

Wyte Yak enrolled in school and for the next two years did nothing but read and study. He aced every test he took and graduated at the top of his class with an associate degree in business management.

He managed to stay out of trouble, and his only friend was Jeffrey Carter. He liked the old man's style and looked up to him like a father figure. Wyte Yak had long talks with Jeffrey and found out that he was once a hit man for the mob and had killed over forty people during his gangsta' days. They played a lot of chess, and Jeffrey showed Wyte Yak how Kings used their Pawns the same way gangsta's are used by Dons.

A year into Wyte Yak's bid, he received a letter from Deuce telling let him how things were going back in Brooklyn. He said he had bought a drum machine and started making beats and that their other homey, D-Ski, had started rapping. Deuce also informed Wyte Yak that he, D-Ski, and Trap had put a few songs together but never made it to the studio. Deuce said they were a team and it just didn't feel right without Yak.

He let Yak know that Rahtiek was chilling but still carried his gun with him every where he went, occasionally busting off whenever he felt it necessary. Deuce brought him up to date on the chicks he had hit since Yak was away and the fact that his old girl Tiesha had started smoking crack a few months after he got locked up.

She had started fucking with some guy from Red Hook who had her sniffing coke. She soon got hooked then started fucking with anybody that would get high. Not too long after that she was smoking. He told Yak that she was so dried up he wouldn't even recognize her if he passed her on the street. He let him know, too, his boy Drizz was still a lush, his boy Dikki Jah was out of town hustling, and niggas was hating on his boy Prince because he had fucked damn-near every bitch in the 'hood. But mostly he just let him know that everything was everything and that his presence was missed.

After the incident in the shower Pooh Berry became one of the most respected inmates in the prison. Although most of the other prisoners only hung with prisoners of their own race, Pooh Berry and Nicky had become very close, like brothers. To repay Pooh Berry for saving him in the shower, Nicky promised to connect Wyte Yak when he was released from Fort Dix with his father down in Miami,

Nicky and Pooh were in the day room playing a game of chess when Pooh Berry said to him, "You know my brother's getting out tomorrow."

"Don't worry, Pooh Berry. I know. Everything is straight. Remember we sent him the ticket to Miami. Once he gets there, he'll be well taken care of," Nicky said.

"Alright, cool," Pooh Berry said, smiling. He wasn't able to say much in the letter he sent Wyte Yak, so he hoped Yak read between the lines and did what he told him to do.

The two men continued their game of chess. Pooh lost three games in a row, focusing more on his baby brother being released from prison.

Back in Fort Dix, Wyte Yak was in his cell packing his belongings. A correction officer walked over to his cell, called him over to the gate, and handed him an envelope.

"I'll be back for you in a minute," the correction officer said. Wyte Yak opened the envelope and found a plane ticket to Miami and a letter from his brother Pooh Berry. The letter read:

What up, brah? First off I would like to congratulate you on receiving your associate degree. You don't know how proud that makes me, and I'm sure mom would have been proud of you, too. As for me I'm doing fine. I can't say as much as I would like to so you're going to have to trust me and read between the lines. When you leave today go straight to the airport and get on the plane to Miami. I have some people who will meet you at the airport. They'll take care of you from there. That's all I can say right now. So be strong do the right thing and take care. I love you, bro. Peace.

As Wyte Yak placed the letter back into the envelope JC called over to him. "What up, JC?" Wyte Yak asked.

"You're on your way out today, huh?"

"Yeah, I'm ghost," Wyte Yak said, nodding his head.

"You mind if I ask you a question?" JC asked, smiling.

"Not at all, JC, what's on your mind?"

"Do you remember the Lucky Luciano story we were watching the other night?"

"Yeah," Wyte Yak said, wondering what JC was getting at.

"In your opinion, out of Lucky Luciano and Miles Lansky, who do you think was the real Don?"

"Luciano," Wyte Yak suggested. "Why do you think they called it the Lucky Luciano story?"

"Because that's what they wanted you to believe. In my opinion Lansky was the Don," JC argued.

"Why would you say that?" Wyte Yak asked, confused.

JC smiled and said, "Although Luciano was a smart man, he was also a loose cannon, and that put him in the limelight a little more than necessary--which is why he went to jail and was later deported.

"Lansky, on the other hand, always laid in the cut, so the authorities didn't see him as much of a threat. He was allowed to conduct business and later was looked at as a respectable businessman. He never went to jail, wasn't gunned down by rival gangsters, and wound up being one of the few mobsters to die of natural causes, like a real Don. I met the man once and, if you ask me, he was a true Don...if I ever saw one."

"That's deep, JC. I never looked at it from that point of view. That's definitely one to grow on," Wyte Yak said.

The C.O. returned and opened Wyte Yak's cell. Wyte Yak gathered his belongings and walked out of the cell. He then walked over to JC's cell, shook his hand, and said, "Take care, JC. I'm gonna miss you. I'll be sure to write whenever I'm able, and thanks for keeping me focused."

"Keep your head up young blood and, always remember, believe none of what you hear and only half of what you see," JC advised his young friend.

Wyte Yak nodded his head in agreement then followed the C.O. down the corridor.

Wyte Yak left Fort Dix and caught a bus to the airport where he boarded a plane for Miami. In less than two hours, he arrived at the Miami airport where a limo driver was holding up a sign with his name on it. He walked over to the driver and said, "I'm Wyte Yak." The limo driver took his bag and opened the door for him as Wyte Yak entered the car. The driver then closed the door behind him and placed his bag in the trunk.

Twenty minutes later the limo drove through a gate and pulled up in front of a huge mansion where Ritchie Latronica, Nicky's twin brother, greeted Wyte Yak as he stepped out of the limo.

"Wyte Yak, it's a pleasure to meet you," Ritchie said, extending his hand. "I'm Ritchie. My brother Nicky is locked down with your brother out in Kansas. Come on in. My father's dying to meet you."

Wyte Yak followed Ritchie through the luxurious mansion still unsure about what was going on. The only time he ever saw a place that big and beautiful was in a movie. Ritchie led him through the house out back to the pool area where his father Raymond Latronica, a well-groomed Italian Don in his early fifties, was sitting at a table smoking a Cuban cigar and reading a newspaper.

There were eight naked women in the pool bouncing around playing a game of volleyball. Wyte Yak pinched himself to make sure he wasn't dreaming. As they approached Raymond he stood to shake Wyte Yak's hand and said, "Wyte Yak, it's a pleasure to meet you. How was your flight?"

"It was pretty smooth."

"Good. You know your brother and my son, Nicky, have become like family in the pen. So I figure you, me, and Ritchie should be like family out in the world."

Wyte Yak nodded his head, saying, "I feel you."

"Have a seat," Raymond said. "Ritchie, have the butler bring us out a bottle of Dom." Then he added, "I'm going to be straight with you, Wyte Yak. Your brother is good people...real good. He had my son's back in the pen when a couple of animals tried to attack him. For that I am forever grateful. To show you how grateful I am, I'm going to front you fifty kilos of raw, uncut cocaine at ten thousand a pie. Since you just came home I'm going to give you a few weeks to handle your business. After that I expect you to buy from me at the low price of thirty five hundred a ki'. Is that alright with you?"

Wyte Yak was caught off guard, his eyes widening, but tried to keep his cool as he said, "With all due respect, Mr. Latronica, I don't know if I can handle that kind of weight."

"Nonsense," Mr. Latronica protested. "Nicky tells me you're smart, got yourself a business degree while you were locked up. Improvise. It's nothing for a smart guy like you. In a few months you'll be moving fifty ki's a day."

"I don't wanna fuck up," Wyte Yak said, sounding a little nervous.

Mr. Latronica tried to reassure Wyte Yak, "You can handle it, relax. I think a man with your intelligence would be good for the family business."

The butler brought a tray with two glasses and a bottle of Dom Perignon and poured the two men a glass of champagne each and walked off.

"To my new family member," Mr. Latronica said, raising his glass.

"To my new family," Wyte Yak replied.

The two men touched glasses and sipped the champagne.

Ritchie then came over with two beautiful, naked, Italian women and said, "This is Crystina and Madilina. They're going to show you a good time--Miami-style."

Although Wyte Yak had never slept with any white women nor ever intended to, he didn't want to insult his new family by turning them down. So he smiled as the two women wrapped their arms around him and led him into the mansion.

"Take it easy on him, ladies. He's a little rusty," Mr. Latronica laughed.

They took Wyte Yak upstairs into one of the many bedrooms and started undressing him. Then they laid him on the huge, king-size, brass bed and started to double-team him, sucking him like he's never been sucked in his life. One had his dick in her mouth while the other had his balls in hers, constantly switching up and giving him the best of both worlds.

After a while Madilina mounted his long, hard penis and let out a pleasurable moan as it entered her tight, moist vagina. He held one hand on her thin waist and the other on her thick, teardrop-shaped ass as she grinded on top of him while Crystina licked his nut sack. Then they switched up again. Wyte Yak, taking control now, made both of them get on their knees side by side with their faces down and their asses in the air and took turns plunging his dick in and out of them, beast fucking them from behind. The women screamed in ecstasy as he pulled their hair and pounded their moist, pink, pulsating pussies. He fucked the two broads silly for the next few hours before collapsing into a deep, coma-like sleep.

The next day Wyte Yak boarded a plane to Virginia and sat down in first class next to a little 11-year-old white boy named Mikey, who appeared to have Down's syndrome. He looked over at Wyte Yak and said, "Hello."

"Hey, Shorty, how you doing?" Wyte Yak asked.
"I'm Mikey."

Wyte Yak shook the kid's hand and said, "What up,

Mikey? I'm Wyte Yak."

"Do you play chess?" Mikey asked as he pulled out a small portable chess set.

"Yeah, a little, but right now I'm just trying to relax," Wyte Yak said, reclining his chair.

"Nobody ever wants to be my friend. That's okay," Mikey complained, frowning.

"Alright, I'll play you a game, but just one," Wyte Yak said, feeling sorry for the kid.

After only playing for five minutes Mikey checkmated Wyte Yak, who was surprised by Mikey's skills.

"You're good, Mikey. Where'd you learn to play like that?"

"I've been playing since I was six years old. My dad says chess is the game of life and if I'm going to be a success in life then I have to know how to play."

Mikey eventually beat Wyte Yak two out of the three. Wyte Yak found out that Mikey was a very bright eleven-year-old who did have Down's syndrome but didn't allow it to keep him back from anything. He attended a special school and usually stayed with his mother since his father was always away on business. He was just coming back from vacationing with his godparents.

Wyte Yak found Mikey exceptional and thought it would be a good idea to hang out with him every once in a while. Knowing that he was about to start living life on a whole other level with his new drug family, Wyte Yak figured Mikey would be his lucky charm.

"You know something, Mikey. I dig you. You're cool. How would you like to meet up a couple of times a month for a game of chess?"

"I'd like that," Mikey grinned, realizing he had just

made a new friend.

"Alright, then introduce me to your mother when we land, and I'll call you in a couple of weeks so we can meet up," Wyte Yak suggested.

The plane landed and, after meeting Mikey's mother, Wyte Yak took a cab to 2636 Princess Ann Road, the home of his Aunt Mattie and Little Ant, his cousin. He approached the white house with the white picket fence, where his Aunt Mattie was inside sitting on the couch and inhaling smoke from the crack she'd just purchase. Wyte Yak rang the door bell, unwittingly disturbing Mattie's high.

"Who the hell is it?" she yelled, walking over to open the door. She was mumbling to herself. When she saw her nephew she screamed, "Franklin!"

Wyte Yak entered the house and kissed his aunt on the cheek. The inside of the house was in very poor condition. In the living room there was nothing but an old, raggedy couch, a badly chipped coffee table, and an old, 12-inch, black & white TV with fuzzy pictures.

"How you doing, baby?" Mattie asked. "I haven't seen you in years."

"I'm fine, Aunt Mattie. Still hanging in there, you know me," Wyte Yak answered.

As they sat down on the couch Mattie tried to hide her pipe, and Wyte Yak pretended he didn't see.
"I thought Anthony told me you was in jail," Mattie said.

"I was. I just got out yesterday," Wyte Yak said, lowering his eyes. Then he asked, "Where is Little Ant?"

"He's upstairs with one of his little girlfriends. He got so many I can't keep up with them," Mattie said. She then called out, "Anthony! Anthony!"

"Chill, auntie. Let me surprise him."

Wyte Yak then crept upstairs where he heard moans coming from Little Ant's bedroom. He busted in the room and found Little Ant having sex with Tammy.

"What the fuck?" Little Ant shouted, reaching for his gun underneath the bed. When he realized who was standing in the doorway, he burst out laughing, "You a funny mother-fucker, cuz."

"Who the fuck is this?" Tammy asked, unamused.

"That's my cousin from New York, baby."

"He don't know how to knock?" Tammy asked, screwing her face at Wyte Yak.

"Chill, baby. Get dressed. Me and my cousin got some business to handle," Little Ant explained.

Tammy wrapped the sheet from the bed around her, picked up her clothes from the floor, and stormed out of the bedroom and into the bathroom to get dressed. LA put on a pair of boxers and walked over to hug his cousin, saying, "I see you made it this time."

"Yeah, I got lucky," Wyte Yak said, smiling. "You got the package I sent you?"

"Yeah, it came a few hours ago," LA said.

LA pulled on a pair of jeans and a short-sleeve Tommy Hilfiger rugby shirt and retrieved a big box from the closet, placing it on the bed. Just then Tammy reentered the room and asked, "Are you gonna drive me home?"

"I can't," LA said, shaking his head. "I got some business to take care of right now." Then he reached in his pants pocket and handed her two twenty-dollar bills, adding, "Take a cab. I'll call you later."

"You better call me," she said, taking the money from LA and rolling her eyes at Wyte Yak before turning and walking out of the bedroom.

"What's in this big-ass box, Yak?" LA asked, looking at his cousin.

"Open it and find out," Yak prompted him.

Little Ant grabbed his pocket knife from on the dresser and opened the box. He reached in the box and pulled out a brick of cocaine wrapped in clear plastic with the words "Coca Cola" printed on the plastic.

"Damn, Yak!" LA exclaimed, eyes bulging. "What's this, a ki'?"

"No doubt!" Wyte Yak said, nodding his head. "And there's forty-nine more where that came from."

"Damn, cuz, you the man!" LA said, impressed. "Nah, cuz, we the men! You know anybody looking?" Wyte Yak asked.

"Only the whole fucking city," LA said after a slight pause. "It's a drought right now. You can get close to thirty thousand a brick. How much do you want per pie?"

"Twenty-five for one, but anybody buying three or more can have them for twenty-two."

"At those prices," LA said, "we can corner the market. How's the product? Is it a head banger?"

"This is the purest shit in America," Wyte Yak boasted.

"In that case I know just who to call," LA smiled.

He then picked up the telephone and dialed seven digits. The phone rang once and was answered by Dazz, one of the largest dealers in Norfolk.

"Hello, Dazz speaking."

"What up, Dazz? This is Little Ant."

"What up, stick man? How you?"

"I'm good. I'm trying to find out if you straight with

that girl yet," LA said.

"Man, I'm dry as a bone. I can't connect on shit, but some garbage. And you know I'll go without before I fuck with some trash."

"Yeah, I know you, but check this out. I came across all the dime pieces you need, bitches so pure you could take one, heat her up, and make another honey that's still knocking the rest of the bitches in the 'hood out of the box," LA bragged.

"Is that right?"

"No doubt!"

"What they running?"

"Twenty-five a bitch."

"If they all that you need to come see me," Dazz said. "I could use a good twenty of them 'ho's right now."

"You know that's a half a man,"

"It's nothing. You know how I get down. Come see me."

"I'm there," LA promised.

LA hung up the phone and turned to Wyte Yak. "We in business, cousin," he said. "Dude ready to spend half a mill for twenty of them joints right now."
"That's what I'm talking about," Wyte Yak said.

LA grabbed a duffle bag from the closet and took twenty ki's from out of the box and stuffed them into the duffle bag. "We don't even have to fuck with nobody else if you don't want to," he said. "This nigga, Dazz, is filthy. He a "willie," for real. He's either got workers or niggas buying weight from him in damn-near every 'hood in Norfolk. Right now we charging him New York prices. Shit! By tomorrow he'll probably buy all we got."

"I'm feeling that," Wyte Yak said.

LA walked over to the bed, kneeled down, and pulled

a suitcase from beneath it, placing it on top of the bed next to Wyte Yak. He then opened the suitcase and revealed an arsenal of guns and ammunition: Two small six-shot Raven 380s, one chromed and the other made of blue steel; four 9mms, two Luger and two Smith & Wesson; one 44 bulldog; three 45s, two automatic and one revolver; one Mac 10; one Mac 12; and one Tec 9.

"Grab whatever you like and let's go get this money," LA said.

Wyte Yak grabbed the two 9mm Smith & Wesson, checked the clips, and placed them in the front pockets of his jeans, saying, "These a work."

LA chose the .44 bulldog. The barrel was empty. He loaded it with bullets from a box in the closet then tucked the weapon in his waist, before closing the suitcase and shoving it back under the bed. He placed the box with the rest of the ki's in the closet, grabbed the duffle bag, and said, "We out."

The two men walked out of the bedroom, and LA locked the bedroom door behind them. They walked down the stairs and out the front door. Then they hopped in LA's Honda Accord and drove to Dazz's condo in Virginia Beach.

Over at Dazz's Condo, Dazz and his bodyguard, Jabba, were in the living room sitting on the couch watching the Mets play the Braves. His brother Dino was sitting at the dining room table with three women doing lines of coke.

The Condo was beautiful with cream-colored everything, the carpet, the wall, the living room set, the dining room table and chairs, and even the marble coffee table. The door bell rang, and Jabba walked over, looked through the peephole, and said to Dazz, "It's Little Ant."

"Let him in," Dazz said.

Jabba opened the door and LA walked in followed by

Wyte Yak. Dazz stood to greet the men, slapping LA five and shaking Wyte Yak's hand.

"This is my cousin Wyte Yak from up top," LA said.

Dino walked over, slapped LA five, and shook Wyte Yak's hand.

"Have a seat," Dazz said, extending his hand towards the couch. "Let's get down to business."

Dazz sat on the couch, and LA sat down next to him. Jabba stood behind the couch with his arms folded. Wyte Yak sat on the loveseat, and Dino stood on the other side of the coffee table in front of the TV.

LA placed the duffle bag on top of the coffee table, pulled out a kilo, and gave it to Dazz, who handed it to his brother Dino. Dino pulled a pocket knife from his right front pants pocket and sliced a hole in the plastic. He then broke off a small rock of coke and called out to one of the girls, "Sandy, bring me a plate from the kitchen cabinet."

Sandy came back with a plate for Dino.

She was a slim, cute, light-brown complexioned female wearing a pair of tight, beige Guess jeans, a red Guess T-shirt, and a pair of red 54.11 Reebok classic women's tennis shoes.

"Stay here a minute. I want you to sample this," Dino told her.

Dino placed the small rock of cocaine on the plate and used the side of his blade to crush it to powder. He then held the plate up to Sandy, who scooped up some with her pinky finger nail and sniffed it. Right away she started choking and nodding her head in approval as her eyes watered. "That's some good shit," she said.

Dino handed her the plate, and she took it over to the dining room table for the other women to sample. Dazz then gave Jabba a signal to go into the back room and looking over at LA said, "I'm impressed. I see you're stepping up in the world. I'm not mad at you. It's a drought and, out of all the dealers in Va., my man Little Ant comes to the rescue. Where'd you get shit like this for such a cheap price?"

"Let's just say, I'm connected," LA said, smiling and looking at Wyte Yak.

Jabba returned from the back with a briefcase, placed it on the coffee table in front of LA, and opened

it to reveal its contents--five hundred thousand dollars.

"Do you want to count it?" Dazz asked.

LA flipped through a few stacks, shook his head, and said, "Nah, I know you don't play no games."

"I'm going to need another thirty of these joints tonight...if you can handle it," Dazz said, looking at Wyte Yak and LA.

"I can handle it. Just hit me. You got the number," LA said.

LA closed the briefcase, and he and Wyte Yak stood up, slapped each of the men five, and walked out of the condo. They walked down the flight of steps and hopped into Little Ant's Honda.

"Damn, cuz, we about to make a million in one day. It looks like your little bid in the Feds done turned out to be a blessing in disguise," LA said.

"You know every adversity has a greater benefit," Wyte Yak agreed.

"So what now?"

"We gone go chill in the crib, get your moms to fix us something to eat, and wait for dude to call and cop the rest of this shit. Then I'm gone jet back down to Miami to check my peoples and give them their five hundred thousand.

Spend another six hundred thou and get us two hundred ki's then we'll really be in business."

"That's what I'm talking about," LA said. "We about to run this city."

The two men slapped each other five as they jumped on the highway and headed back to Norfolk.

LA was well known in Norfolk. So when he put out the word that he was selling pure coke at New York prices it seemed like every dealer in the Tidewater area was trying to cop from him. The drought really did them lovely. His phone rang off the hook. Within three weeks they moved over six hundred kilos. They hooked up Aunt Mattie's house and bought three condos--all in the same building--in Virginia Beach, one for Wyte Yak, one for LA, and one for LA's right hand man, Brock, a 6'3" dark-skinned, baldheaded, muscular black male with two gold fangs. They also purchased a three-bedroom town house.

Everything in Wyte Yak's condo was green the way Dazz's was cream. The only extra feature was the throw rug made out to look like a million-dollar bill, with Wyte Yak's picture on it instead of a president's.

Wyte Yak, LA, and Brock were all in Yak's Condo as LA was stacking cash in the safe in the hallway closet. Brock was watching Yo M.T.V Rapps, while Wyte Yak was on the phone talking to a BMW dealer.

"You have all three sitting there right now...the red, the white, and the blue?" he asked. Then he added, "Alright, I'll be right over to pick them up."

Wyte Yak hung up and called a cab. Five minutes later the taxi was out front beeping the horn.

"Come on y'all we out," Wyte Yak said.

"Where we going?" LA asked, closing the safe in the

closet.

"To the BM dealer to pick up some cars."

"We going car shopping?" Brock asked.

"Yeah, but not for us. We'll pick up our cars once we get to New Yitty," Wyte Yak said.

The three men walked out of Wyte Yak's condo and took the cab to the dealership where they spent two hundred and twenty-five thousand on three brand-new 1992 BMW 740ILs two months before the cars were scheduled to come out. When they rolled out they hopped on the I-95 North and headed for New York.

CHAPTER 4

Seven hours later they were coming off the Manhattan Bridge and entering Brooklyn. They drove on Flatbush Avenue two blocks up, made a left on Myrtle Avenue, then another left at the next corner--Prince Street--down to Johnson Street, and finally a right turn into the Project parking lot, pulling up in front of 48 Fleet Walk, where Rahtiek, Trap, Deuce, D-Ski and Drizz were standing drinking beers.

Their eyes almost popped out when they saw Wyte Yak emerge from the red BMW, and they all rushed over to greet him. D-Ski was the first to get there. "What up, 'White Boy'? When you got out?" he asked Wyte Yak, slapping him five and giving him a hug.

"Three weeks ago."

"What up, my brother? How you?" Drizz greeted him, smiling.

"I couldn't be better."

"I see," Drizz said, making eyes at the red BMW.

Deuce hugged Yak. "Welcome home, my nigga."

Then Trap showed Yak some love, saying, "I missed you, Sun,"

"I missed you, too," Wyte Yak said.

The last to hug Wyte Yak was Rahtiek. He hugged him so tight he managed to lift him off his feet. "Why you didn't let nobody know you was coming home?" he asked, putting him down.

Wyte Yak slapped Rahtiek five and slipped him the

keys to the red BMW.

"What's this?" Rahtiek asked.

"That's you, my nigga."

Rahtiek looked at the gorgeous, apple red BMW then hugged Wyte Yak again, saying, "I love you." He quickly hopped in the car and peeled off, taking it around the block for a test drive.

LA and Brock, each carrying a half-gallon of Hennessy, exited the other two cars and walked over to the crowd, slapping everybody five and introducing themselves. Wyte then told LA to give the keys to the white BMW to Deuce, and Brock the keys to the blue BMW to Trap. Deuce and Trap both smiled and hugged Wyte Yak to show gratitude. They then walked over to their new cars and sat in them checking them out.

D-Ski, not believing what he just saw, said, "Nigga, you just got out of jail and you giving niggas seventy-five-thousand-dollar cars. What the fuck? You hit the lotto or something?"

"If that's the case, where's mine?" Drizz asked, putting his forty to his lips.

"If y'all rolling with me, y'all can get cars, too," Wyte Yak promised the two men. "...Well, then again I don't know about you, Drizz. I don't think you're ready to get behind the wheel of a car."

"I don't think so neither," Drizz confirmed, looking at Yak from the corner of his eyes.

"I'm down for whatever," D-Ski said.

Just then Rahtiek came back from his test run.

"Look in your glove compartments," Wyte Yak said, turning around to face the cars.

The three men looked in their glove compartments

and found ten thousand dollars.

"What's going on, my nigga? Can I be down?" Rahtiek asked.

"You already down," Wyte Yak answered smiling. "Y'all all down. It's on and popping. So let's pop this Henrock and start celebrating. It's a new day. The days of the nickel and dime hustle are over. We out of state moving weight."

LA was about to twist the cap off the Hennessy, but Deuce stopped him. "Hold up. Let everybody tap the bottom."

"Nah, Sun, tap the top," Wyte Yak protested. "We been on the bottom too long."

Everybody tapped the top. LA opened the bottle, poured himself a drink, and passed the bottle around. Once everybody's cup was full, they formed a circle, held up their cups, and made a toast.

"Glad to see you back in the streets," Deuce said to Wyte Yak.

"No," Wyte Yak said. "To us, finally stepping up in the world."

"And who are we?" asked Trap.

"We're CC," Rahtiek chimed in, "career criminals for life."

"I'll drink to that," Drizz said.

On that note, they all gulped down their cups of Hennessy and poured themselves another.

"Tell me something, Wyte Yak," Trap said. "How you only been out of jail three weeks and you come with over two hundred grand in gifts?"

"It's simple, my nigga, but if told you the answer I'd have to kill you. So fuck it. Let's just say, I did my time.

Now, it's time to shine."

"No doubt! Like you said," Rahtiek repeated, "we been on the bottom too long."

"Where that nigga, Prince, at?" Wyte Yak asked.

"He probably in the crib fucking something, you know Prince," Trap said.

"He still got all the bitches?" Wyte Yak asked.

"Too many," Deuce sniffed. "He need to pass some of them broads over here."

"Word! Let me hit a couple of them off with the drunk dick," Drizz teased. They all broke up laughing as Drizz humped the air.

Just then Dikki Jah pulled up in a red BMW 525. He was a skinny, dark-skinned, 20-yr-old, and about 5'11". He hopped out smiling as he yelled, "Wyte Yak! What up, my nigga?"

"Dikki Jah!" Wyte Yak yelled.

They slapped five with the right hand and hugged each other with the left.

"Damn, Whitey, that's you brightening up the PJs with all that fly shit?"

"I guess," Wyte Yak said, smiling. "What's going on with you, Dikki?"

"I'm out in DC doing a little something, but it look like I need to get with you."

"You know you're more than welcome. I could always use a live wire like you on the team. You know we go way back," said Wyte Yak.

"Like Adidas and Pumas?" asked Dikki Jah.

"Further than that."

"British Walkers and Playboys?"

"Further."

"Converse and 69ers?"

"Further."

"Pro keds and Corduroy Skips?"

"Yeah...somewhere around that time," Wyte Yak agreed.

"No diggedy, we were hanging since I was about seven years old!"

Just then Prince came walking up the lane with a slit-eyed, caramel-complexioned cutie with an hour glass shape. He yelled to Wyte Yak, "Is that my brother from another mother?" hugging and lifting him off the ground.

"What up, Prince, lover? What's the deal, baby bro?"

"You know me, same ol' Prince. Ain't nothing changed. No job; but I keep something fly slobbing the knob."

Wyte Yak looked over at Prince's lady friend and said, "Yeah, I see."

"I'll be right back, my nigga. Let me walk Shorty to the avenue to catch a cab."

"Fuck a cab!" Rahtiek said. "Take the red one." He tossed Prince the keys to his red BMW.

"I'll be right back," Prince said, looking over at the cars and smiling. He and his lady friend hopped in. He then backed out of the parking space and sped out of the lot, tires screeching as he turned onto the street.

"Let me kick it with you for a minute, Dikki," Wyte Yak said.

Yak and Dikki walked away from the crowd and

leaned on the parking lot fence.

"So what's going on in DC?" Wyte Yak asked.

"Man, everybody and their mother in DC, them Fulton Street niggas, them LG niggas, them East New York and Brownsville niggas--everybody you don't see out here. If they ain't locked up, they in DC. It's paper out there."

"Can you move some weight out there?"

"Hell, yeah...if the shit is decent and the price is right."

"I got the best coke in America," Wyte Yak boasted. "Niggas cooking my shit, doubling the weight, and it's still better than anything else on the street."

"It's like that?"

"It's like that!"

"What you want a ki'?"

"Twenty-two thousand."

"Twenty-two G's? Man, them joints going for twenty-five and better uptown right now! Thirty in DC!"

"All I want is twenty-two. You can sell them for whatever you want."

"I know damn-near every nigga getting money in DC. I could probably move twenty-five, thirty of them joints a day, even more if that shit come back like you say."

"We rolling out in a couple of days. Roll with us down to Va."

"I'm with you."

"We gone be rolling six sevens deep. So take that money you was about to spend with them Dominicans and upgrade that nervous-ass 525 to a seven series."

Dikki laughed, slapped Wyte Yak five, saying, "Yeah, alright, nigga."

Prince pulled back up in the red BMW, hopped out,

and walked over to Wyte Yak and Dikki Jah.

"You took Shorty home that fast? Where the fuck she from? Clinton Hills?" Dikki asked.

"Nah, Shorty from the east. She didn't like the way I was driving, so I kicked her out and told her to take a cab," Prince said.

Wyte Yak gave Prince a playful punch to the stomach, saying, "I see you still got all the 'ho's."

"I got problems, but pussy is not one of them!" Prince said, sticking out his chest.

"You got any strippers? I was thinking about opening up a strip club in Norfolk."

"Whitey, believe you me, I got over a hundred strippers on the team. We can make it happen. Them country boys ain't seen no freaks like these," Prince said, nodding his head.

"Alright, then. Can you roll out with us in a couple of days, so we can pick out a spot?" Wyte Yak asked.

"I'm with that. What you getting into tonight?"

"Whatever."

"Let's rent a couple of suites over at the Marriott. I'll call over some shorties, and we can do it up big to celebrate your homecoming," Prince said.

Wyte Yak slapped Prince five, "That's what I'm talking about, Sun."

The Career Criminal clique hung out drinking in the Projects for a couple of hours. Then Wyte Yak rented out four suites, which they stayed in for the next three nights partying with twenty of Prince's lady friends.

CHAPTER 5

Although they hated to leave it was time to head back down to Va. Dikki Jah traded in his red 525 for a black 735I and they rode down I-95 seven, Seven series Beemers deep. Wyte Yak copped a lime green, LA copped a canary yellow, and Brock copped a smoke gray. Heads turned in every car they passed as they raced down I-95 South. You would've thought they were famous rap stars, with all the attention they were getting.

Once they pulled up in front of the town house everybody stepped out the cars and stretched before taking their bags in the house. After chilling in the town house for about half an hour, Deuce and Trap went with LA to check out the condos, and Wyte Yak and Prince went to look for a spot to turn into a strip club.

Yak and Prince were driving along the highway when they saw a sign that read, "For rent: Fifty thousand square feet. For info call Henry (804) 797-4113. Prince wrote the number down then called from the car phone, setting an appointment for 10:00 a.m. the next morning to look at the place.

When Wyte Yak and Prince returned to the town house everybody was gone, leaving a note saying they were going to get something to eat then go partying at the "Big Apple" nightclub.

Prince and Wyte Yak had already eaten and both were too tired from the long drive to go out clubbing so they decided to just kick back and relax. Wyte Yak sat on the couch, kicked his boots off, and propped his feet up on the coffee table as he surfed the channels, stopping at the news.

Prince grabbed a Guinness stout from the refrigerator and sat down on the love seat. A shooting took place in the Project across the street from LA's mother's house so Wyte Yak turned up the TV to hear what the reporter was saying:

Two innocent bystanders were shot today in a drive-by shooting in Roberts Park. Police say that Denise Richardson, a 74-year-old grandmother was shot in the chest earlier today by a stray bullet intended for drug dealers while sitting on her porch. Along with Mrs. Richardson, six-year-old Rodney Bell was also shot in the head while playing tag with his eight-year-old cousin. Both victims died at the scene of the crime. The police have no leads other than the fact that the shots were fired out of a blue, four-door Acura legend sedan. If anyone knows who the men in the Acura or have any information about the shooting, they should call the Police at 1-800-596-7732.

Wyte Yak clicked the TV off.

"Damn! Shit buck wild out here, huh, Yak?" Prince asked, gulping down the Guinness like he was dying from thirst.

"You don't know, Sun. It really bothers me when I hear about stupid shit like that," Wyte Yak said, shaking his head in disgust.

"I know what you mean. A seventy-year-old grand-mother and a six-year-old kid get hit, but they don't hit who they were after. That's some bugged-out shit. I know them idiots gotta be feeling it," Prince said.

"They probably don't even give a fuck. But I know one thing: shit's about to change out here," Wyte Yak predicted.

"Ain't shit you can do about that, Yak," Prince said, walking back over to the refrigerator to retrieve another

Guinness. "You know niggas gone be niggas."

"Not as long as I'm supplying these niggas. They gone get their shit together."

"You crazy, Yak. What the fuck you gone do?" Prince asked, sitting back on the love seat.

"Stick around. You'll see."

The next morning Wyte Yak and Prince went to check out the building for rent. They liked the fact that it was nice and spacious and began discussing plans for the club. Henry, the owner, was waiting up front talking on the phone but rushed off when he saw the two men approaching him.

"Is it enough space for you guys?" he asked.

"It'll work," said Prince.

Wyte Yak looked directly into the eyes of the well-dressed business man and asked, "How much we talking?"

"To rent, it's $4,200 a month; to buy, I'll need $15,000 down and $3,000 a month."

"I think I'd rather buy," Wyte Yak said. "Give me your card, and I'll meet you in a few days with the down payment."

Henry handed Wyte Yak his card, and Yak and Prince left the building and headed over to the mall to cop a pair of the latest Timberland before bouncing back to Virginia Beach to meet up with the rest of the "fam."

Back at LA's condo, Deuce was sitting on the couch next to Drizz playing John Madden on the Sega Genesis video game system, while LA, Brock, Rahtiek, Trap, Dikki Jah, and D-Ski were all sitting at LA's dining room table playing blackjack, smoking blunts, and drinking Heinekens. LA was dealing, and the next play was on Trap.

"I feel it, Ant. Hit me," Trap said, holding a six and a seven. Ant turned up eight of spades, and Trap yelled,

"Blackjack! Twenty one!"

Brock who had a queen and a deuce said, "I feel it, too. Hit me." When Ant turned up a ten, Brock turned his cards over and said, "Damn, I'm busted."

"I'm good," Dikki Jah said. He held a queen and an eight and decided to stay.

D-Ski had a nine and a jack and also decided to stay, saying, "Me, too."

Rahtiek had a queen and a king and, all along, planned to stay. "Hmm...should I take another card?" he asked himself, fucking with Ant. "Let me think. Nah, I'm good."

LA had a seven and a four. He hit himself and turned up a three. He hit himself again and turned up a nine then said, "I'm busted." LA paid the winners then continued dealing. Just then the door bell rang, and Deuce walked over to answer the door. It was Wyte Yak and Prince. They both slapped Deuce five as they entered the condo.

"Me and Prince found a spot for the strip club," Wyte Yak said, looking around at everybody. "I'm going to meet with the owner in a couple of days to give him a down payment. So, basically, you can say that's a done deal."

Everybody cheered. He continued, "I also spoke with a construction crew who told me they could have it ready for business in a few weeks. If I like what they do with the club, I'm going to have them build me a crib from the ground up, some ol' fly shit."

"Make sure I got a room in that motherfucker," Drizz said to everyone's amusement.

Wyte Yak then looked over at LA and said, "LA, I need to speak to you in the back for a minute."

As Wyte Yak walked in the bedroom, LA asked,

"Who wanna deal?"

"I'll deal," Brock said.

LA handed Brock the cards and walked into the bedroom to kick it with Wyte Yak. He entered the bedroom and took a seat on the edge of the bed. Wyte Yak closed the door and leaned his back against it.

"What up, cuz?" LA asked.

"Did you see the news last night?"

"Nah, what happen?"

"Some assholes in a blue Acura tried to spray some niggas out Roberts Park and fucked around and killed a old lady and a six-year-old kid," Wyte Yak explained.

"That had to be Keith and them niggas from Bowling Green," LA said, shaking his head. "They got beef with Fat Mike and them niggas from Roberts Park over that 'ho'-ass bitch, Barbara."

"Niggas shooting like that over a bitch?" Wyte Yak asked.

"All over this 'ho'-ass bitch named Barbara, who ain't even worth it. I nutted in that bitch mouth plenty of times and sent her back home to kiss that bitch-ass nigga, Keith."

"That type of bullshit is bad for business," Wyte Yak said, screwing his face. "I need you to bring me that nigga Keith and whomever was in the car with him. We gone make examples out of their asses, cause ain't gone be no more drive-bys out this motherfucker."

"Say no more."

"What y'all got planned for the rest of the day?" Wyte Yak asked.

"Nothing. I was thinking we should head over to the beach to fuck with some bitches," said LA.

"That sounds like a plan. I could use a tan," said

Wyte Yak.

"Nigga, your white ass ain't getting no darker," LA teased.

"You can't call me white. You ain't but a shade darker than me," Wyte Yak said. They both laughed.

Wyte Yak and LA walked back out front to tell the rest of the team they were headed to the beach. They grabbed a few blankets and some towels then walked outside and hopped into their vehicles, stopping at the market to pick up some beer and snacks. They had a lot of fun at the beach, drinking and joking around. They met a group of girls and, while the rest of the crew took most of the women into the water to fool around, Prince was able to convince his honey to go with him under the boardwalk so they could get their freak on.

The lifeguards ran along the beach instructing everyone to get out of the water because of the high tide. The crew got out of the water, but as the lifeguard moved farther down the beach, Wyte Yak and Deuce decided to go back in the water for one last swim. They swam a good distance out then decided to wait for a big wave to ride back to shore.

They jumped into the wave as it came and Deuce rode it back to shore. But Wyte Yak got twisted and wound up farther out into the ocean. Wyte Yak, who was not that great a swimmer, raised his head above the water to see where he was and saw nothing but ocean. He went back under and turned around, but when he came back up still saw nothing but ocean. Just then another huge wave came and twisted him again, and he panicked and lost focus. He kept going under the water and coming up yelling for help but was so far out in the water none of his crew members heard him. Wyte Yak started to think he was ass out of luck and about to drown when suddenly, out of nowhere, a man came floating by on an inflated yellow raft. The man rescued Wyte Yak, allowing him to hold onto the raft, and brought him back to shore.

"You should be able to walk from here," the man said when they reached shallow waters.

The thankful, out-of-breath Wyte Yak said, "Thanks, partner. You saved my life. I have to give you a reward."

"Nah, that's okay. You just be careful out here. Those waves can be dangerous," the man said, paddling back out into the ocean.

Wyte Yak walked up onto the beach and was met by his crew.

"What happen, Yak?" Deuce asked.

"I got twisted in the wave and every time I stuck my head out of the water all I saw was ocean. I panicked and thought I was ass out. The next thing I knew dude came out of nowhere with that raft."

"Where the fuck did he come from? I didn't see nobody on a raft all day," Deuce said.

"That must have been your guardian angel," LA said.

The crew laughed as they headed back over to their blankets. Wyte Yak looked back out into ocean, and the man on the raft, as quickly as he came, was gone.

CHAPTER 6

The following evening Keith and three of his friends got into his Acura Legend outside of his apartment in Bowling Green Projects. Before they could pull off, four BMWs came alongside and surrounded the Acura. LA, D-Ski, Prince, Rahtiek, Deuce, Trap, Dikki Jah, Drizz, and Brock hopped out with guns drawn.

"Get out the car! Y'all niggas coming with us!" LA ordered.

"What for, LA?" Keith asked, petrified. "We don't got no beef with you."

The Career Criminals opened the doors to the Acura and dragged the four men from their car, forcing each one into a different BMW. They blindfolded them and took them to the town house where Wyte Yak was awaiting their arrival. He had clear plastic all over the floor and furniture and two long two by fours lying in the middle of the floor.

The Career Criminals made Keith and his crew lie face down on the floor with their hands extended above their head. They then took the two by fours and laid them across their wrist and ankles. While Dikki Jah, Brock and Drizz stood on the two by four laid across their ankles, D-Ski, Deuce, and Trap stood on the two by four laid across their wrists. Rahtiek and Prince stood up top near their out-stretched hands holding razor-sharp samurai swords.

Wyte Yak who was sitting next to LA on the couch in front of the four men asked, "Y'all like doing drive-bys, killing innocent people, huh?"

"Nah, it wasn't supposed to go down like that," Keith explained. "We was trying to hit Fat Mike and them niggas."

"You got a beef with a nigga and, instead of walking up to him and popping him, you just drive by shooting, not giving a fuck who you hit?"

"It wasn't like that. We didn't mean to hit no innocent bystanders. But drive-bys...that's how we do it down here. Tell him LA."

"I don't know what the fuck you talking about," LA said. "I always step to the nigga I got beef with."
"Motherfucker, this ain't Cali. This is Virginia. We still on the East Coast where you walk up and pop the nigga you beefing with and walk away. We don't shoot kids and old people and nobody else that's not in the game," Wyte Yak said.

"We sorry, man," Keith pleaded. "Please don't kill us. We ain't never gonna do no shit like that again. That's my word."

"We're not going to kill you," Wyte Yak said with a sly grin. "That wouldn't accomplish anything. We gone make examples out of you motherfuckers to make sure nobody else don't do no stupid shit like that again."

Wyte Yak raised his hand. Prince and Rahtiek took the covers from the swords and raised them above their heads. As Wyte Yak dropped his hand, they swung the swords down at the four men's wrists chopping all eight of their hands off. Blood splattered everywhere, and LA had to run over to the entertainment center and blast the system to muffle the screaming and wailing coming from the four men.

The Career Criminals placed their hands in a plastic bag and wrapped the men's wrists with towels. They then drove them back to Bowling Green and tossed them out near their Acura Legend.

What Wyte Yak had done to Keith and his homeboys had him thinking it was time for him to do a good deed. So he called up his little homey Mikey and told him he was coming to pick him up. He took Mikey to the park where they sat at a chess table to play a few games.

They were playing their third game, and Mikey was dominating. Wyte Yak wasn't focused and had already lost two games. He took almost all of Wyte Yak's pawns, his rook, both knights, and both bishops, but Wyte Yak thought he was still in the game because he still had his queen.

"Checkmate!" Mikey yelled. "That's three in a row. What's the matter Wyte Yak? You don't seem focused."

"I wasn't, but I got you the next game," Wyte Yak said, lowering his head.

"I hope so," Mikey said. "You're making it too easy for me."

An ice-cream truck pulled into the park playing the good-humor music, and children rushed over to the truck.

"You want an ice-cream cone?" Wyte Yak asked Mikey.

Mikey nodded his head and said. "Yeah, that'll be swell."

Wyte Yak and Mikey walked over to the ice-cream truck. Mikey ordered a double chocolate cone with sprinkles, and Wyte Yak ordered a double vanilla.   Back at the chess table they started to set the pieces for a new game. "I got your number now, Mikey," Wyte Yak said. "You're not winning any more games!"

"If you say so," said Mikey.

"That's it for you. I'm focused now, watch!"

"You know something, Wyte Yak, your game is a lot different than most."

"How so?"

"I don't know if you noticed, but for some reason you

play a lot better without your queen," Mikey noted.

"You think so?"

"I know so. Most of the games you win I have your queen already captured."

"Now that I think about it, you're right," Wyte Yak agreed, scratching his chin. "Maybe I should just give you my queen from the start."

Wanting to prove to Yak that his game was stronger without his queen Mikey said, "Yeah, let's put our queens aside so you can see how different you play without it."

"Alright."

They both played without their queens for the next three games, and Wyte Yak won all three.

"You see what I mean?" Mikey asked.

"Yeah, but I don't understand. Maybe I play harder once I lose my most valuable piece," Wyte Yak reasoned.

"I'm not sure what it is, but it does seem like you focus better without it."

They put their queens back on the board. This time Wyte Yak barely used his and again he won. He smiled, thinking he found a new strategy. Wyte Yak hung out with Mikey for a few hours then headed back to the town house to check on his crew.

Back in Virginia Beach everybody was busy. The phone was ringing off the hook, and LA was sending different crew members out to meet dealers interested in buying weight.

Drizz was the only one who didn't make any runs. He just stayed in the town house and counted the money the others brought back from their deals. Wyte Yak, noticing that everything was under control, was able to kick his feet up and relax for the rest of the day.

Over in Leavenworth Pooh Berry was in the recreation room knocking out sets on the chin-up bar. As he was finishing his last set, Nicky walked over and sat down at a machine to do leglifts. Pooh got off the chin-up bar and sat down on the weight bench pressing three hundred pounds of steel.

"I just got off of the phone with my dad," Nickie said. "He's really impressed with your brother. He wouldn't stop talking about him."

"Word? What did he say?" Pooh Berry asked, sitting up.

"He said Wyte Yak's moving shit so fast out in Virginia, he was able to double up on his last couple of shipments."

"So my baby brother's out there handling business. I told you he could do it," Pooh said proudly.

"Yeah, man. He's purchasing more coke than anyone else in our organization when my father has people in twenty other states as part of our family for years."

"Wyte Yak's always been like that. Whatever he does, he always strives to be the best. I remember back when we were kids we had started a kool-aid stand, but by the end of the week we were selling chips, cakes, candy bars.... Whatever junk they were selling at the corner store, we had at our stand for a cheaper price."

"So Wyte Yak's always been about business?"

"Pretty much."

"That's a good thing because my father really likes his style. He wishes the rest of the family had heads on their shoulders like Yak."

The two men continued working out, and Pooh Berry's energy level increased as he proudly thought about the way his baby brother was handling business.

The Career Criminal clique was all at the bowling alley with a few of their girlfriends drinking and bowling. It was fall, and everyone, sporting the best 'hood gear available at the time, seemed to be doing real well. They were really shining and having the time of their lives.

LA was in a booth sitting with his arm around his main girl, Angie, whispering in her ear and making her blush. When he looked over at his cousin, Wyte Yak had a calculator and a pad and was writing down numbers.

"Do you ever take a break?" LA asked him. "No matter where we go your mind is always on business. Give it a rest. Have a drink. Bowl a game or two."

"I can't help it, cuz. It's always been about business with me. I have to stay on point. I don't know, maybe I'm a workaholic."

"You gotta live a little," LA advised. "What's the sense of having all this money if you don't take time out to enjoy it?"

"I enjoy making money."

"Nigga, you need a girl. Not none of these chicken heads, but a real woman, somebody to help you unwind and relax."

"You're probably right, but right now I'm focused on this."

Wyte Yak reached in his Gucci tote bag and handed LA a bunch of invitations to a boat ride.

"What's this?" LA asked, looking down at the invitations.

"Those are invitations to the boat ride we're throw-ing. I need you to ride around with a few of the girls and hand them out," Wyte Yak said.

"This say it's on the seventeenth," LA remarked after reading the invitation. "The club opens on the eighteenth. Why would you throw a boat ride the day before we open the club?" he asked.

"The boat ride is exclusive. We're only inviting big willies--no petty hustlers."

"I got you, Mr. Workaholic."

LA looked over at Angie and said, "Baby, we gotta find my cousin a girl. You know anybody you think he'd like?"

"Not off the top of my head," Angie said, "but I could probably come up with somebody."

"What's up with your cousin?" LA asked, snapping his fingers as he tried to remember her cousin's name. "What's her name? Oh yeah, Coretta!"

"I don't think it'll work," Angie said, twisting her lips.

"Well, try to find him somebody. He's driving me crazy with his mind always stuck on business."

"I'll see what I can do," Angie said, smiling.

"You do that," said LA, kissing Angie's lips and nib-bling on her ear.

Wyte Yak continued working, paying no attention to what was going on around him.

A couple of days later LA was riding around with three Mustang 5.0 convertibles filled with strippers handing out flyers to all the major players in Norfolk. He pulled up alongside a white convertible 500SL Mercedes Benz, and Cinnamon, wearing a tight red spandex jumpsuit, hopped out of the car and walked over to the Benz to hand the driver an invite, seductively swaying her hips and showing off her voluptuous body.

"What up, Petey?" LA yelled to the driver. Petey looked over and noticed LA.

"What up, Little Ant?" he asked.

"I'm having a boat ride with a hundred strippers from New York--anything goes--but keep it on the low. Only the elite are invited."

"I got you stick. I'll be there," Petey said smiling.

"And I got you," said Cinnamon, winking and tossing Petey a kiss.

The night of the boat ride Wyte Yak was below deck watching the activities on a monitor. Every major player from the Tidewater section of Virginia appeared to be on the boat. The party was like none other they had ever been to. There were women all over the ship wearing nothing but leather pumps and G-strings, shaking their asses, and rubbing up against the dealers.

Prince and Rahtiek were standing by the steps leading to the lower level. LA, Brock, Deuce, Trap, and D-Ski all walked onto the stage, and the deejay stopped the music. Prince clapped his hands, and all the strippers rushed downstairs to the lower level.

LA grabbed the microphone from the stage and screamed, "Is everybody having a good time?"

The crowd cheered and stomped their feet, letting LA know they were, indeed, having the time of their lives.

"I'm glad to hear that. We aim to please," LA yelled.

"Man, where the bitches go?" Dino, Dazz's brother, asked anxiously.

"Calm down," LA said, looking at Dino. "The honeys will be back in a few minutes. Give me a minute. I have a few issues I want to discuss. First off, I wanna let y'all know that everybody who is somebody in our town is on this boat right now. So I'm sure that everybody here has heard about Keith and his crew from Bowling Green."

"Fuck them stupid-ass niggas! That's what they get!" Petey yelled. "They gone shoot a old lady and a baby. I ain't mad at you. Two of my spots out Roberts Park got raided behind that stupid shit."

"I ain't mad either! They making shit hot over a slutty-ass bitch. I bet every nigga on this ship done fucked that 'ho'," Dazz said.

The crowd laughed, and a voice hollered, "Word Up!"

"So we all agree," LA continued, "that what they did was bad for business." The crowd agreed.

"Well, most of y'all don't know it, but I have a silent partner. And he thinks it's time we got organized."

"Me and my crew already organized," said Sincere, a drug dealer from New York known for his violent nature.

A few of the other dealers said the same.

LA regained control of the crowd, adding, "Everybody is organized to some degree, but I think it's time we get Mafia-type organized. Yeah, we making money right now, but the police can come snatch whoever they want whenever they want. We too open with our shit. It's time to snatch our people off them corners and put them in spots. Get shit from out in the open and stop airing our dirty laundry."

"How the fuck is everybody gone eat off of a spot?" Petey asked.

"Simple, nigga. It's enough money out here for everybody. We can have twenty to thirty spots in each 'hood or a few spots where niggas take shifts, and trust me everybody's gone still eat. It's a lot better than twenty motherfuck-ers on each corner wilding out, causing all kinds of ruckus and scaring the shit out of all the working class people."

"I feel you on that," Dazz agreed. "I'm with it if everybody else down. We would fuck the cops head up if we was organized."

All the other dealers seemed to be in agreement.

"Alright then, cool. I only have one other issue," LA said.

"Come on, man, we with you. Now would you please bring the pussy back?" Dino begged.

"Hold up a minute, nigga. This shit is important! Me and my peoples are going to start putting money together to start opening some legit businesses. We got this one thing in mind that's going to be real big and could use all the help we can get. Y'all know that big old tobacco warehouse off Virginia Beach Boulevard?"

"That shit is big as hell. What the hell y'all trying to do with that?" Petey asked.

"We trying to make that the spot. And when I say the spot I mean the spot. We wanna put a club in there, a bowl-ing alley, a pool hall, a food court, a game room, a roller rink and a movie theater--all in the same building."

"That's gonna take a nice piece of change," Dazz thought.

"It's enough millionaires on this boat right now to make it happen. We doing a lot of dirt. It's only right that we put back if we want to survive the game."

"You've been doing a lot of thinking, Ant. I ain't have any idea you were this smart," Petey said.

"I'm not. I told you I have a silent partner," LA reminded him. All of the strippers below deck looked at

Wyte Yak when LA gave him his props. "You are a smart motherfucker, Wyte Yak," Cinnamon said. "When you gone let me put it on your smart ass?"

"Shiitt," Wyte Yak said, laughing. "You can give me some head right now if you want."

"Don't mind if I do," Cinnamon said, licking her lips. Prince clapped his hands again, and the strippers rushed back upstairs--with the exception of Cinnamon, who kneeled down in front of Yak, unzipped his fly, and started to bless him. The party on deck turned into one big orgy, and by the end of the night the dealers had a new-found respect for LA, nominating him "King of the Streets."

CHAPTER 7

A few days after the Career Criminals and the rest of the big timers had the time of their lives on the boat, Keith, miserable as hell, was at home with his girlfriend, Barbara. He was sitting on the couch with his wrist bandaged and his bottom lip poked out, the same look he had on his face ever since him and his boys were kidnapped and had their hands amputated. His boy Jack walked up to the door and knocked with his elbow.

"Who is it?" Barbara yelled.

"It's me. Jack!"

Barbara opened the door, and Jack walked in and took a seat. Barbara closed the door and sat back down on the couch next to Keith.

"What up, Jack?" Keith asked.

"I know you heard LA got the whole city on some organized shit," Jack said.

"Yeah, I heard. That's fucked up. That motherfucker gone take us out the game then get on some Mafia, Don-type shit. Ain't that a bitch!"

"And he ain't even the Don. He just the front man for that motherfucker, Wyte Yak," Jack fumed.

"That's alright, though, Jack. We gone get them niggas!"

"What the fuck we gone do? We don't even have no hands."

"We still living, right? If there's a will, there's a way. Trust me, they gone get theirs, LA and all them pussy-ass New York niggas he running with."

Barbara cut her eyes at Keith knowing the only thing

he could be thinking about doing was going to the police. Although Keith was her man and she knew it was her fault that he did that shooting in Roberts Park, she liked LA's style and couldn't just sit quiet while her punk-ass man went out like a bitch and ratted on him.

Later that evening Rahtiek and Prince were driving around in Rahtiek's red BMW. They stopped at a light near Young's Park and witnessed two police officers roughing up a Project thug. They had him pinned against a fence.

"Where the fuck is everybody?" the white cop asked.

"I don't know."

The black cop slapped the thug with the back of his hand, saying, "You better tell us something, motherfucker."

Rahtiek and Prince drove up to the next corner, made a right, and pulled over alongside the Projects. Prince hopped out and put a bullet in the chamber of his gun. Then he walked to the corner and let off six shots from his 9mm in the direction of the police. The thug ran off, and the police scrambled behind their patrol car to return fire.

Prince hopped back in the Beemer, and Rahtiek sped off. The police heard the car tires screeching. By the time they reached the corner the Beemer was long gone. The police were pissed. They radioed for back up and, within moments, there were ten patrol cars surrounding Young's Park combing the ground for shells so they could get finger-prints off them.

Rahtiek and Prince hit the highway and headed for Virginia Beach. They were laughing, and the adrenalin was pumping.

"You think you hit something?" Rahtiek asked Prince.

"Nah, I was shooting above their heads. I just want-ed them to stop harassing dude before he cracked and told them what they wanted to know."

Prince picked up the car phone and called Wyte Yak's condo. The phone rang twice then Wyte Yak answered, "Hello."

"Yo, Yak, Po Po still fucking with niggas."

"What happened? Y'all got pulled over?"

"Nah, they fucking with niggas in the 'hood, trying to find out why ain't nobody on the streets."

"Word?" Wyte Yaks asked, his eyes widening.

"Hell, yeah, I just spit at a couple of pigs questioning this kid," Prince said, matter-of-factly.

"That was smart thinking, Prince. I got it from here. Where y'all headed now?"

"We on our way back out to the Beach."

"Alright, cool. I'll see y'all when y'all get here," Wyte Yak said. Wyte Yak hung up the phone and turned to Little Ant who was sitting beside him on the couch.

"I think it's time you had a talk with the chief of police," Wyte Yak suggested.

"Say no more! I think I got his number in my wallet. I had Cinnamon put it on him one night--just for security reasons. She got him open. He be calling her all the time trying to make a date," LA said.

He reached in his back pocket and pulled out his wallet, thumbing through it until he found the chief's number. He grabbed the telephone and dialed the chief.

"Hello, Chief Kobe speaking."

"Hello, Chief. This is Anthony Higgins. I hope you don't mind, but I got your number from a mutual friend. I understand that you're running for mayor, and I was wondering if we could meet tomorrow night around 7:00 p.m. at Shoney's, off Virginia Beach Boulevard, to discuss me, maybe, making a campaign contribution."

The mere mention of a contribution got the chief excited.

"Seven's a good time for me," he said. "I'll be there."

"Cool, I'll be the guy in the back wearing the blue Dodgers cap."

"The meet is set," LA said to Wyte Yak after hanging up.

"Cool. You know what to do. Handle that," Wyte Yak said.

"I got you," LA said.

The next evening LA was sitting at a table in the back of Shoney's Restaurant off Virginia Beach Boulevard sipping on a Pepsi and waiting on the chief. LA himself wore a blue Dodgers baseball cap, a blue silk shirt, a pair of blue Tommy Hilfiger khakis, and a pair of Kenneth Cole casual shoes.

Brock, Trap and Deuce were three tables in front of LA eating dinner. The Chief of Police entered the restaurant wearing a checkered brown sports jacket, a blue button-down shirt, and a pair of black slacks. He walked over to the table where LA was sitting.

LA stood to greet him, "How you doing, Chief? I'm Anthony Higgins."

"It's a pleasure to meet you, Mr. Higgins."

The men shook hands and sat down, and a waitress came over to take their order.

"Are you gentlemen ready to order?" she asked.

"I'll have the steak dinner with collard greens and mashed potatoes and gravy as my sides," ordered LA.

"And you, sir?"

"I'll just have a coffee...black with two sugars."

"First off Chief," LA said, "I would like to say that I

personally believe that you would make a great mayor and that you definitely have my vote."

"Thank you, Mr. Higgins," the chief said.

"On the other hand, I have to let you know that I work hard for my money so I have to make sure that I'm backing the right man for the job," LA said.

"I believe my reputation speaks for itself," the chief said, tugging his collar.

"Don't get me wrong, I do know who you are, but I need to know if you're willing to play ball and if we can play on the same team."

"That all depends."

"On what?"

"On how much of a contribution you're willing to make," the chief pointed out.

The waitress returned with a cup of coffee for the chief and said to LA, "I'll be back with your meal shortly," before walking off.

The Chief took a sip of the coffee as LA continued, "I guess I could contribute somewhere around twenty thousand a week or about eighty thousand a month."

The Chief choked, and his eyes almost popped out of its socket as he asked, "Did you say eighty thousand a month?"

"Yes, I did. Is that not enough?"

Trying to maintain his composure the chief said, "That's a generous contribution. I could do a lot of promoting with that kind of money. So tell me, what's in it for you?"

"I'm going to need you to calm down the police in this city," LA demanded.

"I don't understand," said the chief, fumbling around

in his chair.

"Did you notice that there hasn't been any drug dealers lingering in the streets these last few weeks?" LA asked.

"It has been a little quiet lately," said the chief.

LA stared the chief directly in his eyes and said, "Well, let's just say, I had a talk with a few of the dealers and told them, 'if they pulled the drugs off the streets the police would let up a little.' It didn't work out that way, though. It seems that the police are still busting chops. I was hoping you could have a little talk with them, you know...a favor for a favor."

"I think that could be arranged," the chief said, smiling.

"You know, with all the dealers being off the streets, the tax-paying citizens would feel a lot more comfortable, the elders would be a lot less afraid, and the children could play safely. You could take all the credit for that. It's sure to get you a lot of good press."

The chief nodded his head in agreement and said, "I like the way you think, Mr. Higgins."

"Just to show you my good nature," LA said, pulling a large manila envelope from beneath the table and handing it to Chief Kobe, "I'm going to bless you with a cool fifty grand for starters."

The chief peeked in the envelope then said,
"Thanks for the contribution. You can consider that business with the police handled."

The chief stood to shake LA's hand and quickly exited the restaurant.

"It's a done deal," LA said to Brock, Trap, and Deuce as they turned around to look at him.

LA's food arrived, and the four men finished their meal before heading back out to Wyte Yak's condo to let him know that the meeting was a success.

The same night two drug enforcement agents Kessler and Johnson were sitting in their car on Princess Ann Road waiting to meet with an informant who said he had some information for them. Agent Kessler saw the informant coming, stepped out of the car, and held open the door for Keith, who hopped in the back seat. Agent Kessler then closed the door behind Keith and sat in the front passenger seat.

"Drive off. I can't afford to have anybody see me talking to y'all," Keith said nervously.

"What's so important that you couldn't speak to the regular police?" Agent Kessler asked after his partner drove off.

"I'm about to put y'all up on some big-time drug dealers. I couldn't tell the regular police because they probably have some of them on their payroll. These motherfuckers selling damn-near all the weight in Norfolk. They gotta be making at least a million dollars a day."

"A million dollars a day and we're not already on them. I seriously doubt that," said Agent Johnson.

"I kid you not. They're making a million a day-- every day, except Sundays," Keith whined.

"Every day except Sunday? Why not Sunday?" Agent Johnson asked with a look of disbelief on his face.

"I don't know. Maybe it's for religious reasons. All I know is they don't sell shit on Sundays. Everybody buys their weight from them. Their prices are better than New York, and the product is killer. Ain't no reason for nobody to leave the city. If you look around you'd notice ain't no dealers on the street. They did that. They got the whole city on some organized shit," Keith told the agents

"So who is this 'they' you keep referring to?" Agent Kessler asked.

"Little Ant and his crew from New York. They call themselves Career Criminals," Keith snitched.

"Little Ant?" asked Agent Johnson.

"Yeah, his real name is Anthony Higgins. His mother lives at 2636 Princess Ann Rd. Everybody thinks he's the man, but he's really just the front man. The real man behind their crew is this cat from New York named Wyte Yak. He's the one that had my crew's hands cut off."

"Why did he do that?" asked Agent Johnson, concerned.

"He was tripping," explained Keith.

"Talking about he don't want us hustling in the 'hood. He fucked us all up. Now we can't hustle nowhere. We can't even get jobs. How are we supposed to make a living?"

Agent Kessler looked back at Keith's hands and said, "That's torture. We can put him away for life on that alone."

"Nah, forget about that. I'm not pressing charges. Y'all gone have to knock them on something else. Where am I gonna live if everybody know I went to the police?"

"Alright, then, what else do you have on this Wyte Yak character?" Agent Johnson asked, thinking that probably wasn't the real reason he and his crew's hands were cut off. "Where does he live? What girls do he mess with? We need something to go on. We know of Anthony Higgins, but we never heard of anyone named Wyte Yak."

"I don't know where he stay, and he don't be fucking with none of these chicken heads. He's smart. My girl told me a lot of girls out here been trying to get with him, but he's looking for a good girl...somebody with her shit together.

That's all I got for y'all right now. So y'all can just let me out right here."

Agent Johnson pulled the car over, and Agent Kessler said, "We'll look into this. See what we can come up with. We'll be in touch if we need you."

"Yeah, alright," said Keith, looking around to make sure nobody was around to see him stepping out of the agents' car.

Agent Kessler hopped out of the front seat and opened the door for Keith, who quickly walked back into Bowling Green Projects, and the two agents drove off.

"So what do you think, Johnson?" Kessler looked over at his partner and asked.

"I think we should look into it."

"I agree," said Kessler, nodding his head. "This Wyte Yak character sounds like a real mobster. He must be connected."

"This Wyte Yak character sounds too good to be true, if you ask me. But if Keith is telling the truth, he definitely has his shit together. It's going to be pretty hard to get close to him," Agent Johnson said.

"Maybe not," Agent Kessler said as he paused and scratched his chin. "Keith did say he was looking for a good girl, one that had her shit together. I think I may have just the diva in mind."

"Who?" Johnson asked, with a blank look.

"You remember Mrs. Coretta Wiggins?" asked Kessler.

"How could I not? That's one fine sistah if I ever saw one," Agent Johnson said smiling. "It's a shame what happened to her little sister. You don't think she'd be willing to help us out, do you?"

"I'm not sure," answered Kessler, "but if Wyte Yak is

the man Keith says he is, it's worth a try."

"One thing is puzzling me, though," Agent Johnson said, breaking the momentary silence.

"What's that?" asked Kessler.

"I wonder what's the real reason Wyte Yak cut Keith and his crew's hands off. I'm sure there's something he doesn't want us to know about."

"I don't know. Maybe Keith and his crew didn't want to get down with the organization," theorized Kessler.

"Nah, I think it's deeper than that, much deeper. Something Keith couldn't tell us," Johnson said.

Agent Johnson had a puzzled look on his face as the two agents drove back to their office to see what they could dig up on Wyte Yak.

While Keith was in the agents' car snitching on the Career Criminals his girl Barbara was in Little Ant's car sucking him off. LA was laid back in the driver's seat while Barbara sat in the passenger seat with her face in his lap giving him head. As LA climaxed he held the back of her head until his nut was fully released. Barbara then opened the door, spit the cum out and wiped her mouth with her hand.

LA zipped his pants, raised his seat to an upright position, and started the car. "Damn, Barbara!" he raved as he pulled out of the parking spot and drove out onto the street, "you always do a nigga right."

"You know you my nigga, Ant," Barbara said.

"Yeah, I know how we do. But what's up with your boy, Keith? He still sitting around the house with his lip poked out?" LA asked, pouting mockingly.

"You stupid. I don't give a fuck about that clown, but at the same time you need to watch that nigga," Barbara warned.

"That nigga ain't even got no hands," LA laughed. "What the fuck I need to watch him for?"

"Don't sleep. Him and Jack was talking about getting back at y'all. I don't know what he meant, but he said, 'if there's a will, there's a way.' You know he's a grimy nigga. Ain't no telling what he's up to."

"I hear you," LA said, his smile turning upside down. "Good looking out."

LA dropped Barbara off in Bowling Green Projects and headed back to Virginia Beach. On the way home the words, 'if there's a will, there's a way,' kept repeating itself over and over in his head.

CHAPTER 8

After being up all night trying to figure out what they could come up with on Wyte Yak and coming up blank, Agents Kessler and Johnson decided to go and pay Mrs. Coretta Wiggins a visit to see if they could convince her to help them. They left the FBI offices and headed down to Coretta's office for a surprise visit.

It was 10:25 a.m., and Coretta Wiggins was sitting in her office behind her desk talking on the phone with a client. Once she was finished with the client she hung up the telephone and answered the intercom.

"What is it, Karen?" she asked.

"Two gentlemen are waiting to see you," Karen said.

"Send them in."

The agents entered the office, and Coretta was surprised to see them as she raised from her chair to greet them. She sat behind her desk while the agents sat in the two chairs in front of her desk.

"How are you Mrs. Wiggins?" asked Agent Kessler.

"I'm fine," Coretta answered.

"Yes, you are!" Agent Johnson said with a big smile that made Coretta blush. "How's Tina?"

"Her doctor said it'll be a miracle if she ever fully recovers, but she is doing a lot better."

"We're happy to hear that she's doing better," said Agent Kessler.

"Thank you," Coretta said, leaning back in her chair. "Now I know you didn't come all the way out here to ask me about my sister. So what's really going on?"

"Well, remember you told us you would do anything

in your power to bring to justice the man responsible for what happened to your sister?" asked Agent Johnson.

"Yeah, I remember and I'm still willing to help," she said.

Agent Kessler leaned forward and said, "Well, I think we may have a lead on him. Only, we can't get close to him."

"Do you know Anthony Higgins from Princess Ann Road?" asked Agent Johnson.

"Yeah, I know Little Ant. My cousin Angie be messing with that fool. She tried to get me to go out with her, him, and his cousin. Don't tell me he had something to do with what happened to my sister," Coretta said.

Agent Kessler cleared his throat then said, "We're not saying he actually gave her the drugs, but word on the street is that he and his partner, Wyte Yak, have been supplying eighty-five percent of the drugs in Norfolk."

"So we're pretty sure that the drugs Tina was given came from these guys," said Agent Johnson, "and we were wondering if you would like to help us take them down."

"Did you say Wyte Yak?" Coretta asked.

"Yeah, that's Little Ant's partner," Agent Johnson confirmed.

"That's also the cousin Angie's been trying to hook me up with, knowing I do not date drug dealers. But if it was his drugs that messed my sister up, maybe I should go out with him to see what I could find out."

"That's exactly what we need you to do," Agent Kessler said.

"Okay," Coretta schemed, "then I'll call Angie and have her set up a date."

"You do that and let us know how it turns out," said

Agent Kessler.

Agent Kessler handed Coretta his card, and he and his partner left her office.

Coretta called her cousin and told her that she saw Wyte Yak with LA and found him attractive. Not wanting to let Angie know what she was up to, she then told her cousin to set up a double date so she could meet him.

Two hours later Wyte Yak and LA were sitting in Foot Locker in the mall trying on boots. Wyte Yak posed in a pair of beige construction Tims asking LA, "How these look, son?"

"They look alright."

"I'll take these," Wyte Yak said to the sales woman. "I would also like to you to bring me a pair of Black Chuckers and a pair of blue on white Harlems."

Not knowing what he meant, the sales woman asked, "Harlems?"

"Yeah, Harlems, Flavors, Air Force Ones--whatever y'all call them down here."

The sales woman walked in the back to retrieve the shoes and Yak asked LA, "So what did you get into last night?"

"I was hanging out with your boy Keith's girl last night. She blew me something decent," LA boasted.

"You better leave that fool girl alone," Wyte Yak advised. "You know he luv her."

They both laughed then LA suddenly became serious. "She told me that nigga scheming."

"What the fuck he gone do?" asked Wyte Yak.

"He ain't got no hands."

"I know, but he got a mouth.

"If he was gone tell he would already said something by now," Wyte Yak said, looking at LA. "He know we know he killed that old lady and little boy."

"Yeah, but he might wanna tell something else, you know. Put the Feds on us or something. We did take him and his crew out the game," LA reminded Wyte Yak.

Wyte Yak rested his foot on the stool in front of him and said, "I don't think he's that stupid, but you never know....Better safe than sorry."

"That's what I'm saying."

The sales woman returned with the footwear Wyte Yak requested and handed him the boxes. Wyte Yak took them out of the box and tried them on.

Just then LA's cell phone rang.

"Hello," he answered. It was his girl, Angie.

"Hey, baby, how you doing?" she asked.

"What up, boo?"

"What you doing?"

"I'm in Foot Locker in the mall with Wyte Yak."

Angie was in her house sitting on the couch and polishing her toe nails.

"What's up with Wyte Yak? Is he messing with somebody yet?" she asked, being nosy.

"Not that I know of."

"Good...because my cousin Coretta wanna meet him."

"Who? Stuck-up-ass, 'I-don't-mess-with-drug dealers' Coretta?" LA growled.

"Yeah. I think she seen you with him the other day.

Now all of a sudden she wanna meet him."

"Hold on."

LA held the phone to his chest, turned to Wyte Yak, and said. "Yak, Angie's cousin wanna meet you."

"As long as she ain't no chicken head," Wyte Yak answered.

"Nah, her cousin ain't nothing like her. Coretta's a diva, definitely a class act, the type of woman you need."

"Alright then, I'm with it."

"He with it," said LA, raising the phone back up to his mouth. "I'll hit you up later so we can link up."

"Alright then, I'll see you later," LA said to Angie.

"You gone like Coretta," LA turned to Wyte Yak and said. "That bitch is a dime. I'd love to get with Coretta. I'd make her my wifey and kick all them other chicken heads to the curb."

"Then why don't you holla at her?" asked Wyte Yak.

"She don't want me; she want you."

Wyte Yak had finished trying on shoes. He took the two pair of boots, a pair of Air Force Ones, and a few baseball caps and left the mall.

Later that night Prince and Rahtiek pulled up in Rahtiek's red BMW in front of Keith's apartment. Barbara watched them as they approached the apartment from the window and walked over and opened the door to let them in. Rahtiek handed her a mitt of money, and she grabbed her purse and jacket and left the apartment.

They walked to the bedroom where Keith was sitting up in bed watching TV. He was totally taken by surprise as the men entered the room. Rahtiek shot him in the chest with a tranquilizer gun, putting him to sleep. Prince picked him up, tossed him across his shoulder, and walked out of the apartment and over to the car, dumping him in the trunk.

They drove out to Suffolk, where they entered some woods pulling up next to a huge, six-foot-deep hole they had dug earlier. They hopped out of the car, popped the trunk, and Prince took Keith out of the trunk and tossed him into the hole.

Rahtiek grabbed two shovels from out of the trunk and handed Prince one. They then began shoveling dirt into the hole. As the dirt smacked against Keith's body he woke up and tried to climb out of the hole. Rahtiek shot him again with the tranquilizer gun, and he fell back to sleep. After filling the hole with dirt, Prince sprinkled some grass seeds on top, and he and Rahtiek then jumped back into the Beemer and drove off.

Over in Norfolk, Coretta and Angie were sitting at a table in Red Lobster waiting on LA and Wyte Yak. Before long they arrived at the restaurant and walked over to the girls' table. LA sat down next to Angie and gave her a kiss.

"What up, Coretta? How you doing?" LA asked her.

"I'm fine and yourself?" she greeted him.

"I can't complain. This is my cousin, Wyte Yak," LA said, making the introduction.

Wyte Yak shook Coretta's hand, and their eyes locked. They both seemed impressed with each other: he by her looks; and she by his looks and mannerism. "It's a pleasure to meet you," Wyte Yak said.

"Likewise," Coretta said, as Wyte Yak sat down next to her.

"Did y'all order already?" LA asked Angie.

"Only a couple of daiquiris," Angie explained.

"We were waiting on you guys."

"Coretta, did anyone tell you how beautiful you are

today?" Wyte Yak asked.

Coretta blushed and cleared her throat, saying, "No. I don't think anyone has."

"Then allow me to be the first," said Wyte Yak. "You are very beautiful. I also would like to thank you on behalf of the manager of this establishment for brightening up the place."

"Thank you, Wyte Yak. What a nice thing to say!"

"I told you he was on a whole other level," said Angie, looking over at Coretta.

"Get off his nuts!" LA said to Angie.

"He's definitely not like this one," Angie said, motioning her head towards LA.

The waitress approached the table. "Good evening. My name is Darlene. I'll be your waitress for the evening. Would anyone like something to drink?" she asked

"Bring the ladies another round of daiquiris, and I'll have a Heineken," said Wyte Yak.

"I'd like a forty of Olde English," LA said.

Coretta and Wyte Yak chatted while waiting for the food. She completely forgot about her mission and found Wyte Yak was all her cousin said he was and more.

After dinner LA and Angie walked out of the restaurant hugged up, followed by Wyte Yak and Coretta. LA looked over his shoulder at Wyte Yak and said, "I'll catch up with you later, cuz. I'm going with Angie back to her crib."

"Alright chill," Wyte Yak said.

"I really had a nice time tonight, Wyte Yak," Coretta said to him as he walked her to her car.

"I enjoyed myself also and I was hoping we could get together again some time," Wyte Yak said, gazing into her eyes.

"I'd like that."

"How about tomorrow?" asked Wyte Yak. "We could catch a movie."

"I don't think tomorrow would be good for me. I'm supposed to spend some time with my little sister," Coretta said.

"How old is she?"

"She's twelve."

"I have a little homey around her age. We could all hang out," Wyte Yak suggested.

"I don't know," she said as they reached her car. "My sister isn't mentally stable right now."

"That's alright. My little homey has Down's syndrome," Wyte Yak pleaded. "Come on, it'll be fun."

"Alright, call me tomorrow afternoon, and we'll see," she said, hugging Wyte Yak.

Coretta got in her 190 Benz, and Wyte Yak hopped in his green 740IL BMW as they waved each other good-bye and drove off.

Three hours earlier Trap, Deuce, Third, and Drizz were lounging in the town house. Drizz wanted to go down the street to the bar to have a drink, but nobody wanted to take him. Brock, figuring the bar was only about a mile away, gave Drizz the keys to his gray BMW.

Drizz went to the bar and got smashed. He came out of the bar and hopped in the Beemer, headed for the town house. Wobbling from side to side, he couldn't keep the car straight, and a police car pulled him over. The officer walked over to Drizz and flashed his light in the BMW.

"What did I do?" Drizz asked the officer.

"License and registration, please."

"I don't got no license and I don't know where the hell the registration is," Drizz offered.

Smelling the alcohol on Drizz's breath, the officer asked, "Were you drinking tonight, sir?"

"I might have had a drink or two, but I ain't drunk."

"It's obvious that you had too much to drink," the officer said shaking his head. "Step out of the vehicle, sir."

Drizz stepped out of the vehicle, and the officer cuffed him after a routine search.

"I didn't even do nothing," Drizz complained. "What's this all about?"

"I'm placing you under arrest for DWI," the officer stated.

"DWI? What the fuck hell is that?"

"Driving while intocicated!"

"I'm not drunk," Drizz said, as the officer took him to the back of his squad car and placed him in the back seat.

The officer radioed in for a tow truck to pick up the BMW before taking Drizz downtown to the precinct.

Wyte Yak was driving down the highway feeling good about the date he just had with Coretta when his car phone started ringing.

"Hello," Wyte Yak said.

"Yo, Yak, I'm in jail." It was Drizz's voice on the other end. "They got me on a drunk driving charge. My bail's a thousand dollars."

Wyte Yak's good mood was gone. He was furious.

"What are you doing driving?"

"I wanted to go to the bar and nobody didn't want to

take me. So I drove myself.

"Whose car were you driving?"

"Brock's."

"So where's the car?"

"They impounded it. You coming to get me or what?" he asked, sounding aggravated by all of the questions.

"You bugging, Drizz. I'm not coming to get you. I'll call the crib and tell one of them niggas to come get you," Wyte Yak said.

"Alright."

Wyte Yak hung up the phone and shook his head in disgust. When he arrived at the town house ten minutes later, Trap, Deuce, and Brock were freshening up, about to go to the club.

"Where y'all going?" Wyte Yak asked.

"We about to hit the club," said Trap, putting on his brown leather, Kenneth Cole, fall jacket.

"That nigga, Drizz, is down at the jailhouse. He got caught driving drunk. His bail is a G. I'ma need y'all to go down there and bail him out," Wyte Yak said.

"Alright, we'll pick him up on the way to the club," said Deuce.

"Nah, bring that nigga back here first. He's gotta go. We too big for that petty shit. I can't afford to have no fuck-ups around me," WyteYak said sternly.

"Chill, Yak. Give him another chance. Y'all like brothers," said Trap.

"What the fuck! Y'all niggas think this is a game? We gotta be on point twenty-four seven. Y'all know y'all wasn't even supposed to let that nigga drive by himself to no bar. How that look, a drunk nigga driving a seventy-five-thousand-dollar car?"

"You right, Yak," Deuce said.

"I know I'm right. So drop that nigga back off here before y'all go anywhere," Wyte Yak ordered.

"We got you," Brock said. "Where did Drizz say my car was?"

"At the impound."

Brock shook his head in disgust as the three men walked out of the town house. Just then the telephone rang. Wyte Yak walked into the living room and picked up the receiver.

"That dirt is buried," Prince said and hung up. Wyte Yak walked upstairs to the master bedroom and fell back onto the bed and closed his eyes. Two hours later Drizz was at the foot of the bed tapping him.

"Yak, wake up," he said.

Wyte Yak opened his eyes.

"What up, Drizz?"

"They said you wanted to talk to me," Drizz said, looking like a sad puppy.

"Yeah, Drizz, I hate to do it, but you gotta go. I'm gonna set you out with some cash and all, but I can't afford to have you around."

"How you sound, Yak?" Drizz protested. "We brothers!"

"Yeah, I know, but your drinking is a bigger problem than you're aware of," Wyte Yak noted.

"I can stop anytime I want to," Drizz said, like a true blue alcoholic.

"Don't you think you should have wanted to stop by now?" Wyte Yak asked. "We were all alcoholics growing up, but you the only one who still drink like that."

"So that's how you gone treat me after all we been

through?" Drizz said, twisting his lips.

"Cut it out," Wyte Yak said, his face screwed. "Stop being selfish and look at the big picture. Nigga, you my brother from a different mother. We closer than anybody else in the crew, but I'm not going back to jail for nobody. So until you get your shit together and cut out all the drinking, you're not going to be around me. I love you and the whole nine, but I love me more.

"I hear you, Yak," Drizz said, feeling embarrassed. "I just like to drink but, if you feel like I might fuck something up, I'll leave. Ain't no love lost. We always gone be brothers."

Yak stood, and they slapped each other five and hugged.

CHAPTER 9

The next afternoon Wyte Yak, Coretta and her sister Tina, and little Mikey all went to the movies to check the latest Disney movie. After the movie they stopped off at Wendy's to have lunch then took the kids to the park as it was a pretty warm fall day. Wyte Yak and Coretta sat on the bench conversing while Tina and Mikey ran around playing.

"Look at Tina," Coretta said. "She's having a ball. I haven't seen her this happy in a while. She and Mikey seem to be getting along well."

"Mikey's a good kid," Wyte Yak added. "I knew she'd like him."

"Who is Mikey? Where did he come from?" Coretta asked.

"Honestly, he's just a kid I met on a plane. He beat me at a couple of games of chess, and I took a liking to him. Ever since that, we've been hanging out every other week."

"Has Little Ant met Mikey?"

"Nah, he doesn't know about him. Nobody does. You're the first person I ever brought around Mikey," Wyte Yak confessed.

"Why me?"

"Because Mikey's special, and I think you might turn out be pretty special yourself," Wyte Yak said, gazing into Coretta's eyes.

"You think so?" Coretta asked with a big smile.
"I hope so, but you never know. You might turn out to be a chicken head in disguise."

Coretta laughed and punched Wyte Yak in the arm. "Shut up," she said.

They continued conversing on the bench while they

watched Mikey and Tina run around and enjoy each other's company. Coretta really started to like Wyte Yak, forgetting all about the reason she decided to go out with him in the first place.

Everything was going good for the Career Criminals down in Norfolk. They were the most respected clique, and whenever they hung out the honeys would surround them like they were stars. The other dealers didn't hate on them because they were cool and actually protected them from the stickup kids. Robberies in Norfolk had pretty much been put to a halt until Tommy and Red from Diggs Park started hitting spots. They stuck up a few of Dazz's and Petey's spots and were planning on hitting a few of the other dealers' spots until Petey called LA to put them in check.

Dazz and his bodyguard, Jabba, were over at Petey's house discussing Tommy and Red. Uptight about being robbed, they were trying to remain calm about the situation and had not yet made a move on them out of respect for the Career Criminals. But they were growing impatient as they sat around in Petey's living room waiting for LA to arrive.

"One way or another," Petey said, "this shit is gone to stop. These motherfuckers ain't gone keep robbing my spots."

"That's what I'm saying. I'm ready to have Jabba split their fucking wigs," Dazz added, gritting his teeth.

The door bell rang, and Petey walked over to open the door. LA walked in, slapped everybody five, and sat down on the couch.

"What's up?" LA asked.

"Yo, Ant, these stickup niggas out here bugging,"

Dazz said.

"What stickup niggas? Who you talking about?"

"I'm talking about them niggas, Tommy and Red, from out Diggs Park. They stuck up three of my spots yesterday," Dazz complained.

"They robbed two of mines the day before," Petey added, shaking his head. "They pistol-whipped my boy, Dee, and knocked out three of his teeth. I can't stand for that. I'm ready to tear them niggas out the frame."

"Them niggas tripping," LA said, alarmed.

"I was about to have Jabba run through there and blow their fucking heads off. The only reason they still breathing is because you got us in chill mode," Petey said.

LA looked up at Jabba, who was standing with his arms folded holding two .44 Magnums, one in each hand, and said, "Y'all niggas just chill. I got this."

"How much they took?" LA asked.

"They took about thirteen thousand in drugs and money from my spot." Dazz moaned.

"They took close to nine from me," added Petey.

"Alright, cool. The next time y'all holla at me I'll toss you a extra half, Dazz, and give you a extra quarter, Petey. That way the loss ain't on y'all; it's on me," LA assured them.

"Fuck that, Ant!" Jabba interrupted. "Just let me do what I do best."

"Nah, chill, Jabba. I got this. Let me handle it," LA said.

"Then let me come with you," Jabba said.

"No, Jabba. Just chill with your boy, Dazz. I'll take care of these cowards my way," LA schemed.

"Yeah, alright, but call Dazz if you need me," said

Jabba.

"Alright, my nigga," LA agreed.

LA then slapped the three men five and walked out the door. The next day the Career Criminals were driving around in four of their BMWs searching for Tommy and Red. They spotted them in line at a Hardies' drive-through sitting in Red's black convertible BMW325.

LA hopped out of his vehicle and instructed the rest off his crew to go around the back. He walked over and jumped in the back seat of Red's Beemer and tossed a mitt of money to the guys up front. He then started taking off his jewelry and tossing it up front.

"What the fuck you doing, LA?" Tommy asked, surprised by LA's actions. LA screwed his face at them. "I heard y'all out here robbing my peoples' spots. Y'all robbing them; y'all might as well be robbing me."

"Nah, nigga, you know it ain't even like that. We ain't even know they was fucking with you like that," Red said.

"Y'all know niggas showed me respect and cut all that bullshit out so we could eat in peace. From where I'm sitting it looks like y'all trying to start some shit up."

Tommy and Red started handing LA his money and jewelry back. He put his money in his pocket and put his jewelry back on as Tommy started copping a plea. "Nah, stick man, we ain't trying to have no problems with you. We still got most of the shit we took. If it's like that we'll just give it back."

"Nah, nigga, y'all took it so y'all earned it," LA said, handing Tommy his card. "But what y'all need to do is come see me for a brick and open up y'all own spot. Get off that robbery shit because I ain't having that in my town."

"Alright, dog, I feel you," said Tommy. "We gone holla."

"Alright then, y'all niggas enjoy the rest of the day," LA said.

LA jumped out of their vehicle, and the Career Criminals pulled up back to back in their Beemers. LA hopped back in the passenger seat of his yellow BMW, and they drove off.

Tommy and Red watched the four BMWs pull off. They knew that the Career Criminals could've killed them right then and there. So the next day they brought LA everything they took, and he fronted them a ki' so they could open their own spot and get on their feet. From that day on they started making their own money and retired from the stick-up game.

The Career Criminals just wanted to make an example of what could happen to stickup kids. But Wyte Yak had informed his crew that they should only kill in self-defense or a member of the crew was harmed.

There were other thugs scheming on sticking up spots but, after the way LA handled the situation with Tommy and Red, they figured it would be easier to just contact LA and ask him to put them up.

LA helped out every thug who came to him, never turning down a soul. He fronted them weight, and they all paid what they owed and started buying weight from him-except Fizz and Flip, two known stick-up kids who used heroin. LA fronted them some weight, and they fucked up his money, going around bragging that they weren't going to pay him shit.

One night the Career Criminals caught them in

Casablanca, a bar just off Princess Ann Road. They stripped them butt naked, taking their clothes and setting them on the doormat with a note saying "SAY NO TO DRUGS," tossed them into the trunk of one of their BMWs, and drove them down to a huge cornfield in North Carolina. They broke their arms and legs with baseball bats and with a straight razor carved the same words into their chests. The Career Criminals then told them they were barred from Virginia. Everybody in Norfolk assumed they were dead, and nobody else ever took LA's kindness for weakness.

After spending the day with Wyte Yak and the kids, Coretta was lying in her bed thinking about the date she had earlier. She had never met a man like him and was definitely looking forward to seeing him again. Then the phone rang. "Hello," she answered.

"What up, cuz? What you doing? Angie asked.

"Nothing, I'm just laying in the bed, relaxing."

"So how was your date with Wyte Yak?"

"I really enjoyed it. Tina had fun, too."

"She did?"

"Yeah, Wyte Yak brung his little homey, Mikey."

"Mikey? Who's he?"

"Don't tell Anthony, but Wyte Yak has this little white friend of his that has Down's syndrome. He and Tina got along real good."

"So what did y'all do?"

"First we took the kids to the movies to see "Snow White." Then we stopped off over at Wendy's to get some lunch and spent the rest of the afternoon in the park. We sat on the bench talking while Tina and Mikey ran around playing" Coretta told her.

"So when y'all going out again--just the two of you-so y'all can get y'all groove on."

"I don't know yet. He said he was gonna call me later on tonight. I can't wait," Coretta said eagerly.

"Listen to you. You all open," Angie teased.

"To tell you the truth if I was like you I'd call him over right now and put it on him."

"That's definitely what I'd do," Angie said as she nodded in agreement.

"Yeah, but you know me, I'm a lady. I have to wait and let him make the first move."

"Girl, you better get you some. You know you ain't had no dick in almost two years," Angie reminded her.

"Don't remind me."

Coretta's other line buzzed. "Hold on, girl," she said. "Somebody's on my other line."

"It's probably Wyte Yak."

"I hope so," she said and clicked over to the other line. "Hello."

"Hello, Mrs. Wiggins. How are you doing?" the caller asked. Coretta's mouth dropped as she recognized the voice on the other end and remembered why she even went out with Wyte Yak in the first place.

"Mrs. Wiggins, is there something wrong?"

"Oh, I'm sorry Agent Kessler," Coretta said, coming back to her senses. "I was expecting someone else. Could you hold on a minute I have someone on my other line?"

"Yeah, sure."

Coretta clicked back over to Angie and said, "Angie,

I'm going to have to call you back."

"Is it Wyte Yak?"

"No, just some business I have to handle."

"Alright then. Call me back."

"Alright, bye."

Coretta switched back over to Agent Kessler. "Hello, Kessler."

"Yeah, I'm just calling to see if you met up with Wyte Yak."

"Yeah, I met up with him. We went out to eat last night and we went to the movies earlier today."

"So what's up with him? What is he like?" Kessler asked.

"Actually he's really quite charming."

"Hold on now. You're not falling for this guy, are you? You know he's a drug dealer," Kessler reminded her.

"He sure don't act like one," Coretta came back.

"That's just what he's doing, putting on an act. Don't fall for it. Stay focused."

"I got you."

"Remember, he's the enemy."

"Okay, I got you," Coretta said, getting agitated. "I have to go now. Good-bye."

Coretta hung up the phone and buried her face in her hands, saying to herself, "What am I doing? Wyte Yak's a drug dealer. I hate drug dealers. I can't be falling for him. Am I? Nah, he's just another smooth talking dealer. I have to stay focused and complete my mission. Put a stop to Mr.Wyte Yak before his drugs mess up some other kid's life. I told the Agents I would help them, and that's just what I'm going to do. But he did make a damn good impression. I guess all work and no play have made me a very lonely girl.

Damn! I'm so confused I don't know what to do."

Wyte Yak had the construction crew that hooked up his strip club build him a minimansion on the beachfront. Two huge fountains on each side of the path led to the beautiful house with nine bedrooms, each with its own bathroom. The bedrooms had thick plush carpet to match the color of the room. The bathrooms all had marble floors, marble sinks, and bathtubs and showers with 24kt gold faucets.

The living room had a 20-foot high ceiling with a huge chandelier. There was a game room with a pool table and video and computer games hooked up to a huge 60" screen TV. The indoor pool led to the outdoor pool. The library had a bookshelf which doubled as a secret passage way leading to an escape route--in case he ever needed one.

Almost everything inside and outside of the house worked by remote control, from the monitors, the TV, the blinds, and even the automatic weapons installed above the windows to protect himself from intruders that somehow managed to get past the front gate. Surrounding the house was a twelve-foot concrete wall topped off with barb wire.

Wyte Yak called Coretta up and invited her over to check out his new home. Her mouth hung from the moment she arrived at the front gate. He gave her a tour of the premises, and by the time they made it to the master bedroom she was like putty in his hands. As they stood at the foot of his king-sized, 14kt gold-framed bed, he pushed a button on his remote, and the mirrors on the side of the wall changed into an entertainment center blasting the sweet sounds of the Temptations.

Coretta was hypnotized and completely forgot that Wyte Yak was the enemy as they passionately kissed. She loosened his pants as he unzipped the back of her skirt, and both items of clothing dropped to the floor. She pulled his shirt over his head and tossed it to the floor. While he unbuttoned her blouse and peeled it off of her, he licked her neck and she fell back into the bed pulling him on top of her. He unfastened her bra and she slipped out of it. He then kissed and caressed her breast and slowly licked down her smooth sexy stomach as he removed her panties then his boxers. He gazed into her eyes then kissed her lips as she spread her legs for him to enter. She tilted her head back and let out a pleasurable moan as she sank her nails into his back. He raised her right leg and kissed the back of her calf as he drove his third leg into her deeper and deeper. He rolled over, pulling her on top of him, and she grinded on top of him as he massaged her butt cheeks.

Her eyes rolled to the back of her head as she took him deep into her and climaxed while driving her nails deep into his chest and nearly puncturing his skin. She rolled back over, pulling him on top of her, and her legs shook as he placed them on his shoulders. He pumped for a little while then tossed both of her legs to the right side of her body and slipped down behind her. She rolled over onto her stomach with him on top of her and leaned her head back and passionately kissed him as he climaxed.

He must have been eating his Wheaties because after he came he was still turned on. Instead of softening, he became even harder and continued to give Mrs. Coretta Wiggins a session she would remember for the rest of her life.

CHAPTER 10

Dikki Jah was making a killing out in DC, selling weight at New York prices, and quickly became the man. He took a lot of customers from the other big-time dealers. Tim Spoon, one of the largest dealers in DC, didn't like the competition and wanted Dikki Jah out of the picture. He had two of his boys follow Dikki this particular day when Dikki Jah and his right hand man, Butch, a DC native, pulled up in front of a convenient store in Dikki's black BMW735I. Butch stepped out of the vehicle and as he walked towards the store Dikki yelled

"Don't buy no Phillies. We smoking Optimos tonight, and grab a six-pack of Heinekens."

Once Butch entered the store, a dark-green Toyota Land Cruiser pulled up beside Dikki Jah's Beemer and bullets flew from out of the Land Cruiser into the BMW. Dikki Jah was struck by four slugs. One hit him in the right thigh, another hit him in the left arm, another, his left shoulder, and the last one hit him in the neck. The Land Cruiser sped off, and Butch ran out of the store busting at the fleeing Cruiser.

Once he emptied the gun he ran over to the Beemer and saw Dikki slumped over. He opened the door and started to shake Dikki asking, "Dikki, you alright? You alright, Dikki?"

The injured Dikki managed to say, "Nah, Sun, I'm fucked up. Get at my peoples in Va."

Butch then grabbed the car phone and dialed 911.

"This is 911. Is there an emergency?" asked the operator.

"Yeah, I need a ambulance on Benning Road and G street. Quick! Someone's been shot," Butch yelled. Butch hung up the phone and held Dikki in his arms saying.

"Don't die, my nigga. Be strong, Dikki. Don't die."

Butch held Dikki in his arms until the police and ambulance attendants arrived and rushed Dikki off to the hospital. He then rushed home to change his clothes, hopped in his car, and headed out to Norfolk, Virginia.

Over at the strip club in Norfolk, the Career Criminals were spread out patrolling the club, while the dancers entertained the customers. Butch entered the club, walked up to D-Ski, and asked, "Is Wyte Yak here?"

D-Ski, guessing Butch must be a friend of Wyte Yak, said, "Nah, he don't come to the club. Why what's up?"

"I need to talk to him. I'm Butch. I run with Dikki Jah out in DC."

D-Ski shook Butch's hand realizing that he was a friend of the family. "Follow me," he said.

Butch followed D-Ski into a back room where LA and Brock sat drinking with two strippers. D-Ski introduced Little Ant to Butch, "LA, this is Butch. He runs with Dikki Jah out in DC."

"What up, Butch?" LA said, shaking his hand. "Where my nigga, Dikki Jah?"

"Dikki got shot up real bad. I don't think he's gonna make it," Butch said.

LA got up and walked over to his desk to press a button. The rest of the Career Criminals rushed into the back room, and Rahtiek asked.

"What's wrong, Sun?"

"This is Dikki Jah's boy from DC. He said Dikki got shot up real bad," LA said. Everybody got upset and started cursing and punching walls.

"Y'all niggas calm down," LA said. "We gotta call

Wyte Yak."

"Hell, nah. You don't wanna do that. Whitey gone lose it," said Prince.

"We gotta tell him," LA insisted.

"Butch, do you know who shot Dikki?" Prince asked.

"Yeah, two pussy-ass brothers name Greg and David. They did the hit for this nigga named Tim Spoon. He was mad because Dikki was taking all of his customers."

"Let's go snatch them niggas and cut their fucking heads off," said Rahtiek.

"We just gone roll out to DC without saying nothing to Yak?" LA asked. Prince placed his hand on LA's shoulder and said, "Listen, Ant, you don't know your cousin the way we do. Whenever anybody fucks with his peoples he goes crazy. We don't want him to do that. We need him to stay calm and keep this organization running smoothly. So we got to go handle them niggas ourselves then we'll tell him about what happened to Dikki."

"Alright, I feel y'all." LA then turned, looked at Brock and D-Ski, and said, "Brock, I'm gonna need you and D-Ski to stay here and close the club. Then I want y'all to head out to the woods and dig a hole six feet wide and six feet deep.

They both nodded their heads in agreement. Then he turned to Prince and said.

"Prince, grab Cinnamon, CoCoa, and Peaches. We need them to roll with us."

"I got you," said Prince.

The men exited the club and waited in the parking lot for the girls to get dressed. The three sexiest strippers on the team came out of the club and hopped in Cinnamon's convertible Mustang 5.0. They followed the Career Criminals out to Washington DC. Two hours later they arrived in DC and rented a room at the Motel 6. The rest of the crew stayed in the room while LA and Butch took the girls to find Tim Spoon, Greg, and David.

All of the clubs had let out, and Butch knew that Tim Spoon and his two sidekicks would be at the Waffle House.

LA pulled his yellow BMW alongside Cinnamon's 5.0, and Butch, who was in the passenger seat, pointed into the Waffle House, saying, "There they go at the table in the back. That's Greg and David with the baseball caps on, and that's Tim Spoon with the corn rows."

"Alright, ladies, y'all know what to do," LA said, looking over at the girls.

Little Ant drove around to the back of the Waffle House and waited for the women to get acquainted with the DC dealers and lure them back to their hotel room.

Cinnamon parked her car in front of the Waffle House. All heads turned as the women entered the Waffle House in their skimpy, alluring outfits. Cinnamon strutted in first with her head held high and wearing a tight spandex dress that hugged her thin waist and big round booty, her huge breasts nearly bursting through the top.

She was followed by Peaches, 5'1" shorty with a plump ass. She had on the most clothes--a tight Guess Jeans suit with an open jacket that revealed a bikini top beneath.

The last to enter was CoCoa with her dark, shining, chocolate skin. She wore a see-through dress showing her long sexy legs and luscious butt as well as her black bra and thong. The women ignored all of the gawking eyes and men commenting as they walked straight to the back and set up at the table next to Greg, David, and Tim Spoon.

Greg said, "Damn! Y'all off the motherfucking

chain!"

"I don't think I ever seen three more perfect bodies in my life," said David. He drooled so hard his bottom lip was nearly touching the floor.

"Me neither! Where y'all from?" Tim Spoon asked. He was the only one who was able to maintain his composure.

"New York," said Cinnamon, trying not to seem too interested.

"I knew y'all wasn't from DC, or we woulda already met," said Tim.

"And you are?" asked Peaches, looking Tim up and down.

"Tim Spoon. I run this city. These my boys, Greg and David."

"Nice to meet y'all. I'm Tasha, and these my girls, Pam and Kim," said Cinnamon. "We were out here looking for some action, but all we keep running into is broke-ass niggas."

"Y'all strippers?" asked David, a huge grin on his face.

"Something like that," CoCoa answered in a smooth, sexy tone.

Greg flashed a mitt of money and boasted, "Our money is long, and our dicks are strong. So let's hit the telly and get the party on."

"Oh, you a rapper? CoCoa asked, not liking the way Greg came off..

Before he could respond, Peaches asked, "Y'all got some weed?" holding her fingers to her mouth like she was puffing a blunt.

"I told you this my city. I got whatever you need," said Tim Spoon, recognizing that his homeboy, Greg, had almost fucked up their chance of getting laid.

"Finally, some real niggas," said Cinnamon, soothing the three men's egos. "We with y'all. Let's roll."

The ladies got up and started to walk out, and the guys followed. The waitress was walking over to the guys' table with their food when David said, "Cancel that order," and placed a hundred-dollar bill on the tray she was carrying.

The three men followed the women to the hotel in Tim Spoon's S600 Mercedes Benz. When they got out of their cars, the women wrapped their arms around the men to assure them they were about to get their freak on and throw them off guard as to what was really about to happen next.

Prince and Rahtiek were hiding behind the door, while Trap and Deuce hid in the bathroom. The three men walked in completely unaware of the setup...until Cinnamon closed the door and they heard the clicking of hammers being cocked on the guns now pointed at their faces.

"What the fuck is this?" Tim Spoon asked. "I don't even know y'all niggas."

"Yeah, but you know our man, Dikki Jah, don't you?" asked Rahtiek, closing the gap between him and the men and placing his gun in Tim Spoon's mouth.

The Career Criminals then handcuffed the men and duct taped their mouths, taking the money out of their pockets and giving it to the women. Butch walked in and gave the women instructions on how to get to the hospital to see Dikki, and they headed out to check on him. The Career Criminals then escorted the men out of the hotel room and put each of the DC dealers in a different car trunk.

LA picked up his car phone and called Brock. The

phone rang six times.

"Hello," Brock answered, out of breath.

"What took you so long to answer the phone?" LA asked.

"We out here digging a fucking hole," said Brock, wiping the sweat from his forehead.

"Y'all almost finish?"

"Yeah."

"Good. Because we on our way back."

"How long before y'all get here?"

"We just snatched them dudes. We still in DC. We'll be there in about a hour and a half," LA said.

"Alright."

LA hung up the phone, and the Career Criminal clique raced to Virginia. They didn't drive too far above the speed limit since they didn't want to get pulled over with the extra baggage in the trunk.

They arrived in the woods where Brock and D-Ski were waiting for them in a little more than two hours. They snatched the DC dealers from the trunk, and Rahtiek and Prince grabbed their Samurai swords from the trunk of Rahtiek's Beemer.

They placed David in front of the hole and Rahtiek swung his sword like a Chinese Ninja and chopped David's head off. His body and head fell into the huge hole. Then they placed his brother, Greg, in front of the hole. He was pleading for mercy when Prince chopped his head off. His body fell into the hole, but his head rolled forward. The Career Criminals treated it like a soccer ball. It rolled in front of Trap, who kicked it to Deuce, who kicked it to Brock, who kicked it to D-Ski, who kicked it into the hole and raised his hands above his head like he just scored the winning goal.

Tim Spoon got spooked and tried to run, but Deuce and Trap picked him up and placed him in front of the hole. Rahtiek and Prince stood on each side of him and he closed his eyes as they pulled their swords back and swung at the same time at his legs chopping both his legs off. His body didn't fall into the hole so Trap and Deuce picked up his body and tossed him into the hole face up. Then they tossed his legs in on top of him. Tim was crying and in a lot of pain. The Career Criminals gathered around the hole and pissed on Tim and his two headless home boys. After relieving themselves on the DC dealers they filled the hole with dirt, burying Tim Spoon alive.

After a long night of passionate lovemaking, Wyte Yak and Coretta walked down the steps of his minimansion holding hands and with plans to meet up for lunch. He gave her a kiss, and she hopped into her car, waved good-bye, and drove off. Wyte Yak opened the front gate with his remote control, and Coretta drove through.

Before he could close it behind her, he noticed his crew coming through in four BMW's. They rode up to the front of the house where Wyte Yak was standing in his silk robe and pajamas. They hopped out of the vehicles with their heads down, and Rahtiek said, "Brace yourself, Wyte Yak. We got some bad news."

"What happened?"

"This is Dikki Jah's boy, Butch, from DC," LA said, pointing at Butch.

"Where's Dikki?" Wyte Yak asked. "Don't tell me he got knocked."

"Dikki Jah is in the hospital. He got shot out in DC,"

said Butch.

Wyte Yak became furious, asking, "What? Is he alright? What the fuck happen?"

"Some jealous-ass pussies shot him because he was taking all of their customers. Cinnamon, Peaches, and CoCoa are with him at the hospital right now," said Prince.

"I'm gone cut off their motherfucking heads!"

"Too late. We already done that," said LA.

Wyte Yak took a deep breath then asked, "How's Dikki? Is he going to be alright?"

"Cinnamon just called a little while ago. She told me the doctor said he's paralyzed from the neck down but lucky to even be alive," LA said.

"Damn! I knew I shoulda sent somebody out there with him to hold him down," Wyte Yaks said, teary-eyed.

Butch took responsibility and said, "That was my job. He sent me in the store to get some beer and blunts and niggas rolled on him just that quick. We had no idea we were being followed."

"I don't blame you, Butch," Wyte Yak said. "I'm sure y'all didn't even know niggas was scheming." Wyte Yak looked at the rest of the crew and said, "Now y'all see why I sent Drizz home. We gotta stay on point twenty-four seven. We don't know what the fuck niggas be thinking. Come on, let's go in the house."

The crew entered the house, and Wyte Yak said, "Make yourselves something to eat. I'm gone go upstairs to get dressed, then we headed to DC to check Dikki."

LA, Brock, Rahtiek, D-Ski, Trap, and Butch all took seats in the living room and put on the big screen TV while Prince and Deuce walked into the kitchen to make the team something to eat.

Dikki Jah was lying in the hospital bed hooked up to a respirator, an IV stuck in his left arm. Peaches and CoCoa were sitting in chairs with their heads down feeling sorry for Dikki Jah. Cinnamon came out of the bathroom with a wet rag, which she folded and placed on Dikki's forehead. Dikki Jah opened his eyes.

"Are you alright, Dikki?" Cinnamon asked. Dikki nodded slightly.

"I just talked to Prince. He said everybody's on their way out here to see you. I'm sorry for what happened to you, but you know we took care of those bastards that shot you," Cinnamon said.

"Hey, Dikki, how you feeling?" Peaches asked.
"Is there anything you want us to do for you?" Cocoa asked.

Dikki spoke softly. They couldn't hear him so Cinnamon put her ear near his mouth and he muttered, "Strip."

Cinnamon laughed then asked, "You want us to strip for you?"

Dikki nodded his head yes, and Cinnamon said, "Come on, girls, we got a special request."

Cinnamon pulled a small portable radio from her purse and turned on some music. The girls started dancing and coming out of their clothes, turning around so Dikki could see them shake their asses. By the time they were down to their G-strings Dikki's doctor walked in. He cut off the radio, saying, "What the hell are y'all doing? This man is ill. You girls can't be carrying on like this. Put your clothes back on, or I'm going to have to ask y'all to leave."

Peaches rolled her eyes at the doctor. "We were just

trying to cheer him up," she said.

"I understand that, but you're going to have to try and cheer him up without taking your clothes off. This is a hospital, not a strip club."

"Alright, we heard you. Sorry, Dikki," said Cinnamon.

As the girls put their clothes back on the doctor checked Dikki's blood pressure and temperature and made a note of it. Everything seemed normal and he left the room.

Right quick the girls put the music back on and continued their performance. Twenty minutes later the Career Criminals walked in and found the women completely naked, dancing, and showing their goods to Dikki. As they entered Deuce yelled, "Dikkiii! What up, my nigga?"

"Don't they know they can't kill you?" Rahtiek said. "You're a Career Criminal. We don't die we multiply."

Wyte Yak looked at the girls and shook his head, "What up, Dikki? How you feeling?" he asked, walking over to Dikki and kissing him on the forehead.

The girls rushed into the bathroom to get dressed.

"I'm alive," Dikki said softly.

Wyte Yak didn't hear him so he leaned over and asked, "What was that?"

"I'm alive."

"You damn right. You're alive, and you gone stay that way!" Wyte Yak said.

"That's more than we can say for the niggas that shot you," said Trap, motioned his hand in a cutthroat signal.

"What's up with this dude? He good peoples?" Yak asked, pointing at Butch.

Dikki nodded, and Yak said, "Alright, then. We gone look out for him on the strength of you, my nigga."

Dikki's doctor walked back in the room with a specialist and a neurosurgeon and said, "Excuse me, people. I'm going to have to ask you guys to step out of the room for a little while. We need to run a few tests. We'll be done in about twenty minutes. You can return then."

The crew started to exit the room, and D-Ski looked back at Dikki and said, "We'll be right outside, Sun."

CHAPTER 11

Back in Norfolk, Coretta was sitting in her office behind her desk talking with agents Kessler and Johnson.

"I'm sorry, gentlemen, but I don't think I can be of any use to you," she said.

"What are you talking about? You said you've become pretty good friends with Wyte Yak," said Kessler.

"Yeah, but he doesn't talk business around me."

"The more you're with him, the more comfortable he'll become. He's bound to slip up sooner or later," said Johnson.

"Honestly, I think you're barking up the wrong tree," Coretta said.

"Nah, he's the man. We're sure of it," said Kessler.

"It just doesn't feel right," Coretta whined.

"He's the bad guy," said Johnson.

"Maybe to you guys, but he treats me with more respect than any man I ever known."

"Don't fall for it. He's a lousy dope pusher. Think about your sister," said Kessler, trying to keep Coretta focused.

"Tina loves him," Coretta added.

"He's the reason Tina isn't mentally stable. Remember, it was one of his people that gave her the drugs," said Johnson.

"You don't know that for sure."

"We're almost one hundred percent sure. He and his people supply eighty-five percent of the drugs in the city. There's only a fifteen percent chance that the drugs didn't come from him. So make up your mind. Are you with us or not?" asked Kessler.

Coretta put her head down and ran her fingers through her hair. "I'm with you," she said.

"Alright then, Mrs. Wiggins," Kessler then said, "you have to do your part and keep your eyes and ears open. So far you haven't given us anything to go on.

Do you even know his real name?"

"Yeah."

"What is it?" asked Kessler.

"Franklin Whitehead."

"Do you know what city he was born in?"

"Brooklyn."

Johnson wrote down Wyte Yak's government name and the city of his birth.

Kessler stared Coretta in the eyes.

"That's a start," he said. "Now remember, keep your eyes and ears open. We're counting on you to do the right thing."

The two Agents stood, shook Coretta's hand, and exited the office.

Later that day the two Agents were to be found in their office. Kessler was talking on the telephone to an old detective friend of his from Brooklyn, trying to find out if he knew of a Wyte Yak or Franklin Whitehead. Agent Johnson was sitting in front of his computer running a background check on Wyte Yak. Kessler hung up disappointed his friend didn't have anything on Wyte Yak. Johnson on the other hand found out that Franklin Whitehead, better known as "Wyte Yak," was convicted for drug trafficking and had spent some time in the Fort Dix Federal Penitentiary.

Agent Johnson printed out the information and handed the sheet to Kessler, saying, "It seems Mr. Whitehead's done some time in Fort Dix."

Kessler smiled as he read the printout. "It says here he got five years for drug trafficking but the judge suspended three. Him and another man named Harold Cortland were caught with nine ounces on a Greyhound bus headed for Virginia. He was just released July second. We got his MO, Johnson. The pieces to the puzzle are starting to come together. He was only caught with a quarter ki', so he must have, somehow, gotten connected on the inside."

"That's the part that's puzzling me. How do you go from being a petty hustler to supplying a whole city?" asked Johnson.

"I don't know, Johnson, but that's what we're going to find out."

"We have one problem."

"What's that?" asked Kessler.

"If he was just released in July then those weren't his drugs that were given to Mrs. Wiggins' sister," Johnson said.

"So what? asked Kessler. "He's still a lousy drug dealer. Mrs. Wiggins should still be happy to help us take him down."

"I don't know, Kessler. She does seem to like the guy. She's only helping us because she thinks he's responsible. I think she might have a change of heart once she finds out he didn't play a part."

"And how is she going to find out? asked Kessler. "You're not going to tell her, and I'm sure as hell not going to say anything. Wyte Yak doesn't seem like the kinda guy who talks about his past. We need her to find out who's his connect. So what she doesn't know won't hurt her."

"But if she was to somehow find out," said Johnson,

"I think she'd be pretty pissed."

"Who cares? By that time we would already have the information we need. So there's nothing to worry about."

Kessler continued looking over Wyte Yak's rap sheet, while Johnson scratched his head as he walked back over to his desk and sat down.

While at the hospital Wyte Yak called Coretta to let her know he couldn't make their lunch date but promised to make it up to her. He picked her up after work and surprised her with a trip to Vegas where they spent the weekend.

After seeing Dikki Jah's condition he felt like he needed a vacation and he made sure not to tell Coretta about what had happened because he didn't want her to know about his problems.

They enjoyed Vegas and really had a good time at the Casinos, where they lost a few thousand dollars at the slot machines. They saw a few shows and even met a few celebrities. But mostly they enjoyed each other's company, spending a lot of time in the Jacuzzi and heart-shaped bed in Wyte Yak's suite at the MGM Plaza.

Once they returned from Vegas, Coretta spent the night with Wyte Yak every night for three weeks. She was really falling for him but fought off any feelings she had because she knew he was a dealer and thought it was his drugs that had crippled her sister, leaving her mentally retarded. She had to constantly remind herself that her loyalty was to her sister.

One morning as they were sleeping in bed the phone rang, waking them from their sleep. Coretta's back was turned to Wyte Yak, and he didn't realize she was awake. He was having a conversation with Raymond Latronica.

"Hello," Wyte Yak said.

"Good morning, Wyte Yak."

"Hey, Mr.Latronica, how's it going?"

As soon as Coretta heard Wyte Yak say the Italian name, she figured it had to be his connect and kept her ears open.

"Everything's lovely. I just called to let you know I appreciate the way you've been handling business. So I'm sending you an extra thousand potatoes I need you to get rid of for me."

"An extra thousand? On top of the thousand I already ordered?"

"Yeah, and I'm going to need ten dollars a potato."

Wyte Yak knew that ten dollars a potato meant ten thousand a ki'. This made him scratch his head as he got up and started to pace the room, wondering how he would get rid of the extra product.

"I don't know if that's a good idea, Mr. Latronica. How soon do you need the money?"

"I could hold off about a month."

"That might be more than I can handle right now, you know, with the prices being back to normal and all."

"Nonsense. If I didn't know you could handle it, I wouldn't of asked you for the favor."

"Yeah, I know, but right now's not a good time. I just lost my partner out in DC. He got shot up pretty bad and is now a paraplegic."

Coretta was shocked to hear what happened to Wyte Yak's friend.

"I'm sorry to hear about your friend, but you're a smart man, Wyte Yak. I know if anyone can handle this for me, you can. Do this favor for me, and I promise I won't ask for another for at least six months."

Wyte Yak was unsure whether he could handle the weight but said, "Alright, Mr. Latronica, I got you."

"That's what I needed to hear. I'll see you in thirty days. I'm sure you won't disappoint me," Mr. Latronica said. Then he hung up.

Wyte Yak walked over to his dresser for his address book and thumbed through the pages until he found Butch's phone number out in DC. He dialed the number. The phone rang a few times then Butch picked up the receiver, "Hello," he said.

"What up, Butch? This is Wyte Yak. How you?"

"I'm alright."

"How's the streets out there in DC?

"Pretty dry without Dikki and Spoon holding shit down."

"You ready to make it happen?"

"Hell, yeah!" Butch said, getting excited.

"Alright, then come check me tomorrow. I'ma set you out real nice."

"I'm there!"

"Cool."

Wyte Yak hung up the phone and walked into the bathroom. He then put on the shower, stepping out of his robe, and got in. Once Coretta heard the water running in the shower, she quickly hopped out of the bed, walked over to the telephone, and pressed *69 to get the number of the last incoming call. She wrote the number down, placed it in her purse, and climbed back in the bed.

The next day Coretta was in her office contemplating on whether or not she should give the phone number of Wyte Yak's connect to the FBI agents. She picked up the phone, started to dial then hung up--twice. The third time she picked up the phone she decided to tell them.

"Federal Bureau of Investigations. Kessler speaking."

"Agent Kessler, this is Coretta Wiggins."

"Hello, Mrs. Wiggins. How's it going? I was starting to think you switched sides."

"No, I'm still on your team. I have a number for you. I think it's the number to Wyte Yak's connect. The number is (305)235-7513."

Agent Kessler wrote the number down and said, "Thanks, Coretta. You've done good."

Just as Coretta hung up the phone, her secretary walked in carrying a bouquet of roses. Karen smiled and handed her the flowers. "Somebody has an admirer," she teased.

Immediately Coretta started feeling guilty and began to feel nauseous. She ran into the bathroom attached to her office and vomited into the toilet.

"Not again," Karen said, running into the bathroom behind Coretta. "Are you alright?"

"I'll be fine," Coretta said, holding her head up from the toilet. Then she started vomiting some more.

Karen walked over to the water fountain in the office and filled a cup with water. She handed it to her and asked, "Are you pregnant?"

"Hell, no, I can't be. At least, I don't think I am."

"Did you take a pregnancy test?" Karen asked, hands akimbo.

"No."

"Then how do you know?"

Karen walked out of the bathroom and through Coretta's office out front to her desk and searched her purse for a pregnancy test. She found one, walked back into Coretta's office, and handed it to her. "It's time you found out if you're pregnant or not," she said, closing the bathroom door.

Coretta took the test and slumped down onto the floor crying when she saw the results.

That same afternoon Wyte Yak was lounging in his living room as he watched the Chicago Bulls play the New York Knicks on his big screen TV. His remote buzzed indicating that someone was at the front gate. He switched the channel on the TV to channel seven and saw Butch on the passenger side of a blue, four-door, Acura Legend. He pressed the intercom and asked, "Butch, is that you?"

"Yeah, Wyte Yak, it's me."

"Who's that you got with you?"

"This is my boy, Rick."

"Yeah, alright. Tell him he has to wait outside."

Wyte Yak pressed the button on the remote to open the gate, and Rick drove up to the front of the house. Butch stepped out of the car and walked up to the front door, and Wyte Yak opened the door to let Butch in.

"Dikki told me you know mostly all of his customers," Wyte Yak said.

"Pretty much. I was usually there during each transaction."

"That's good. Then I guess you know Dikki Jah used to move somewhere between a hundred and a hundred and fifty bricks a week. Now that your boy Tim Spoon's out of the picture, you should be able to move an extra hundred, don't you agree?"

"Yeah, something like that."

"Once the price dropped I started giving them to him

at eighteen thou a ki'. I got a little more than I can handle right now, so I'm going to let you have them for fifteen."

Butch got excited and asked, "Fifteen thousand a ki'? Get the fuck out of here. Are you kidding me?"

"Not at all. I'm giving them to you cheap because I need you right now. I got a thousand bricks I need to get rid of, and you and my boy Murt up in Richmond are the only two people I'm fucking with right now. So I need you to move as much as possible as quickly as possible."

"That shouldn't be a problem. I'll just sell them for twenty thou. That'll stop niggas from going to New York."

"That's what I need you to do. I know some of the big boys aren't going to be too happy about that. You got some people to hold you down."

"Yeah, I got my boy Rick that's out front in the car and my cousins, Ted and Josh, back in DC."

"They get busy?"

"They're gorillas! Ain't nobody fucking with us!"

"I believe you, but I can't take any chances. So I'm sending Prince and Rahtiek with you to be sure."

"No problem."

Outside the house Prince and Rahtiek, each carrying a briefcase, walked up to Rick, who was sitting in his Acura Legend. "Pop the trunk," Prince said. Rick popped the trunk, and they put both briefcases in the trunk then sat in the back seat of the Acura.

Meanwhile back in the house Wyte Yak said to Butch, "Alright then. They're outside waiting on you. You got two hundred and fifty bricks in the trunk. Holla at me once it's gone."

"Cool."

Butch stood and slapped Wyte Yak five and walked

out of the front door.

Wyte Yak picked up the phone to call Coretta. He tried to reach her office, but her secretary said she had left for the day. He then tried her at her home. The phone rang four times then the answering machine came on saying, "You've reached the home of Coretta Wiggins. I'm not available to take your call right now, but please leave your name and number and I'll be sure to return your call."

Wyte Yak left a message, "Hey, Coretta, this is Wyte Yak. The construction crew just finished hooking up the spot. I was headed over there to meet up with a few of the other investors to celebrate. I was hoping to bring you with me. I'm sorry I missed you, but give me a ring as soon as you get this message. Peace. I'm out."

Coretta was sitting on her couch with her head on Angie's shoulder, crying. "What are you going to do, Coretta?" Angie asked.

"I'm having an abortion."

"Yeah, right. You don't even believe in abortions. What are you going to tell Wyte Yak?"

"Nothing."

"You have to tell him. Don't you think he has a right to know?"

"Yeah, but he's going to want me to keep it. And I can't do that."

"Why not?"

"I just can't."

"There has to be a reason. There's something you're not telling me. Now what's going on?"

Coretta wiped at the steady flow of tears running down her cheeks and said, "Nothing. I can't tell him, and I can't have his baby."

"I don't understand you, Coretta. Wyte Yak's one of the few good guys left. You can't just get rid of his seed without him knowing. That's not right."

"I know."

"Then why would you do it?"

"Because he's a drug dealer!" Coretta yelled.

"You knew that before you even got involved with him. So why did you even sleep with him? You tripping, girl."

Coretta paused and wiped at her tears again. "I heard Wyte Yak and Little Ant distribute eighty-five percent of the drugs in Norfolk," she said.

"They probably do. So what?"

"I also heard it was probably their drugs that messed Tina up."

"Now whoever told you that is a lying son of a bitch!" Angie said, pointing her finger at Coretta.

"How do you know?"

"Because Little Ant just blew up six months ago when Wyte Yak got out of jail. So it couldn't have been their shit."

"Wyte Yak was in jail?" Coretta asked, surprised.

"Yeah. He didn't tell you? He did two years in the Feds."

"No. Why you didn't tell me?"

"I thought you knew by now and didn't think it mattered."

"Damn, girl, you should have told me that. Fuck!"

Coretta sat back on the couch, holding her head in her hands and crying. Angie looked on with a puzzled look on her face.

CHAPTER 12

Butch was in the passenger seat, and Rick was driving. Rahtiek was sitting in the back behind Butch, and Prince was sitting in the back next to Rahtiek and behind Rick. They were in Rick's brand-new 1992 Acura Legend, driving on the I-95 North and headed for DC. Rick was doing about sixty miles per hour.

"Slow down, Rick," Butch said.

"I'm only driving sixty miles per hour," Rick protested. "No cop ain't gone pull us over for that."

They rode past a police car equipped with radar and lying in the cut. The police car pulled out onto the highway behind the Acura and flashed its lights, signaling them to pull over. "What the fuck I told you! Now look!" Butch yelled.

"Calm down," Rahtiek said, trying to keep everybody cool. "He's not going to do nothing but give Rick a ticket for speeding."

"I don't know about that. My license is suspended," Rick whined.

"Ah man! We fucked," Prince said, shaking his head. "He's gonna wanna search the car."

"I told your stupid ass to slow down!" Butch repeated.

Still trying to keep everyone calm Rahtiek said, "Fuck it. Just chill. They probably gone just take Rick and let the rest of us go about our business."

Prince pulled his gun from his waist and said, "Yeah right! He gone see four niggas in a brand-new Acura Legend then call for back up so they can search the car. Fuck that!

120

It's not going down like that."

The officer stepped out of his vehicle and approached the Acura. As soon as he reached the back of the vehicle Prince hopped out of the back seat with his 9mm in his hand and shot the state trooper right between the eyes. The officer fell to the ground and was dead before he even hit the pavement. Prince hopped back in the Acura and yelled, "Let's get the fuck outta here!"

Rick put the car back in drive and sped off.

Rahtiek looked over at Prince and asked, "What the fuck you do that for? We're really fucked now."

"Nigga, don't you know all state trooper cars got cameras on the dash?" Butch asked.

Right then Rick went into panic mode and started to shake, saying, "Man, we fucked. Man, we fucked. Oh my God, I don't believe this."

Prince looked over at Rahtiek, who held his hands in the air and shook his head. They both knew right then and there that Rick was a weakling. Prince put his gun to the back of Rick's head and said, "Pull the fuck over."

Rick pulled the car over and Prince jumped out, opened Rick's door, and said, "Get the fuck out of the car, bitch."

Prince grabbed Rick by the arm and snatched him out of the car, bringing him around to the passenger side of the vehicle. He shot Rick twice in the face killing him instantly. He kneeled down and took Rick's wallet from his back pocket then ran back around and hopped in the driver's seat.

"Sorry, Butch, but your man was acting like a bitch. I had to kill him. He woulda snitched on us, and you know it," Prince explained.

"He was acting like a bitch," Butch said, nodding his

head.

"Whose car is this, Butch?" asked Prince.

"It's Rick's."

Rahtiek leaned forward and asked, "Did you look back when Prince shot that trooper?"

"Hell, no. I knew the trooper's car had a camera on the dash," Butch said.

"I didn't turn around either," Rahtiek added. "So this is what we gone do. We gotta get off the highway, ditch the car, and take a cab the rest of the way. Prince, you gone have to get low. Your best bet is to take a cab to the nearest Greyhound bus station and hop on a bus headed out west because your face is going to be all over the news on every channel along the East Coast."

"I know. Damn! I fucked up!" Prince said.

Prince got off the highway at the next exit, and they followed Rahtiek's plan. Prince took a cab to the nearest bus terminal while Rahtiek and Butch took a cab to DC.

Agents Johnson and Kessler were sitting in their office. Kessler was talking on the telephone while Johnson, who was channel surfing, paused on the news.

"That was John Adams from the agency down in Miami," Kessler said after he hung up. "I had him check on the number Mrs. Wiggins gave us, and you wouldn't believe whose home address it was."

"Whose?"

"Raymond Latronica."

"The Don himself?" Johnson asked, shocked.

"Yep, the king of Miami, Mr. Mob Boss himself. Adams said they already have surveillance around his home and trucking company. Now guess how our Mr. Whitehead became connected with Latronica."

"I don't know. How?"

"Remember Mr. Harold Cortland, the guy who was arrested with Wyte Yak?" Kessler asked.

"Yeah."

"He got ten years and is over in Leavenworth. Well, it turns out that Mr. Cortland is Wyte Yak's half brother. Now guess who's also in Leavenworth."

"Nickie Latronica, Raymond's son, who got caught with the truckload of kilos a couple of years ago," Johnson said.

"Bingo. Mr. Cortland saved Nickie's ass in the pen and, out of gratitude, Raymond allowed Wyte Yak to join their family."

"Wow!" said Johnson. "This is turning out to be bigger than we ever expected. I wonder what ever happened to Keith. This tip he gave us is sure to take us to the top of the Bureau."

"I don't know. He probably decided to leave town," Kessler said.

"I sure would like to thank him."

"You and me both," said Kessler.

The phone rang and Agent Kessler answered it, "Federal Bureau of Investigations. Kessler speaking."

"Agent Kessler, this is Coretta. I need for you and Agent Johnson to meet me at my office in an hour."

"At this hour?"

"Yes, it's very urgent," she said and hung up.

"Who was that?" Johnson asked.

"Mrs. Wiggins. She wants us to meet at her office in an hour. She says it's urgent," Kessler said.

Chief Kobe appeared on the news speaking at a campaign rally. Johnson turned the volume up, and they listened to the chief.

"It was I who cleared all of the drug dealers off the streets," he bragged. "It was I who put a stop to all of the drive-bys and neighborhood shootings. It was I who made it safe for our children to play in the playgrounds and for the working class citizen to feel safe coming in and out of their neighborhoods. A vote for Rodney Kobe is a vote for peace, justice, and a safe, drug-free environment."

The crowd went wild with praise for the chief and soon-to-be mayor.

Agent Johnson turned to his partner and said, "Would you listen to this fool. I wish I could be there to see his face tomorrow morning when he opens the envelope I left on his desk."

"Yeah, I can see him now, sitting there with his mouth open," said Kessler.

The Agents walked out of their office laughing at Chief Kobe and were happy that they had enough evidence to arrest Wyte Yak and the rest of the Career Criminals.

Wyte Yak went over to the spot, which, after just four months of fifty million dollars worth of day and night construction, was now ready to open. He put in a little more than half of the fifty million, making him the majority stockholder. The rest of the Career Criminals made large investments of at least five hundred thousand. Petey invested three million, and Dazz and his brother Dino together invested close to five million. A good thirty-five other dealers made investments of over a hundred thousand or more. A few black businessmen made investments, and, to make it appear all legal, Wyte Yak had paid a few crooked preachers as front men to pretend they put the whole thing together.

The dealers were proud of their achievement as they walked through the various departments admiring their money. There was a bowling alley with thirty lanes. There was a billiard room with over fifty pool tables, a game room consisting of over a hundred and fifty different video games. They were two huge clubs with 1500 capacity, one for adults and the other for teenagers. There was a roller skating rink, a food court, and a huge movie arcade with twelve separate theaters.

All of the proud young black investors gathered around in the food court and popped bottles of champagne to celebrate the opening of one of the first multi-million dollar, black-owned establishments. For Wyte Yak, it was a dream come true. But although most of his crew was there, he still wished Coretta was at his side.

Wyte Yak, sensing that something was wrong, left the festivities early. He went home and checked his telephone messages to see if Coretta had called. She didn't, and he was sad as he sunk into the comfort of his off-white, five-thousand-dollar leather couch. He clicked on the big screen television and started to watch the news. Same time the telephone rang, and he turned down the TV and rushed to answer it, hoping it was Coretta.

"Hello," he said.

"We ran into problems on our way out to DC, Yak," Rahtiek said.

"What happen, Rah? Is everybody alright?"

As Wyte Yak was being brought up to speed on what happened, he saw Prince on the news shooting the trooper.

"Me and Butch are cool," Rahtiek said, "but Prince

had to get low. I'm gone need you to send Brock out here."

Wyte Yak sat there for a moment with his mouth open in disbelief at the headline news. Then he put his head down and said, "I understand. He'll be there tomorrow."

Wyte Yak hung up the telephone and turned the volume up on the television. The newscaster said, "The police are asking anyone who knows the man in this video to please call 1-800-Cop Shot. Any information you give will be kept confidential."

Wyte Yak turned off the TV and buried his face in his hands.

Coretta was in her office sitting behind her desk. The two agents entered and took seats across from her on the other side of her desk.

"What was it you needed to see us about?" Kessler asked.

Coretta attempted to protect Wyte Yak. "I had a talk with Franklin and found out that he's not a drug dealer at all," she said. "His parents died and left him a trust fund. He invested in some stocks back in New York, and they're really starting to pay off."

"Mrs. Wiggins, what's gotten in to you?" asked Johnson, seeing through her game. "Wyte Yak's not only a dealer, but he's also connected to the mob."

"In fact," Kessler added, "the number you gave us was none other than that of Raymond Latronica, Mr. Mob Boss himself."

Coretta blew her cool and said, "Then he must be an investor because Franklin's no drug dealer."

With pity in his eyes, Johnson said, "Don't tell me you fell for this guy. He's a drug dealer, Mrs. Wiggins. He's not good enough for you.

"He's the greatest man I've ever known, and I'm madly in love with him," Coretta said, tears flowing down her cheeks.

"I told you it was his drugs that hurt your sister," Kessler said, trying to bring her back on their side.

"You're a liar, Agent Kessler. You knew he had nothing to do with that. He was locked up at the time. You knew how I felt about drug dealers so you used me, and that wasn't right. You have to leave him because I love him and I'm going to have his baby."

"We can't do that, Mrs. Wiggins," Johnson said, shocked to hear that Coretta was pregnant. "We have a strong case against him. So I don't think it would be wise for you to have his child."

"You don't think it would be wise for me to have his child? Fuck what you bastards think! You set me up not caring what happened to me," she screamed. Coretta was losing it. "Get the hell out of my office. I hate you redneck bastards. The first time I find a man that I believe is worthy of me you have me destroy him."

"Mrs. Wiggins, please be reasonable," said Johnson.

"Get out!" she screamed, pointing towards the door. The two agents got up and hurried out of the office as Coretta dropped her head to her desk and cried a waterfall.

Outside of Coretta's office the two agents looked at each other. "We fucked up big time," Johnson said.

Agent Kessler, with no consideration for Coretta's feelings, said, "We did what we had to do to get our man."

"But she's pregnant, Kessler."

Kessler shrugged his shoulders. "She knew what she was getting into," he said. "She should have been more careful."

Johnson shook his head as they exited the building, entered their vehicle, and drove off.

CHAPTER 13

Prince had boarded a Greyhound bus to Seattle, Washington and was dozing off. A middle-aged, white woman who was watching the news on her portable TV kept looking back and forth from Prince to the TV as they showed the video tape of a man shooting the state trooper. When she was absolutely sure that the man in the video was sitting next her, she went to the bus driver and told him that guy she was sitting next to had killed a state trooper back in Spotsylvania, Virginia. The bus driver called the police, and fifteen minutes later they pulled the bus over and arrested Prince.

The following morning Chief Kobe received a standing ovation as he walked through the precinct. A female officer handed him a fresh cup of coffee as he proudly entered his office, closing the door behind him. He placed the cup of coffee on his desk and picked up a large manila envelope. When he opened the envelope his mouth dropped as he pulled out a bunch of dated, 8x10 photographs.

The pictures were of him accepting money from Little Ant. The pictures were accompanied by a note which read: We know who's been funding your campaign as well as who really cleared the drugs off the streets.

He sat behind his desk for a moment with a look of disbelief on his face. He had no idea who took the pictures. He picked up the telephone and dialed Little Ant's home number. LA was lying in bed with Angie as the phone rang continuously.

"Hello," LA answered.

"Somebody's watching you," the chief said calmly. "They left pictures on my desk of me accepting money from you."

"What?" LA said, wiping the cold from his eyes.

"We can no longer do business with each other," the chief said, hanging up abruptly.

LA stood there with a puzzled look on his face.

Thirty minutes later LA was banging at Wyte Yak's front door. LA walked in upset and extremely paranoid, saying, "We got problems, cuz."

Wyte Yak, thinking LA saw Prince on the news said, "Yeah, I know they caught Prince last night riding the bus on his way to Seattle."

"What the fuck are you talking about?" asked LA, confused by what Wyte Yak said.

"Prince....He shot a state trooper yesterday. Isn't that what you're talking about?"

"Hell, no, I didn't even know about that," LA said. "I'm talking about the Feds. They're onto us, cuz."

"What the fuck you talking about, Ant?"

"I just got a call from Chief Kobe. He said we could no longer do business because I'm being watched. Somebody left pictures on his desk of me handing him cash."

"So what? That don't mean shit! Just calm down and hold your head," Wyte Yak said.

"What the fuck you mean 'calm down'? They don't have no pictures of you doing shit!" LA said.

Wyte Yak walked over to the bar and poured two glasses of Hennessy. He handed LA a glass and ushered him over to the couch, where they both sat.

"First off," Wyte Yak said, "we don't know what the fuck they got. If they're watching like that, they coulda just followed your ass here. But you don't see me panicking, do you?"

"Nah, you're calm as hell. I don't understand that," LA said.

"Panicking won't do anything but have us tripping and making mistakes. So what the fuck are we supposed to do? We don't know what they have on us."

"That's right. So we can't flip out, slip up, and give them more than they already have. It's time to sit back and analyze and figure this thing out. Now think. Since we've been in business has anyone other than Prince been arrested?" Wyte Yak asked.

"No, what? You think Prince sold us out?" LA asked.

"Hell, no. Sun can hold his own. What I'm saying is there's not a person close enough to us, with enough information on us, to do us any harm. Our shit is airtight," Wyte Yak boasted.

"So what the fuck is up with those pictures?"

"I don't know. It could be anything. Maybe they were clocking the chief to see where he was getting all of his support from. They clock you handing him money, do a background check and find out that you never had a job in your life. So they automatically tag you a criminal. What type? I'm sure they don't even know. So all you have to do is stay clear of any poison and in January when we file our taxes from the spot, we'll look like legitimate businessmen and they'll have to get off of our backs.

"I never looked at it like that," LA said smiling.

"Trust me, they have nothing. Just hold your head. After January we'll be made men. They won't be able to fuck with us. At the same time, if you're trying to get low, do you. I can't make that decision for you in a situation like this. You have to do whatever is in your heart. I'm alright.

You know if you stay here you'll be alright."

"I feel you."

The two men touched glasses and gulped down their drinks. Feeling reassured, LA said, "I guess I was tripping, Yak. I'm alright now."

"You sure?"

LA slapped Yak five and said, "Yeah, I'm cool. You brought me back to my senses. I'm gone jet back to the crib. I left Angie there. I didn't even bother to wake her up. I just jetted over here as soon as Chief Kobe hung up.

LA walked over to the front door and opened it. Coretta was standing in the doorway about to ring the bell. She was looking sad. "Hey, Coretta, what's wrong?" LA asked.

Coretta ignored him, and LA just looked over at Wyte Yak, shrugged his shoulders and walked through the door. Wyte Yak hopped up off the couch as Coretta walked towards him. He kissed her on the lips and, noticing her sadness, asked, "What's wrong, Coretta? And where have you been for the last two days? I've been trying to reach you."

Coretta paused. "I'm pregnant, Franklin," she said, looking deep into Wyte Yak's eyes.

"For real?" Wyte Yak asked, getting excited and hugging Coretta.

"Yeah."

He held her tight, saying, "Coretta, boo, I love you. I'm going to be the best father in the whole world."

Coretta, choking on her words, said, "I know you will. You're the best man a sistah could ask for."

Tears started pouring down her face, and Wyte Yak asked, "What's the matter, baby? This is supposed to be a happy moment."

Coretta pulled away from Wyte Yak and said, "I have something to tell you, but you're gonna hate me once I tell you."

LA exited Wyte Yak's house and hopped into his yellow BMW740I. He drove through the front gate which was, for some reason, left ajar. As soon as he drove out onto the street his car was surrounded by a fleet of police cars. Right then and there he realized that he had good reason for being paranoid. The police hopped out of the vehicles and pointed their guns at him, instructing him to step out of the car with his hands up.

Wyte Yak had a puzzled expression on his face as he wondered what was it that Coretta needed to tell him. "Whatever it is you need to tell me just spit it out," he said.

"I'm sorry Franklin," Coretta said, crying.

"Sorry for what?" asked Wyte Yak, confused.

"When I met you I was working for the Feds. They're on their way here now to arrest you."

Wyte Yak became furious. He charged Coretta and wrapped his fingers around her neck, choking her. After a few seconds, he remembered that she was carrying his child and released her, saying, "I can't even kill your ass, you're carrying my seed."

"I'm sorry, Franklin. I'm so sorry. Please forgive me," Coretta pleaded as she weeped.

"How could you do this to me? I showed you nothing but love."

"I'm sorry. They tricked me into thinking you were responsible for what happened to my little sister, Tina."

"What are you talking about?"

"They told me that you distributed eighty-five percent of the drugs in Norfolk and that it was your drugs that had messed her up."

"Your sister was messed up way before I even came to Norfolk."

"I know that now, but I didn't know that you had just got out of jail in July."

Suddenly the sound of sirens could be heard as the police surrounded the premises. Wyte Yak ran to the window and saw dozens of police cars spread out on his front lawn.

Kessler put a bullhorn to his mouth and said, "We have the place surrounded, Franklin Whitehead. Come out with your hands in the air."

Wyte Yak jumped back from the window and grabbed his remote control. He hit a switch, and automatic weapons appeared above all of the windows. The police saw the weapons and started to duck behind their squad cars. Wyte Yak pushed another button, and the weapons started to release fire. He grabbed Coretta and walked over to the door and cracked it. He stopped the weapons from firing and yelled, "I have a hostage. Get your vehicles off of my property, or she dies."

Johnson immediately instructed the officers to move their vehicles behind the gate. Once Wyte Yak saw that the officers were retreating, he took Coretta over to the library, moved a certain book on the shelf, and the secret passageway opened. It led to a tunnel beneath the house, where there were two briefcases containing two million dollars each as well as a hovercraft. He grabbed the briefcases and started the hovercraft. Then he hit another switch on his remote control, and a bomb under the house started to count down.

"Come on!" he yelled at Coretta. "We have two minutes to get the fuck out of here."

She hopped into the hovercraft, and they sped through the tunnel, which led directly into the ocean. They hit the water and made a clean getaway.

Once all the officers cleared the premises, Kessler started to talk into the bullhorn. "Whitehead, let's be reasonable," he said. "There's no way out. So let Mrs. Wiggins go and come out with your hands up."

Then BOOM! The house blew up. The officers all hit the ground and covered their heads.

Coretta turned around and looked at the exploding minimansion as Wyte Yak steered the hovercraft across the ocean.

A few hours later Wyte Yak and Coretta boarded a plane to the Florida Keys. Wyte Yak told Coretta they could never be together and paid her two million dollars to give him custody of the child once it was born. They stayed in the Florida until the baby was born.

CHAPTER 14

Coretta gave birth to a beautiful baby boy, which Wyte Yak took back to Brooklyn to raise, while she went back to Virginia two million dollars richer.

The agents assumed that Wyte Yak and Coretta had died in the explosion. And although Agent Kessler wanted to pursue an investigation, Agent Johnson, feeling sorry for the way things turned out for Coretta, convinced him to drop the investigation, saying, "If the couple had somehow survived then they were meant to be together."

The Feds raided the three condos and the town house, where they found Brock, Deuce, and D-Ski, and confiscated over seven million dollars in cash. Although no drugs were ever found, LA, Brock, Deuce, and D-Ski were all charged with conspiracy and sentenced to life in prison.

Trap would have been arrested along with Brock, Deuce, and D-Ski. Only, he had just left the condo to go sell two kilos. On his way back with the cash he saw the Feds surrounding the building. As he drove by the condo his body shook when he saw his crew being escorted out in handcuffs. He hopped on I-95 and headed straight for Brooklyn. He laid low in the Projects for a few months, but once he realized the Feds weren't looking for him, he started hustling in the 'hood and got a girl pregnant a year later. She gave birth to a healthy baby boy named Daequan.

After surgery, Dikki Jah was moved to Mount Sinai Hospital in Manhattan. He stayed in the hospital and went through therapy for a year before moving back in with his mother for a few years until he got his own apartment in 1995. He got married in 1999, but his wife left him after she walked in on him being ridden by his home attendant. Although he doesn't feel anything, his dick stays hard, and he enjoys just watching women ride him.

The Feds arrested Rahtiek five months later in Washinton, DC and, after holding him for a year, they were unable to get a conviction and had to release him for lack of evidence.

Six years later, Rahtiek was arrested for armed robbery and sentenced to six years in prison. His girlfriend, Sandra, was five months pregnant at the time of his arrest and gave birth to a beautiful baby girl named Quanesia, born on the same day Rahtiek was sentenced. The FBI also raided Raymond Latronica's mansion and trucking company down in Miami and didn't find anything illegal. Raymond sued them, and they had to pay him ten million dollars-- which was exactly what Wyte Yak owed him.

A year later Wyte Yak contacted Raymond to try and figure out a way he could pay him back the ten million he owed him. Raymond told Wyte Yak that the Feds had paid his debt and that he would always be family, but right now he should just continue to lie low.

Once Wyte Yak was back in Brooklyn he stashed a million dollars beneath his sister's house for his brother, Pooh Berry, which he gave him when he came home on his release from prison in 1999. He laid low for the next twelve years, never putting anything in his name since he couldn't work, and he and his, son, Jeremy lived off the money.

He did a little hustling here and there, but nothing major--just enough to keep him from putting too much of a dent in his stash. He sent LA, Brock, Deuce, and D-Ski a hundred-dollar money order once a month and made sure they received anything else they needed. He also wrote letters to them from time to time to let them know that although they were locked down, they were not forgotten. Chief Kobe was elected Mayor of Norfolk, Virginia, and Agents Kessler and Johnson made him pay them $250,000.00 to destroy the evidence they had on him. During the four years he was mayor, the crime rate soared two hundred percent, making him the worst mayor in the city's history.

The spot opened and, without Wyte Yak's presence, the crooked preachers and legitimate businessmen were the only ones who profited. They didn't acknowledge any of the dealers, and after six months the dealers burned the spot down. The preachers and the legitimate businessmen still came out ahead because they collected the fifty million from the insurance company.

Wyte Yak laid low in the Projects and watched his homeys back in the 'hood go in and out of jail. Some days he sat in his apartment all day in the dark just thinking, hoping to come up with a plan to blow up him and his new crew- a bunch of thugs from the 'hood that grew up under him.

Wyte Yak didn't really get into too much trouble throughout the years, but he was shot in the back in 1998. He was in a building on the middle side of the Projects shooting dice, and a guy came running in the building when this other dude started shooting at him. Wyte Yak was headed to the door to let the dude outside know that he was in the building and, as he reached for the doorknob, bullet holes started to appear in the door. He turned around to run but was struck in the back. He went into the hospital under a fake name and left the following day, afraid that the Feds might come through asking questions, once he realized he was alright.

Wyte Yak allowed Jeremy to visit his mother on holidays and his and her birthdays but really didn't converse too much with Coretta, other than to let her know that he was sending their son to see her or to find out when he should pick him up from a visit. Jeremy often asked his parents why they didn't get along, but neither one of them ever gave him an answer.

Coretta missed Wyte Yak and prayed that one day they would all be a family. Twelve years passed and, although Wyte Yak missed Coretta, he couldn't find it in his heart to forgive her. Although he was miserable without her, he was content knowing he had custody of their child.

Twelve years later, Rahtiek was lying in his bunk sleeping. He was dreaming that he was in bed with two equally sexy, gorgeous women. One was a gorgeous light-skinned hottie wearing a hot pink thong and her fat, red ass sticking up in the air as she sucked Rahtiek's dick while he was sucking on the pretty, brown-skinned sister with juicy red lips and big breasts. He snatched the light-skinned one by her hair and started sucking her pretty yellow titties with the red nipples as he pushed the brown-skinned cutie's head down so she could give him a little head action. He guided the brown-skinned cutie's mouth down to his nuts as the light-skinned one slowly mounted his nine inches of man-hood. Then suddenly a loud clang was heard. Rahtiek's dream was interrupted by the sound of his prison cell being opened.

"Damn, man! What the fuck? I was just about to get some pussy!"

"Pack your shit, Davis! Your time's up. You're being released today. You can go home and get some pussy for real," the corrections officer said, placing a large black garbage bag at the foot of Rahtiek's bed.

"Man, that dream seemed so real, I forgot I was still

in this motherfucker. Thank God, I'm getting out today."

"I'll be back to get you in five minutes, Davis. Be ready or I'll leave your ass here for another day or two," the CO warned. Rahtiek chuckled and said, "I'll be ready. You don't have to worry about that."

The CO walked down the corridor, leaving the cell door open. Rahtiek stretched, got out of bed, and grabbed his rag and toothbrush. He walked over to the sink and freshened up. After drying his face he put on his green prison pants and shirt, took the black bag from the bottom of his bed, and placed two pair of Timberland boots in it along with a black pair of Air Force One's. He reached under his bed for some books and magazines and stuffed them in the bag. He then stripped his bed down to the green, state-issue mattress and folded the sheets and cover and stuffed them into the pillow case. Then he took his pictures off the wall, three pictures of his crew back home and one of his daughter.

"Don't worry, baby girl. Daddy's coming to get you," he said, kissing his daughter's picture. He placed the pictures of his friends in the bag and held his daughter's in his hand as he sat on his bunk waiting for the CO to return.

"Are you ready, Davis?" the CO asked when he returned.

"Yeah, I'm ready."

"Then let's go."

Rahtiek grabbed his bag and pillow case and walked out of the cell. The CO closed the cell, and they began walking down the corridor. All the prisoners were asleep, except for Jay, a short stocky dark-skinned brother with a mouth full of gold teeth.

"Yeah, my nigga," Jay said. "I see they finally letting

you up out this joint."

"No doubt!"

Rahtiek stopped in front of Jay's cell and shook his hand. Jay held on to Rahtiek's hand and said, "I'ma see you, Sun. I'll be home in another fourteen months."

"I hear you, baby bro. I should be straight by then. Come holla at a nigga down in Fort Greene so I can help you get on your feet," Rahtiek said.

"No doubt! Leave a nigga a little something," Jay begged, looking down at Rahtiek's bag.

"I got you," Rahtiek said.

Rahteik reached in his bag and pulled out three magazines: The Source, Vibe, and Double XL; and a Donald Goines' novel, Black Girl Lost. He handed them to Jay then reached back in the bag and pulled out the pair of all black Air Force One's.

Jay smiled as Rahtiek handed him the sneakers through the bars.

"I won't be needing these," Rahtiek said. "I don't wear kicks in the street."

"Good looking out, my nigga," Jay said thankfully. The two men slapped five, and Jay said, "One."

"Hold it down, Sun," Rahtiek said.

Rahtiek followed the CO down the corridor and was led to the receiving room, where he changed into civilian clothes. He put on his blue Tommy Hilfiger jeans and a wife beater and noticed that his shirt was missing. The sergeant called Rahtiek to the front desk and handed him his personal property, while looking over Rahtiek's paper work. As Rahtiek was putting his daughter's picture into his wallet, the sergeant said, "I see you turned down parole and you're leaving here, today, a free man."

"No doubt!" Rahtiek said, puffing out his chest

proudly.

"That don't mean you won't be back," the sergeant said, cutting his eyes at Rahtiek .

"Not in this lifetime, I won't," Rahtiek said confidently

."We'll see," said the sergeant as he handed Rahtiek a bus ticket.

"What happen to my shirt?" Rahtiek asked.

"I don't know. You want me to see if I can find one that fits you?"

"What's the weather like?"

"It's about seventy degrees."

"I'm alright then. Fuck it."

Rahtiek then stuffed the rest of his property into his black bag and was escorted out of the building to the front gate by two COs, one black, the other white. The white CO swiped his shield across the monitor, and the gate opened. As Rahtiek started to walk through the gate he said, "See you later."

Rahtiek looked at the CO and said, "You won't never see me again!"

"That's what they all say," he answered.

Rahtiek walked out of the gate and put on a show for the corrections officers. He dropped his bag, stretched his arms, bent down and kissed the ground and said, "Free at last, free at last. Thank God Almighty, I'm free at last!"

The COs laughed, closed the gate, and reentered the building.

Now over at Wyte Yak's apartment, his twelve-year-old son, Jeremy, was sitting at the foot of Wyte Yak's bed watching cartoons looking back at his father who was lying in bed constantly tossing and turning in his sleep. Wyte Yak was dreaming about his "near-death" experiences. He was in a Project building walking towards the front door as shots were being fired and bullet holes appeared in the door. He reached the door and had his hand on the knob about to open it to let the shooter know he was in there but changed his mind and turned around and ran away, taking a slug in his back.

The scene changed....and Wyte Yak was in the ocean drowning. It was high tide and Wyte Yak couldn't seem to swim back to shore and he panicked and went under water. Each time he came up to look for land he saw nothing but ocean. He was yelling for help when out of nowhere a man on a yellow raft paddled over and rescued him.

Next, Wyte Yak was sitting on the bench with Trap, Deuce, and Rahtiek, Shakim came running around the corner with a 9mm in his hand shooting. Trap and Deuce ran off while Rahtiek ducked behind a tree. Shakim shot Wyte Yak twice in the belly and was standing over him about to finish him off when Rahtiek stepped from behind the tree with a .357 Magnum and emptied the slugs into Shakim's back. Shakim fell onto Wyte Yak and Yak woke up in a cold sweat.

Jeremy looked back at his father and asked, "You still having those nightmares, huh, dad?"

Wyte Yak, realizing he was just dreaming, said, "They won't go away. I guess they're just reminders of the past."

Wyte Yak sat up in his bed and stretched. He pulled back his Tommy Hilfiger sheet got out of bed and stepped into his Ralf Lauren slippers. Wearing nothing but a pair of Tommy Hilfiger boxers he walked into the bathroom. He grabbed his tooth brush from the tooth brush rack, put some tooth paste on it and began brushing his teeth and washing his face. Once he was finished washing his face, he poked his head out of the bathroom door. "Did you eat yet, Jerm?" he asked his son.

Jeremy shook his head no and said. "Nah, I just got up. All I did was take a shower then came in here and put on the TV.

"Well, go fix yourself something to eat. I'm about to jump in the shower. As soon as I get dressed, we out."

"Alright, Dad."

Wyte Yak put on the shower stepped out of his slippers, took his boxers off, and entered the shower. Jeremy walked into the kitchen, pulled out a big salad bowl and poured half a box of Super Sugar Crisp into it. He then reached in the refrigerator for a gallon of milk and poured some milk into the bowl of cereal and sat down to eat.

Wyte Yak stepped out of the bathroom dripping wet with a huge red white and blue Tommy Hilfiger towel wrapped around him. He walked over to the dresser, opened the top drawer, and took out a white T-shirt and a pair of Ralph Lauren socks. He closed the top drawer then opened the second drawer and pulled out a fresh pair of Hilfiger boxers. He dried himself off, put on his underwear, walked over to the closet, and pulled out a pair of blue Polo jeans and a red and blue Tommy Hilfiger long-sleeve rugby shirt. After putting on his shirt and pants he put on a pair of dark blue construction Timberlands.

Jeremy was in the kitchen cleaning out his bowl when Wyte Yak entered and asked, "You ready, Jerm Dogg?"

Jeremy looked over at his father and said, "Yeah, I'm ready."

He placed the bowl on the dish rack and followed his

father out of the front door.

Wyte Yak and Jeremy walked out front and entered his Ford Expedition. Wyte Yak hopped in the driver's seat and Jeremy the passenger's. They put on their seat belts, and Wyte Yak started the car. He then reached in his CD case and pulled out Eric B and Rakim's "Paid in Full" CD and put it in the CD player. He handed Jeremy the case and told him to check out the picture on the back as he drove off.

Jeremy looked down at the CD and asked, "Man, who are these dudes with all this jewelry?"

"I don't know all of them, but that little dude down at the bottom with the big horse shoe hanging from his chain, that's Fifty Cent. He died in the late eighties."

Jeremy frowned, looked over at his father, and said, "That's not Fifty Cent. Fifty's not dead. I just saw his video the other day."

Wyte Yak laughed and said, "That's the original Fifty Cent, the one the rapper got his name from."

"Oh, I thought he was the original."

"Nah, a lot of rappers get their names from old school gangsta's. But they usually pick old, white gangsta's. That's why I fuck with Fifty because he chose a black gangsta' to name himself after. I'm feeling that."

"Me, too. Fifty's the man."

The two sat back and listened to the sounds of Eric B and Rakim's "Paid in Full" CD until Jeremy turned down the music, looked over at his father, and asked, "Dad, can I hang out with you today?"

Wyte Yak shook his head and said, "Sorry, Jerm Dogg. I'm going to be busy today. We can hang out tomorrow. The disappointed Jeremy lowered his head and said, "Man, you always say that. Then when tomorrow comes you say, 'Sorry, Jerm Dogg, we gotta hook up later.' Which never comes, and I wind up spending all day with Aunt Rosie."

"Come on Jerm, I gotta make that money. We gotta eat. We need a roof over our head, and I know you like wearing Rockawear, Sean John, Timberland and Jordans."

"Truthfully I don't care about none of that stuff-- except for, maybe, my Jordans. I don't need none of that. I not trying to impress nobody. I'm Jerm Dogg. I got Don status. Everybody's gonna love me regardless."

"And why is that?"

"Because I'm that dude."

"No doubt! You the man."

"I'm not the man; you the man. I'm that dude."

Wyte Yak laughed as he pulled over in front of his sister's house on Green and Franklin. He beeped the horn and sister, Rosie, opened the door. Yak and Jeremy slapped five and hugged.

"Now get out. I'll see you later."

Jeremy stepped out of the car and said, "Alright Dad, chill."

Jeremy walked up to the front door and his Aunt Rosie stepped out and hugged him. She waved to Wyte Yak and her and Jeremy entered the house. Wyte Yak beeped the horn and drove off.

He drove down Myrtle Avenue and as soon as he reached the beginning of the Projects on Carlton he saw Mia, a short, sexy, thick, brown-skinned sister, crossing the street. Yak beeped his horn and waved, and Mia yelled, "Hi, Wyte Yak."

He continued driving down the Ave until he reached Myrtle and Prince St, where he pulled over the Expedition and walked into the corner store. He said, "What up, Ak?"

and slapped the teenage Arab five as he passed him.

He walked over to the refrigerators and grabbed a kiwi strawberry drink. The Arab man behind the counter said, "What up, Ak Man?" and shook Wyte Yak's hand.

"I'm chilling, Ak. How you?"

"I can't complain."

Wyte Yak handed him a dollar for the Mystic and said, "Cool out, Ak," as he walked out of the store. Once he stepped out of the store he saw Lisa, a sexy light-skinned female with long hair, wearing a red, business skirtsuit and red high-heel shoes.

"What up, Lisa G?"

"Hi, Wyte Yak."

"Where you going looking all divalicious?"

As Lisa hurried past Yak she said, "I'm on my way to work and I'm late."

Wyte Yak held out his hand attempting to slow her down.

"Hold up a minute. I'll drive you to work."

Lisa held her hand up and said, "Thanks for the offer, but the train's faster."

"Alright, 'Booger Woman."

Wyte Yak walked over to the pay phone, picked up the receiver and dialed Yiddo's crib. The phone rang twice, then was answered by Yiddo.

"Hello."

"What up, Yiddo?"

"What's good, Wyte Yak?"

"Ain't nothing. You heard from Rahtiek this morning?"

"Nah, he'll probably be through in a hour or two."

"No doubt! Who you in the crib with?"

"Just Web right now. J-Bigg called and said him and

Little coming through after they snatch up Sugar."

A fine brown-skinned sister with a fat ass, wearing a tight, light-blue Baby Phat sweatsuit walked by. Once Wyte Yak saw the total package he yelled to her, "Damn, boo, you looking bootylicious. You mind if I tailgate?"

The girl smiled and kept walking.

Yiddo asked, "Where you at?"

"I'm at the pay phone on the corner watching all the gorgeous creatures head to work. I'll be up there in a minute."

"Alright, Sun, the door is open."

Meanwhile in the 'hood J-Bigg and Little were exiting 107 Navy Walk, a building in the Projects that's right next to the green bridge that leads to the middle side of the Projects and the first building on the right side of the basketball courts. J-Bigg, a dark-complexioned, six-foot three, two hundred and seventy pound, handsome gorilla, was with Little, a dark-skinned, five foot four, stocky player, with his low-cut hair greased and waves spinning 360 degrees. They stopped at the bench in front of the building and an old lady walked by with an eleven-year-old boy pushing her shopping cart filled with groceries. Little tapped J-Bigg and said, "Dig, look at Sun out here early in the morning getting that money."

J-Bigg nodded his head and said, "You know Sun a hustler."

"He gotta be. You know his moms smoked out. She don't take care of him. He don't even go to school."

The two men sat on the bench, and J-Bigg pulled a Dutch Master cigar from his jacket pocket. He licked the cigar to moisten it. Then with his thumbs he split the cigar down the middle and asked, "Why he don't go to school? I was kicking it with that Little nigga the other day. Sun mad smart."

Little looked over at J-Biggs and said, "You know why. The same reason you dropped out."

K-Bigg pulled a nickel bag of weed from his pocket and sprinkled it into the cigar while saying, "Yeah, I was a bum. I feel for Shorty. It is hard to concentrate on your schoolwork while the other kids are joking you because your gear ain't up to pah."

As Bigg was rolling the blunt and sealing it, Little said, "That's why all schools should have uniforms. You go to school to learn, not for no fashion show."

"You right, but I doubt that will ever happen. You know everybody ain't gone look at the overall picture. People too selfish."

"You finished?" asked Little.

"Just about."

J-Bigg used his lighter to dry the blunt then lit it. They stood and walked through the baketball courts and started calling Sugar from the window.

J-Bigg yelled, "Awwooo!"

Little yelled, "Aaaayyyo!"

As they passed the courts and were standing in front of 85 Fleet Walk, Sugar's building, Little said, "He hear us. Sun just acting dumb."

J-Bigg took another puff on the blunt, inhaled the smoke, and passed it to Little as he said, "I know. He always do that. Now watch."

Sugar opened the eighth floor window looked down and yelled, "Oooweee!"

The two men looked up and Bigg yelled, "Come

down!"

"I'm coming right now!"

Little held the blunt up and yelled, "You better hurry up, if you trying to hit this blunt."

Within two minutes the legendary Sugar, known for his exquisite ball handling skills, five-foot eight, slim, light brown, sporting a low cut, came rushing out the building and said, "Pass that, stupid face."

Little passed Sugar the blunt, and they started walking through the 'hood towards the store on Prince and Johnson. Little looked over at Sugar and asked, "Why you always do that?"

Sugar laughed and said, "Do what?"

"You know what you be doing. Don't act dumb," said Little.

Still laughing Sugar asked, "What you talking about?"

J-Bigg screwed his face and said, "Don't say nothing, Little. He know what he be doing. He just acting stupid."

They arrived at the front of the store and Sugar, who was slightly ahead of the other two, paused before opening the door and said, "It's too early in the morning for this bullshit. I don't know what the hell y'all talking about. So if y'all ain't gonna tell me, fuck it."

J-Bigg looked down at Sugar and said, "Alright then, fuck it. But you know what we talking about."

In agreement with J-Bigg, Little said, "Word!"

Sugar said, "Whatever" and entered the store followed by J-Bigg and Little.

Once they entered the store Sugar walked up to the counter and said, "Let me get three cigars."

The middle-aged, male, Arabian cashier asked,

"What kind?"

Sugar didn't hear him as looked to the left at J-Bigg who was walking over towards the refrigerators to retrieve a beverage.

Sugar yelled, "Sun, grab me a fruit punch Snapple."

Little, who was at the newsstand looking through the Daily News yelled, "Me, too, Bigg."

The cashier asked Sugar again, "What kind of cigars do you want?"

Sugar twisted his lips and sarcastically replied, "It's a boy! Sun, you know what I smoke. Stop playing."

"Yeah, I know. You smoke Dutch Masters. I was just fucking with you, Sun."

The cashier then grabbed three Dutch Masters out of the box behind him and placed them on the counter. Little walked over by the door still reading the newspaper, and J-Bigg walked over and placed two Snapple drinks and a Tropicana orange juice on the counter.

The Arab asked, "Ring it all up together?"

Sugar said, "Yeah, the newspaper, too."

The cashier rang up the merchandise and said, "That'll be six seventy-five," then placed the items in a black plastic bag.

Sugar handed him a twenty dollar bill, and the cashier handed him a ten, three singles, and a quarter. J-Bigg grabbed the bag off the counter, and the three men were about to leave but were frozen in their tracks when they heard a flurry of gunshots go off. First there were sixteen consecutive shots, followed by another twelve, and then six more which were a lot louder than the others.

With a surprised expression on his face, J-Bigg asked, "Who the fuck shooting like that this early in the morning?"

"It sounds like somebody just got laid out." Sugar said.

"The last six sounded like a four four," said Little.

"Word!" said J-Bigg, in agreement with Little.

They waited a few minutes to make sure the shooting was over. No more shots were fired so the three men walked out of the store and back into the Projects. As they were walking to Yiddo's crib Sugar's cell phone started ringing and he answered it, "Yeah."

"Yo, Shoog, what up?"

"Who this, AG?"

"Yeah, Sun. Where you at?" asked AG, sounding concerned.

"I'm on the other side."

"You heard all that shooting."

Curious, Sugar asked, "Yeah, who was that?"

"That was little Ryhiem and them niggas from over here shooting out with some little niggas from the far side."

"Did anybody get hit?"

"Nah, them stupid-ass niggas was shooting like the A-Team."

"Them niggas need to chill."

"Fuck them niggas. I was just checking to see if you was alright 'cause I know you usually be walking on this side taking your daughter to school every morning."

"I'm good! My daughter moms took her to work with her today."

"Alright then. Holla."

"Alright chill."

Sugar hung up the cell phone and him, Little, and J-Bigg continued walking to Yiddo's crib.

CHAPTER 15

Rahtiek was reading a book as he was riding the Greyhound bus. He had his bag of personal items sitting next to him in the chair. Other than Rahtiek there were about twenty other people on the bus. The bus made a stop in Poughkeepsie, New York, picking up five more passengers. A white couple who appeared to be in their late fifties was the first to enter and was followed by a husky white male in his late thirties with a shaved head and thick mustache. After him a nineteen-year-old black guy entered with a knapsack on his back and a walkman on his ears.

They all walked pass Rahtiek and took seats in the rear of the bus. The last person to enter the bus was Nikki, a twenty-five-year-old, light-skinned, sexy female wearing a perfectly fitting mint-green business suit that definitely showed off the curves of her voluptuous body. Her hips swayed seductively as she walked with the grace of a well-bred stallion. Rahtiek was unaware of the woman's presence since his head was down and he was reading a book.

The woman noticed Rahtiek's huge chest and biceps since he was shirtless, wearing only a tank top. Although there were many available seats on the bus she chose to sit in the seat Rahtiek had his bag in. Bending over and reveal-ing the top of her cleavage she tapped Rahtiek to gain his attention and said, "Excuse me. Is this seat taken?"

Rahtiek stopped reading to move his bag, and there appeared in front of him the sexiest creature he'd seen in six years. As she sat down Rahtiek stared deep into her eyes.

"Is something wrong?" Nikki asked.

"No, I'm sorry I didn't mean to stare, but I haven't seen a woman as sexy as you in quite some time. Six years

153

to be exact."

"Six years? That's a long time. You must be on your way home from prison."

Rahtiek nodded his head and said, "No doubt!"

Curious to find out if Rahtiek had a girl, Nikki said, "I bet your girl can't wait for you to get home."

"Nah, boo, the only girl I got waiting for me to get home is my baby girl, Quanesia."

Rahtiek reached in his back pocket for his wallet and pulled out a picture of his daughter. He handed it to Nikki, who smiled and said.

"She's a cutie. She has your eyes."

"Thanks."

Not wanting the hassle of a baby mother, Nikki asked, "Where's her mother? I'm sure she'll be glad to see you."

"She's deceased."

Although she was really relieved, not wanting to be disrespectful, Nikki said, "I'm sorry to hear that."

Feeling sad, Rahtiek lowered his head and said, "It happened a few years ago while I was locked up. She was at a party in the Projects down in Fort Greene Brooklyn. A beef broke out, and dudes just started shooting. She wound up taking one to the head."

"That's messed up," said Nikki, thinking to herself this sure is one fine thug here, and he's single. Hmm...if I play my cards right, I just may be able to lock this nigga down.

"Yeah, it happens. Now my daughter is in foster care, and once I get home I'm going to see if I can get her in my custody."

"I wish you the best. I hope everything works out for

you. I know you miss her."

"No doubt," Rahtiek said, livening up. "But enough about me, what's your name? Where you come from? I know your fine ass don't live up here in these mountains."

"My name is Nechemiah, but everybody calls me Nikki. I'm an assistant manager of a bank up here in Poughkeepsie. I have an apartment up here but right now I'm going to visit my moms on the lower east side of Manhattan."

Rahtiek said, "Nice to meet you, Nikki. I'm Rahtiek. I find you extremely sexy and was wondering if the feeling is mutual."

"Thank you, Rahtiek. And to be honest with you," Nikki said lustily as she paused to bite her bottom lip, "once I saw your fine ass sitting here, I knew I had to meet you."

Rahtiek laughed and looked around at the other available seats. Realizing he was the one being bagged instead of the other way around, he said, "Damn, it's like this in the new millennium?"

"Like what?"

"Honeys be bagging niggas now?"

"Please…I always go after what I want. I was taught if you see something you want, you better go out and get it because if you don't the next chick will."

"I hear that," Rahtiek said smiling.

Nikki licked her lips and said, "And ugh, being that you just did six years I know what's on your mind. You don't even have to worry about that because as soon as we reach the city I'm gone get us a room so you can release some of that tension you built up over the years."

Rahtiek got excited and said, "Damn, shit got real in

New Yitty while I was away!"

"Don't you think it's about time?"

Rahtiek nodded his head in agreement and said, "No doubt!"

They both smiled as they looked into each other's eyes. They conversed all the way to the city. Once they got off of the bus, they found a hotel and rented a room for four hours.

Yiddo was in the kitchen cooking some grits, eggs, and turkey bacon. Little was sitting on the edge of the couch playing N.B.A. live on the Play Station 2 against J-Bigg, who was sitting on the same couch two seats away with a blunt in his mouth. Sugar was sitting in between them two rolling a blunt, and Web was at the end. J-Bigg took the blunt out of his mouth and said, "Yiddo, come get this Neatho. Hurry up so I can finish busting this nigga ass."

Yiddo quickly walked over and took the blunt from J-Bigg and asked, "He busting your ass, Little?"

Little twisted his lips and said.

"He only up four."

"Yeah, but look how much time is left," Bigg said.

Sugar interrupted, saying, "Shit, it's thirty seconds left. I seen dudes make a comeback in less time that."

As he walked back into the kitchen, Yiddo said, "Word!"

"Don't tell him nothing," said Little.

J-Bigg poked out his chest and said, "Niggas can't tell me nothing! I'm busting your ass! You know it, I know it, and they know it!"

Somebody knocked at the door.

Web looked back and asked, "You got that, Yiddo?"

"Yeah, I got it."

As Yiddo walked over to answer the door, Sugar said, "Hook me up with some eggs and turkey bacon, Yiddo. You know I get hungry after I had my breakfast blunts."

"You don't want no grits?"

"Nah, you know I don't fuck with no grits."

Yiddo opened the door, and Dikki Jah rolled in, followed by Trap and Pooh Berry. Everybody greeted each other with fives and "what ups" then Pooh asked,
"Rahtiek didn't get here yet?"

"Nah," said Yiddo.

Dikki Jah and Trap entered the living room with J-Bigg and them while Pooh Berry sat at the kitchen table kicking it with Yiddo.

Rahtiek and Nikki were in a hotel room in midtown Manhattan. Nikki was at the bottom of the bed in her bra and panties. Rahtiek was standing in front of her wearing nothing but a pair of boxers with his head tilted back inhaling the sweet fragrance of Nikki's perfume as she seductively kissed his neck and slid her tongue down the front of his broad chest. She sucked his right nipple and twirled her tongue around it for a few seconds then proceeded to licking down his stomach.

Turned on by his tight six-pack she ran her tongue along his stomach muscles. She then pulled his boxers down and was slapped in the face by his enormous erection. She looked up at him and smiled letting him know that she was pleased with the size of his dick. She licked the tip then placed all nine inches deep into her mouth, her bottom lip almost touching his nut sack. This drove Rahtiek crazy and he almost lost control.

Though he didn't want to, he stopped her. He knew he woulda busted off if he didn't. So he lifted her head up and grabbed a hold of her pretty plump breast. He reached into her bra, grabbed the nipples and pulled her titties out above the bra. He lowered his head and began sucking on them like a newborn baby then pushed her back on the bed and snatched her panties off. Nikki's pussy was already soaked and awaiting him as he mounted her and placed her legs onto his shoulders. He inserted his manhood into her vagina and her toes immediately curled as she moaned and dug her fingers into his back.

Nikki let out moans of pleasure, screaming, "Fuck Me, Fuck Me," with her legs wrapped around his waist. Her head was twisted up against the headboard since Rahtiek forced her to the top of the bed thrusting in and out of her, pounding her pussy like the gorilla he is. He grabbed her right leg and tossed it to the left so he could take her from behind. Nikki, the obedient servant, got on her knees so he could hit it better, which he did. He grabbed a hold of her hair and aggressively pumped. Nikki's eyes rolled to the back of her head as she released the first of many orgasms. She screamed, "Oh Daddy, fuck the shit out of me."

Her pussy juice soaked his testicles and again he got that tingly feeling like he was about to bust a nut. He pulled out and lay back on the bed. Nikki slowly sat on him took in every inch of his manhood. Once comfortable she started bouncing.

Everybody was in the living room watching Sugar and K-Digg play the game, except for Pooh Berry and

Yiddo, who were sitting at the kitchen table talking. Pooh Berry said, "I wonder what's taking Rahtiek so long to get here. They usually let you out at six in the morning. He should have been here by now."

"I don't know. When they let me out, I was here before ten o'clock. I hope he's alright," said Yiddo.

Sugar yelled from the living room, "Rahtiek's not you, Yiddo! He alright. He probably beating up on some pussy."

Agreeing with Sugar, J-Bigg said, "Word! Sun probably blowing some bitch back out."

Wyte Yak drove into the 'hood and parked in the parking lot in front of 48 Fleet. He reached in the glove compartment and grabbed two handguns, an automatic sixteen-shot, 9mm Glock and an eight-shot, automatic .38 with infrared beam attached to it. He looked around making sure he didn't see any police since dudes were just shooting in the 'hood. He stuffed both guns into his pants and stepped out of the vehicle. As soon as he stepped out of the vehicle he was called by Pillsbury--always in good spirits and was one of the most-loved thugs in the neighborhood--from his window on the fifth floor.

"Wyte Yak!"

Wyte Yak looked up at the window saw Pillsbury and said, "What up, Pillak?"

"Ain't nothing. Where you headed?"

"Yiddo crib. You know Rahtiek coming home today."

"Oh yeah, that's right. I'll be up there in a few."

"Alright."

Pillsbury left the window, and Wyte Yak walked out of the parking lot and headed towards 340 Hudson Walk, Yiddo's building. As he was walking to the building he saw his young homey, Phil Boy, sitting on the bench in front of 342 Hudson Walk the building connected to 340. Phil Boy had his head down and appeared to be in deep thought. Wyte Yak walked up to Phil Boy and said, "What up, Phil Boy? What you thinking about?"

Phil Boy raised his head, saw Wyte Yak, smiled and said, "What up, Wyte Yak? I was just thinking about you."

"What about me?"

"I was hoping you hurry up and come up with a plan to blow us up. I'm tired of being broke."

"Nigga, you better take your ass to school or get a job or something."

Phil-Boy frowned as he said, "You know I not with that school shit, and I ain't never had a job in my life."

"You got to do something. You can't be sitting around waiting for me or nobody else to do nothing for you. You're not my responsibility. How about if I never come up with a plan to blow us up? You gonna blame me for the way your life turns out?"

"I wouldn't blame you, but I'd probably be mad at you."

With a look of disbelief, Wyte Yak asked, "You will, huh?"

Phil-Boy looked up at Wyte Yak and said, "Ugh huh, probably."

Wyte Yak shook his head,

"Then I guess I better come up with that plan to blow us up then, huh?"

Phil-Boy nodded his head and said, "Mmm hmm."

"Alright, Phil, I'm out."

Wyte Yak slapped Phil five and started to walk off but was called by DY from a second floor window in 342

Hudson Walk.

"What's good, Wyte Yak?" DY asked.

Yak looked up at the window before responding

"Ain't nothing, DY. How you?"

"I'm good. Where you headed?"

"To Yiddo crib."

"I'm coming up there."

DY exited the window, and Wyte Yak walked over to 340 Hudson Walk. He opened the door and was about to enter but was called by Nite, who was walking from around the corner with a big-butt stripper. Nite yelled, "Wyte Yak, hold the door!"

Wyte Yak held the door for Nite. Although he was five-foot eight he appeared to be shorter because his ankle was twisted owing to a gunshot wound and he walked with a limp. He had a "ruff" look and was a true thug for life. They slapped five, and the three of them entered the building, walking up the first flight of stairs before entering the elevator.

Nite pressed the number five button and said, "This is Butter. She's a welcoming home present for Rahtiek."

Wyte Yak looked Butter over, smiled and said, "He gonna like that present, but I got two he's gonna like even better." He pulled the two guns from his waist.

Nite took them from Yak and said, "What's this, a trey eight auto? Oh yeah, Sun gonna love this. And you giving him a Glock, too?"

"No doubt!"

The elevator stopped on the fifth floor, and Wyte Yak exited. Nite tucked the two guns in his waist, then him and Butter walked out of the elevator. Wyte Yak walked over to Yiddo's door, twisted the knob, and entered, followed by

Nite and Butter.

After three hours of fucking and eleven of the most pleasurable orgasms Nikki had ever had, she laid her head across Rahtiek's chest smiling, thinking to herself, "I really picked a winner this time." She was wondering what was this man really about and how could she be on his team. Although she was more comfortable lying across Rahtiek's chest than she had been in a long while, she got up and searched her pocketbook for a cigarette. She found her pack of Newport and pulled one from it. She lit it, inhaled, and held the pack out towards Rahtiek.

"Nah, I don't smoke," Rahtiek said, waving his hand.

He then got out of bed, put on his boxers, and walked into the bathroom. He cut on the shower and got in. Nikki turned on the TV and lay back on the bed puffing her cigarette. When Rahtiek walked back in the room Nikki was lying on her side watching the news, still completely naked with her sexy, firm ass sticking out.

"Should I hit it one more time or chill?" Rahtiek asked himself. He fought the temptation and decided to put on his clothes. He put his pants on and, once he put on his wife beater, he sat down on the bed and started to put on his boots.

Nikki looked back at Rahtiek and asked, "You leaving already?"

"Yeah, I gotta go. My peeps waiting for me back in the 'hood. I don't want them to think something happened to me."

Nikki turned her body around so that she was facing Rahtiek and said, "When will I see you again?"

"Write your number down. I'll give you a ring. We can hook up the next time you come back down because you know I'm not going back up to them mountains for nothing."

Nikki smiled and seductively said, "Not even if you had a good reason?"

Rahtiek looked down at Nikki and said, "Nikki, you'se a hottie and the whole nine, but I can't see myself traveling all the way up state for no ass."

Nikki was offended but tried to play it off, saying, "That's not what I'm talking about."

"For what then?" asked Rahtiek.

"I think I might have something else you might be interested in. What were you locked up for?"

"Armed robbery. Why?"

Nikki, wanting to be with Rahtiek more than any man she had ever met, decided to lay the best cards she could think of on the table and said, "I'm sure your MO hasn't changed, and I do manage a bank."

Rahtiek had finished tying his boots, stood and asked, "So what you saying?"

"I'm saying maybe you want to come stick it up. It's easy as hell to hit. We don't have but one old-ass security guard and on the last Thursday of every month, this Colombian drug family drops off anywhere between twenty-five and fifty million dollars that my bank launders for them."

"And you'd set it up for me?"

Nikki stood and walked over to Rahtiek. She placed her arms around his waist, looked up into his eyes and said, "I have to be honest with you. No nigga has ever rocked me like that in my life. I'm open. I'll do whatever you want me to do, whenever you want me to do it."

Rahtiek smiled, kissed Nikki on the forehead, and said, "I knew you was my kind of girl."

Rahtiek hung out a few minutes with Nikki listening

to her talk about the bank she worked in. She wrote down her cell phone number, and he promised to give her ring. Then he left the hotel and hopped on the train to Brooklyn

CHAPTER 16

It was a quarter to two in the afternoon, and all of Rahtiek's homeboys were still awaiting his arrival at Yiddo's apartment.

"Y'all sure this nigga got out today?" J-Bigg asked.

"He coming, Sun. I talked to him last night," said Wyte Yak.

"Sun taking forever," said Little.

A knock was heard at the door, and Pillsbury walked over to answer it. He looked through the peep hole and said, "Here he go. Pillsbury opened the door and Rahtiek walked in, hugged Pillsbury, and everybody started yelling.

Pillsbury said, "What up, Sun? Welcome home."

As Pillsbury closed the door Yiddo hugged Rahtiek.

"What up, Yiddo?" Rahtiek asked.

"Chillin', Sun. How you?"

"I'm good."

Yiddo walked off, and Rahtiek hugged DY.

"What the deal, Rah? I missed the shit out of you."

"The feeling's mutual. I see you putting on a little weight. What, you working out?"

"Yeah, you know I did a couple of years up north. I still be working out, hitting the chin-up bar."

"That's good. Gotta stay in shape."

DY walked off, and Wyte Yak hugged Rahtiek.

"What up, dummy?"

"What up, you white nigga?" Rahtiek said laughing. "You the reason I got knocked. Talking about drink the drizzy, PO's don't check for alcohol."

"Shut up, dummy. You ain't get violated, you caught a new case."

"Yeah, but I was drunk when I robbed dude."

Wyte Yak walked off, and J-Bigg hugged Rahtiek.

"What up, you dumb dog? Welcome home."

"What up, stupid face? You still be illing?"

"Nah, I be chilling now. No more wilding out."

Rahtiek had a surprised look on his face when Nite hugged him. He hadn't seen him in over ten years because whenever Rahtiek was home Nite was locked up and whenever Nite was home Rahtiek was locked up.

"Damn! What up, my nigga?" Rahtiek asked. "I ain't see you in forever. What's good?"

"I'm maintaining. It seems like we always miss each other."

"No doubt!"

"It's all good, though. We both here now. We gone hook up and make something happen."

"That's what I'm talking about."

After Nite walked off Web hugged Rahtiek.

"What up, baby boy?"

Surprised to see Web, Rahtiek said, "Damn all my niggas is home. You went down a couple of years before me. I'm suprised we didn't bump heads up north."

"I did most of my time in Green."

"Damn! I was in Attica. So what up?"

"I got out two years ago, but I got violated and had to do another six months. I got back out about a month ago. I'm finish with parole. I don't owe them crackers shit. They can suck my dick!"

"I hear you. That's why I turned down parole."

Trap hugged Rahtiek.

"What up, Rah?"

"What up, Trap? How you?"

"I'm good."

Next Rahtiek was hugged by Little.

"What up? You dumb, dirty, desert dog from Denver driving a Datsun."

"What's the deal, Little?"

"Ain't nothing. Chillin', laying low."

Little walked off, and Rahtiek was hugged by Sugar. "What up, Rah? Welcome home."

"What the deal, Sun?"

"Ain't nothing."

"I heard they did a movie about you."

"Yeah."

"So what up? You should be blown."

"They beat me, Sun. It's all good, though. I'm about to head down to Miami in a couple of weeks to shoot this other flick."

"That's what's up."

Pooh Berry walked up, and Rahtiek was shocked as hell because he hadn't seen Pooh Berry since he got locked down by the Feds in 1989. Pooh Berry hugged Rahtiek.

"What's the deal, my nigga?"

"Chillin', brah. How you?"

"Man, I ain't seen you since the crazy 80's. How long you been home?"

"It's been about a few years now. Got a little strip club in East New York. Every kinda pussy you could imagine. Come through. I'll lace you."

"No doubt, you know I'm coming through."

As Pooh Berry walked off, Dikki Jah rolled up.

"What up, Dunn? What's good."

Rahtiek smiled and hugged Dikki's head then kissed him on the forehead.

"Damn, Dikki, I hate to see you like this!"

"It's all good. I hate to see me like this. At least I'm still breathing."

"No doubt!"

As many dudes I done deaded, I supposed to have been dead. I guess God ain't want me to die. He wanted me to suffer, but I'm alright. I still got bitches, my money's just a little low right now."

"Get the fuck out of here, nigga. You ain't got no bitches."

"Yes, he do," said Bigg.

"The 'ho's love Dikki," said Sugar.

Nite led Butter from the back room, and she walked over to Rahtiek, dropped to her knees, and attempted to unzip his pants. Rahtiek grabbed her wrist and said, "Hold on, Yohon."

He raised her to her feet and escorted her to the back room saying, "Chill back here for a minute. I'ma get with you. I need to kick it with my peeps for a minute."

Rahtiek walked back into the living room, and Trap said, "What's wrong, Sun? Don't tell me prison done changed you."

"Nah, never that! I already tore this bitch back out I met on the bus on my way home."

"You fucked a bitch on the bus?" asked Yiddo.

Rahtiek hung his head in disgust and said, "I see this

dude still dumb. No, Yiddo, I met her on the bus. I fucked her in a hotel."

Pillsbury said, "Y'all know Rah a player for life. I told Nite you ain't need no stripper."

"Oh no, don't get me wrong. Shorty got a fat ass. I'm definitely gone hit that, but first I wanna find out what's up with my niggas."

"Niggas is fucked-up, Sun. Other than Pooh Berry and Wyte Yak, we all in the same boat--broke, undisciplined, and unorganized," said J-Bigg.

"Word, Sun!" Web said, agreeing with J-Bigg. "I'm tired of going to prison for bullshit, coming home to nothing, getting violated for some petty shit, laying up for a minute to come back home to nothing."

Rahtiek looked at Web and asked, "So what kind of changes have you made?"

"None yet, but I'm about to make something happen.

"Ain't no opportunities out here for us," J-Bigg said. "All niggas know how to do is hustle and rob niggas. And niggas don't really know how to hustle because dudes is ass-backwards.

"So basically all niggas really know how to do is stick ups," said Nite.

Everybody agreed with Nite.

"The way I see it," Rahtiek said, "we gotta do what-ever we do best to get us paid in this new millennium. So if all we know how to do is rob motherfuckers, I guess it's time for everybody and their mother to get stuck."

Everybody shouted in agreement with Rahtiek, except for Wyte Yak, who said, "Yo, hold up! Y'all know motherfuckers ain't letting nobody rob them these days. Either they bringing the drama or they telling."

"Nah, baby, if we organized we'll be wearing mask

and gloves. So even if the people we rob know who we are they can't prove it. And if somebody decides they want the beef, fuck it. We'll be more than happy to bring it to them. Shit, nigga, with all the heat you packing, I know you ain't worried about nothing," said Rahtiek.

"I'm not worried about me. I just hope everybody can hold their own once shit heat up. Speaking of heat, we got a little something for you."

Nite reached in his waist and pulled out the two automatic handguns and handed them to Rahtiek. Rahtiek held both guns up, admiring them.

Wyte Yak said, "The trey eight with the infra red, that's Bernadette. And the Glock, that's Murder Avenue Milly."

"Good looking out. These bitches are pretty as hell. They gone be my American Express cards."

"They better be, if we gone be robbing everybody and their mother."

Rahtiek kicked it with his crew for about a half hour, catching up on what he missed. Then he went in the back room and smashed Butter. He punished her pussy like there was no tomorrow. She worked for herself, but after the way Rahtiek fucked her, she handed him the three hundred dollars she made the night before at the club and said she wanted to work for him. He took the money, telling her he wasn't a pimp but would consider the offer. In an attempt to persuade him, she sucked him off for the next two hours.

CHAPTER 17

The next day was beautiful. The sun was shining brightly as Rahtiek walked through the Projects. Laughter could be heard, as the children played in the playgrounds and adults sat around on the benches near checkerboard tables, playing cards and dominoes, drinking beer and smoking blunts.

A group of women in their early twenties called out to Rahtiek and stopped their card game to stand and give him a hug, welcoming him home. He smiled, returned the love, then continued walking towards 340 Hudson Walk. When he arrived there he approached the bench, where some of his young homeys were sitting. Although they were all grown up, they didn't recognize Rahtiek because they were all pre-teens when he got locked up.

"What up, Tank, Rob, and Tim," Rahtiek said.
The three looked up at Rahtiek, and Tank frowned, asking, "Who you, duke?"

"Rahtiek. Tank, you don't remember you use to always go to the store for me?"

Rob recognized Rahtiek and stood, slapped him five, and gave him a hug.

"What up, Rah? I didn't even recognize you. You got big as a house."

"You get like that in the pen."

"When you came home?"

"Yesterday, little Rob. Pardon me, I mean big Rob. You seen Sugar?"

"Yeah, he around the corner at the chess tables."

"Everybody around there. They're ranking," said

Tim.

"Good looking out. Chill, young thugs."

Rahtiek walked around the corner, and Tank asked his brother, Rob, "Who's that?"

"Rahtiek. You remember Rahtiek that used to hang with Wyte Yak all the time?"

Rob looked at Tim and said, "I know you remember him, Tim."

Tim shook his head and said, "No!"

"You don't remember when Creepy Sha from the middle side pulled a gun out on Rahtiek down the basketball court? He took it from him, beat him down, took the bullets out of the gun and gave it back."

"Oh yeah, now I remember. He told Sha next time don't walk up on him, 'just shoot from a distance."

"Yeah, that's him."

"That nigga crazy. I thought he was dead."

Rahtiek reached the chess tables where his boys were laughing while Yiddo and Trap ranked on each other. He slapped all of his friends five. There was Phil Boy smoking a blunt, sitting next to Web at the checkerboard table on the left, along with Nite, who was sitting across from Web and next to Pooh Berry.

Sitting on the single bench to the left was DY, who was sitting next to Trap, while Yiddo and Little was sitting on the single bench to the right. At the checkerboard to the right, there was Pillsbury sitting across from J-Bigg, with Sugar sitting next to him, while Dikki Jah sat in his wheel-chair about a foot away from Sugar.

He kissed Dikki Jah on the forehead and said,

"What's good, Dikki?"

"I can't call it. Every time I call it I spoil it."

"Same here."

Then he looked over at Sugar and said, "Walk me downtown, Shoog."

"Hold up a minute. These niggas bugging."

Rahtiek paused for a few and listened to Trap and Yiddo go off on each other's mother then said, "Come on, Sun. Let's bounce."

"Alright, come on."

Sugar stood, and him and Rahtiek headed downtown. They entered the Metro Mall through the parking lot and took the elevator to the top floor. They looked through the window of a few sports stores comparing the prices of the Timberland boots. They were heading towards the escalator when Rahtiek saw a fine, well-shaped, pretty, brown-skinned sister. She was wearing a pair of ankle-length, burgundy, Prada stilettos, a pair of tight jeans showing off her fat apple bottom, and a tight, blue Baby Phat T-shirt cut off at the belly to show off her sexy navel ring, and a short-cut burgundy leather spring vest.

The girl and Rahtiek were staring into each other's eyes, so Rahtiek grabbed her hand and said, "Hello, beautiful. Am I your type, am I suitable? If not, trust me, you need a change from the usual."

The girl smiled and said, "I don't have a type but, if I did, I'm sure you'd be it."

Rahtiek grinned, "Yeah, that's what I wanted to hear,

sweetness. What's your name?"

"Tameeka."

"I'm Rahtiek. What's good with you, Tameeka?"

"Ain't nothing. I'm chilling, doing a little shopping."

"What you shopping for?"

"Some jeans and, probably, another pair of boots."

"What kind of jeans you got on right now?"

"Apple Bottom."

Rahtiek looked behind Tameeka to get a better view of her butt then said, "Oh yeah, then I think you need to buy another pair of those because they definitely got that ass looking right."

Tameeka giggled and said, "Thank you."

"You welcome, sexy. I like your style, Tameeka, but I'm kind of in a rush. If you feeling me like I'm feeling you, fuck the small talk. I just came home from up north yesterday. I don't have a girl. So if you trying to make it happen for yourself write your number down for me, and I'll hit you a little later to see what's really good."

"Alright."

Tameeka reached in her purse for a pen and pad and started to write down her number.

"How old are you?" Rahtiek asked.

"Nineteen."

"Where you from?"

"Far Rockaway?"

Surprised that Tameeka was from Queens and shopping in Brooklyn, Rahtiek said, "Oh, you from Queens. Who you live with?"

Tameeka handed Rahtiek her phone number and said, "I live with my mother, but she's going to work in a couple of hours and won't be home until six in the morning.

So if you trying to see me later, it's all good."

Rahtiek smiled, thinking to himself, "I'm hitting that tonight."

Rahtiek looked back at Sugar, who was gazing into the jewelry store window and said, "You ready, Sun?"

"If you finished," Sugar said.

"Yeah, I'm good."

Rahtiek turned his head back around to face Tameeka. He spread his arms and Tameeka hugged him. He tapped her on her behind as she started to walk away and asked, "What's this you gave me?"

"My cell."

"Alright, cool. I'll hit you later."

"Alright, bye."

Tameeka walked off, and Rahtiek and Sugar headed down the escalator.

"What happen, Dunn? You bagged that?"

"Ain't nothing changed, Sun. You know my stizzy."

"She was on your dick."

"They all are," said Rahtiek, his head held up high like he's the man.

"You a funny nigga," said Sugar as they walked off the escalator.

Once they reached the main level of the mall Rahtiek exited through a door on the left and locked eyes with another cutie, but lets her pass, his eyes lowering his eyes to her ass for a few seconds, saying to himself, "I can get that."

Sugar exited through the revolving doors and was greeted by a fan wearing a white gold, barrel-link, chain with a white gold, Virgin Mary piece that was flooded with diamonds.

"Theodore Sugar Richards," the fan said, shaking Sugar's hand. "I saw you playing in the West Fourth Street tournament last summer. What's up with you? You're not going to the NBA or nothing?"

Before Sugar could answer him, Rahtiek walked over and snatched the fan's chain. The fan was about to defend himself, but Rahtiek gritted his teeth and gave him a stare like, "Front, and your ass dead," as he held his hand on the 9mm on the back of his waist. Then he said, "Get the fuck outta here," and the fan ran off.

Sugar had a disturbed look on his face as he and Rahtiek walked down Fulton Street. Rahtiek looked at Sugar and asked, "What's wrong with you?"

Sugar screwed his face up and asked, "What you gone rob that nigga for when you see he know me?"

"Fuck that nigga! He ain't your man."

"I know he ain't my man, but he know me."

"Fuck that! He shouldn't be running up dick lapping niggas. I bet he won't do that shit no more. Besides, you don't like nobody calling you Theodore, anyway."

Sugar shook his head in disgust as the two men continued walking downtown. They walked in and out of stores for about two hours looking for a sweatsuit for Rahtiek. They couldn't seem to find anything to his liking so they stopped in the pizza shop on Fulton Street and ate a couple of slices. Once they finished eating they decided to head back to the PJs. Instead of cutting back through the mall they walked along the side, down Albee Square Street. As they approached the mall parking lot, they saw a dice game on the outskirts of the parking lot. There were nine young black males playing dice, sporting jewels, and holding shopping bags.

Rahtiek and Sugar looked at each other then headed over to the dice game. The banker--the one who everyone was betting against--had a hot hand. They were playing Ceelow. The banker had just rolled a six and was collecting his winnings. After each player had paid him, he started to take bets on the next roll.   "What's   bank?"   Rahtiek asked.

"Bank is money!" the banker said.

"Don't tell me 'bank is money,' then when I drop two G's on you, you tell me you paying as far as you can go."

"Oh, you's a big baller. In that case bank is..." The banker started to count up the money in his hand, and Rahtiek stopped him.

"You ain't gotta count it. Just shoot it."

"Shoot what? Everything in my hand?"

"Did I stutter?"

"Alright, big baller."

The banker looked at Rahtiek, backed up, kneeled down and shot the dice. He released three dice: a red, which stopped at 4; a white, which stopped at 5; and a green, which went into a spin and stopped on 6, the highest point you could possibly roll. The banker yelled, "Ceelow" and started counting the bank as he walked up to Rahtiek. To his surprise he was met by Rahtiek's 9mm, pointing at his face. The banker said, "Fuck that!" and attempted to grab the gun from Rahtiek, but was slapped to the ground by the .38 automatic in Rahtiek's left hand.

Rahtiek continued to pistol-whip the banker while Sugar pulled his .357 Magnum and told the rest of the crowd, "Nobody move! Y'all know what this is. Put all y'all money and jewels in the bags. Toss y'all bags towards me and get on the ground face down. Anybody try to grab my gat, they getting shot in the face!"

The other gamblers were shook by Sugar's words and started placing their money and jewels in their bags and tossed them over to Sugar. Rahtiek was standing over the banker, whose face was bleeding and lumped up. He put his .38 on the back of his waist, took the money from the banker's hand and what was left in his pockets then said, "If you ever disrespect my iron again, I'll blow your mother-fucking head off and mail it to your mother. You hear me?"

The banker nodded yes. Then Sugar told Rahtiek, "We out, Sun!"

The two jogged through the mall parking lot and exited on the Flatbush Avenue side. As soon as they made the right on Prince Street, Wyte Yak and his nephew, who was driving a black S500 Mercedes Benz with tinted windows rolled up beside them. Rahtiek started to reach for his gun, but Wyte Yak rolled down the passenger side window and yelled, "Get in!" They jumped in the Benz, and Bryan sped down Prince Street, running the light on Myrtle and swerving and almost hitting a jipsy cab that had the right of way. The car skidded as he turned into the Project parking lot at the corner of Johnson Street.

They parked the car and jumped out. Sugar and Rahtiek started arguing as they all walked towards Yiddo's building.

"Nigga, you better start letting me know what you up to so I can be on point."

"You better stay on point. You never know when opportunities going to present itself."

Wyte Yak interrupted and asked, "What happen?"

"Ain't nothing. We just stuck up the dice game downtown."

Sugar screwed his face and said, "Nigga, you know that's not what I'm talking about."

Rahtiek pulled Sugar's fan's chain from his pocket

and said, "This nigga mad because I yapped one of his fans."

Rahtiek dangled the chain in front of Wyte Yak, who took it from his hand and examined it. "This is hot," Wyte Yak said.

"You like that? That's you. We got some more shit to show you when we get upstairs. By the way, who the fuck is this?"

"This my nephew, Bryan."

Rahtiek twisted his lips as he looked at Wyte Yak and said, "Nigga, I know your whole family. This ain't your nephew."

Sugar interrupted saying, "Yes, it is. He's married to his niece, Keisha.

"Oh, word? My bad. What up, Pah?" said Rahtiek, extending his hand.

"What up?" said Bryan as he shook Rahtiek's hand.

"That's a phat-ass Benz," Rahtiek said. "What year is it?"

"Two thousand and two."

"I like that. You gotta let me whip that some time."

"Whenever you ready."

They entered 340 Hudson Walk, took the elevator to the fifth floor, and knocked on Yiddo's door. In a few seconds Yiddo opened it and let them in. Yiddo, Wyte Yak and Sugar all sat down at the table. Rahtiek tossed the money he took from the banker on the table, and they emptied all the bags out on the kitchen table. There were three boxes of Timberland boots, two Rockawear sweatsuits, two pairs of Rockawear jeans along with three Rockawear shirts, three pairs of Sean John jeans, and five Sean John shirts. There was an iced-out diamond bracelet, four different style white gold chains with four iced-out pieces, two gold rings, four-iced out white gold rings, one iced-out platinum pinky ring, and a lot of cash.

Wyte Yak picked up the platinum pinky ring and asked, "This me?"

"If you want it," said Rahtiek.

"How you know I don't want it?" Sugar looked at Rahtiek and asked.

"Nigga, shut the fuck up! All this shit we got here and you crying about a ring."

"You want it, Shoogs?" asked Wyte Yak.

"Nah, you can have it. This nigga bugging giving shit away without even asking me...like he just stuck shit up by hisself.

Rahtiek looked through all the clothes searching for something his size. "Damn! All this shit too small for me," he complained. "Y'all can split this up."

He grabbed the telephone and walked into the living room and took a seat on the couch. Bryan also walked into the living room and took a seat on the couch.

"Thanks for letting us know that, Rahtiek," Sugar said sarcastically.

Sugar split the clothes up between himselk, Wyte Yak, and Yiddo.

"Who the fuck y'all caught for all this shit?" asked Yiddo as he held up a chain admiring it.

"We stuck a dice game on the side of the mall," said Sugar.

Wyte Yak picked up a mitt of money and said, "Let's count up this money, Shoog."

"Hold on," said Sugar.

"Yo, Rah, you ain't trying to help us count up this money?" Sugar yelled in the living room to Rahtiek.

"I'm on the phone. Y'all can handle that."

Sugar, Wyte Yak and Yiddo separated the money into three piles and begin counting. Rahtiek continued talking on the phone, and Ryan cut on the TV and flipped through the channels.

Five minutes later Wyte Yak said, "I counted twenty-seven fifty. How much you got, Sugar?"

"Hold up....ninety-eight, ninety-nine, a hundred. I got eighteen hundred. What Yiddo got?"

"I got eleven seventy-five."

"All together that's five thousand seven hundred and twenty-five dollars," said Wyte Yak, gathering all the money. He deducted twenty percent for the fam and placed it in his right front pocket. "Y'all got four thousand five hundred and eighty dollars."

Sugar screwed his face up and asked, "What the fuck you mean twenty percent for the 'fam'?"

"That's how it's going down. Everything anybody takes, twenty percent goes in the stash for the "fam." Me and Rahtiek talked about that last night."

"Oh, alright."

Wyte Yak handed the rest of the money to Sugar, who walked over to Rahtiek and said, "Get off the phone, Sun. We gotta split this money up."

"Hold on a minute, Meeka," Rahtiek said, resting the phone on his chest. "I don't gotta get off the phone. I heard everything that was said. Give them three eight hundred a piece. Take a G eighty for yourself and give me the last eleven hundred."

Bryan was amazed by Rahtiek's math skills. He looked back into the kitchen at Wyte Yak and asked, "Damn, Yak! Where did you find this genius at?"

"Rah ain't no joke when it comes down to them dollars," said Yiddo.

"No doubt! That's one of the reasons I love that nigga. He one of the smartest thugs I know."

Rahtiek continued his phone conversation, while Sugar distributed the money. He handed Bryan eight hundred then gave Wyte Yak and Yiddo the same. Then went over to Rahtiek and handed him eleven hundred dollars. Rahtiek, ending his phone conversation said, "Alright, baby girl, I'll see you in about a hour."

Rahtiek walked over to the table and put on some of the jewelry they took, saying, "Since everybody straight, I'm out."

"Where you headed, Sun?" Yiddo asked.

"I'm going to check this chick I met earlier in the mall."

"I know you ain't going all the way out to Queens for no ass," Sugar said.

"Hell yeah, nigga, you seen Shorty."

"What part of Queens you going to?" Wyte Yak asked.

"Far Rockaway."

"Alright, me and Bryan gone drop you off."

"Good looking out."

Wyte Yak looked Rahtiek in the eyes and said, "You just make sure you get in a cab coming home. Don't fuck with the train. Too many gangsta' rappers be on them trains."

"Gangsta' rappers?" asked Rahtiek.

"Gangsta' rappers, play play gangsta's--whatever you wanna call them."

"Yeah, alright," Rahtiek laughed and said.

"Man, you stupid going all the way out there to see

that bitch. She probably won't even give you no ass."

"Go 'head, nigga. You know I'm a player for life. I lays the G down thick. Stick with me, you'll learn."

"Get the fuck outta here, nigga," Sugar said screwing his face, "I got plenty of 'ho's."

"Yeah, but only because you Super Star Ted Sugar Richards, but once they meet me they gone be my 'ho's."

"Yeah, alright," Sugar looked over at Yiddo and said, "You hear this nigga, Yiddo?"

"Yeah, I hear him. He don't know they only sweating him because he got that fresh, "from-up-north" glow. It'll wear off in a few weeks."

"Yeah, whatever," said Rahtiek as he, Wyte Yak, and Bryan exited the apartment. They went downtown to Junior's restaurant to have a few drinks and get something to eat. Then they took Rahtiek out to Queens to see Tameeka. Bryan's Benz pulled up in front of Tameeka's house, and Rahtiek slapped Wyte Yak and Bryan five and hopped out the vehicle.

Wyte Yak rolled down the passenger side window and said, "Remember, don't fuck with that A train."

"Alright, I heard you the first time," said Rahtiek as he walked up to Tameeka's house and rang the door bell. After a few seconds Tameeka opened the door wearing nothing but a purple bra and thong. Rahtiek smiled and said, "Turn around so my boys can see that ass."

She turned around, and Rahtiek stepped to the side so Wyte Yak and Bryan could see Tameeka modeling her thong.

Wyte Yak said, "Damn! She got a fat ass."

"I don't know what Sugar talking about," Bryan said smiling. "Sun definitely hitting that!"

Wyte Yak held up the peace sign as Bryan beeped the horn and drove off. Rahtiek entered the house and closed the door behind him.

"What took you so long?" Tameeka asked. "I was starting to think you wasn't coming."

"We stopped at Junior's to get something to eat. I was hungry as hell."

Tameeka smiled, looked down at Rahtiek's crotch, and said, "So you ready to feed me."

"No doubt," Rahtiek chuckled.

Tameeka grabbed Rahtiek's hand and led him upstairs to her bedroom. She closed the door, pushed him on the bed, kneeled down in front of him, and unfastened his pants. She pulled his pants and boxers down to his ankles and looked into his eyes as she grabbed his dick and massaged it and kissed it. Then she lowered her mouth onto it and started sucking.   Rahtiek was overenthused by the pleasure Tameeka was giving him. He leaned up and attempted to stop her. Tameeka pushed him back down, and Rahtiek lost control and climaxed. Once Tameeka tasted his cum, she closed her eyes and let the rest splatter all over her face.

Tameeka's mother walked in the bedroom, saying, "Meeka, I'm not feeling well. I had to leave early."

Tameeka jumped up trying to wipe her face, and Rahtiek quickly pulled up his pants.

Her mother flipped. "Girl, what the hell are you doing? I know you wasn't in here sucking this punk-ass nigga dick."

"Nah, Ma, it wasn't even like that."

"What the hell you talking about, you little fucking freak? You got sperm all over your face!"

Tameeka rushed past her mother and ran into the bathroom to wash her face. Her mother was steamed. She looked over at Rahtiek and said, "Nigga, you better get the hell out of my house before I cut your dick off and shove it down your throat. As a matter of fact, where's my machete?"

Tameeka's mother rushed out of the room to find her machete, and Rahtiek dashed out of the bedroom, down the stairs, and out the front door. Tameeka's mother then ran out of the house yelling and cussing and waving her machete as Rahtiek rushed down the block laughing.

Rahtiek walked down Rockaway Boulevard searching for a cab. Every time a car rolled by that looked like a cab, he held his hand up for it to stop but it was just a regular car that kept on going. He walked ten blocks without seeing one cab. He walked into the train station paid his fare and walked upstairs to the platform. He pulled the Donald Goines' novel, "Black Gangster," from his back pocket and sat on the bench reading.

Within ten minutes the A train arrived and he got on the last car. The only other passenger on the last car was an old homeless man sitting in the far right corner. Rahtiek took a seat in the middle of the car and continued reading.

Everything was cool up until the train stopped on Nostrand Avenue, better known as NA Rock, where four thugs entered the train. Their ages ranged from twenty to twenty-five. Although they were noisy Rahtiek didn't lift his head from his book. The leader of the group of thugs noticed Rahtiek's jewelry and made a gesture to his friends, who all looked over at Rahtiek. The leader then lifted his shirt and tucked it behind his gun, making his 9mm visible. The others did the same. Then they all walked over to where Rahtiek was sitting and sat around him. The leader sat one o'clock in front of him, another sat eleven o'clock in front of him, and the last two sat right beside Rahtiek. The leader said, "My, my, you sure got on some nice jewels there, homey."

Rahtiek raised his head, smiled, and said, "Thank you," and continued reading. The men were startled by Rahtiek's reaction. Their leader realized that Rahtiek was not the average thug but figured, no matter who he was, he would be no match for the four of them, with the artillery they were packing.

So he said, "I see we got us a tuff guy here."

Rahtiek paid him no attention, and he started to get frustrated.

The agitated leader said, "Listen here, duke. I see you gangsta' and all, but you gone have to come off those jewels. You know what this is. Let's not make this into a homicide."

Rahtiek then stood and took a step forward. He lifted the front of his shirt and scratched his belly to make the men think he was unarmed. Then he said, "Nobody never told y'all about the thug sitting on the train reading the book?"

"Nah, what was they supposed to tell us?" asked their leader.

"He's not only gangsta', he also smart..." Rahtiek dropped his book and, as the four men watched the book fall to the floor, reached on the back of his waist and pulled both of his guns at the same time. Without even looking behind him he shot the two thugs who were sitting beside him and were now behind him. The one on his left was struck in the face right below his left eye, and the one on his right was shot in the forehead. Blood slowly dripped from their wounds as they died instantly.

The two men in front of him quickly grabbed the automatic weapons from their waist and attempted to cock them, but it was too late because Rahtiek crossed his guns in front of him so that his 9mm was facing the thug on the left and his .38 with the infra red was facing the leader. He shot the thug on the left twice in the chest, one of the slugs piercing his heart and killing him instantly. He grabbed his chest and tumbled over onto the floor. The leader finally had his gun cocked and was raising it to take aim, but Rahtiek's .38 had the infra red shining right into his open mouth, where Rahtiek shot him. He gagged for a minute then slumped over and died. Finishing his sentence Rahtiek said, "...and he's not to be fucked with, stupid face!"

He put his guns back on his waist, picked up his book, and looked over at the old man in the corner. He pulled out his money and peeled off five hundred dollars. He walked over to the old man, who was shaking in his boots, and handed him the five hundred dollar bills. Then he looked over at the dead men and said, "You see these assholes, Pop. They gone try to rob me, knowing I'm as gangsta' as it gets. What the fuck is this world coming to?"

The train stopped at Hoyt and Schemerhorn. When the doors opened, Rahtiek calmly exited.

The next day at 9:00 in the morning somebody was banging on Yiddo's door. Yiddo was tired and tried to ignore it. But the knocking kept getting louder and louder. Finally Yiddo got out of bed half asleep and walked to the door, wearing nothing but a pair of boxers. Aggravated by the disturbance, he yelled, "Who is it?"

A voice on the other side of the door yelled, "Me!"

Yiddo recognized Wyte Yak's voice so he opened the door. Wyte Yak and Trap walked in. Yiddo closed the door and said, "Damn, Yak! Why you banging on my door like that? I thought you was my PO."(Parole Officer)

"Fuck that! You see this?"

Wyte Yak held up the Daily News showing Yiddo the cover. Yiddo read out loud, "Four armed robbers were shot to death on the A Train by a mysterious man."

Wyte Yak pulled the paper back down to his side and asked, "Where's Rahtiek?"

"He's in the bed. You don't think Rah had anything to do with this, do you?" asked Yiddo.

Wyte Yak rushed into the other bedroom where Rahtiek was sleeping and slammed the door. Rahtiek was rudely awaken by the noise and said, "What the fuck?"

"This is what the fuck!"

Wyte Yak tossed the newspaper into Rahtiek's face. Rahtiek sat up and, clearing the cold from the corners of his eyes, looked at the cover page. "Damn, Yak, how you knew this was me?" he asked

"Who the hell else was it? Bernhard Goetz?"

Rahtiek tried to defend himself, "Chill, Sun. Shit, I wasn't trying to hurt nobody."

"You didn't hurt nobody; you killed four people!"

Rahtiek continued to explain, "I was chillin' minding my business, reading my book when these shitheads tried me. What the fuck was I supposed to do?"

"You were supposed to get in a fucking cab!"

"Man, as soon as y'all left, Shorty took me upstairs to her bedroom. She dropped to her knees and just started sucking the shit out of my dick. I tried to stop her because that shit was feeling too good. I knew I was about to bust, but Shorty wouldn't stop. So I nutted all in her face. Right while I was nutting-man, you ain't gone believe this..."

"Try me."

"Her moms walked in."

Wyte Yak chuckled. "Get the fuck outta here."

"On the real, Sun. The bitch got my dick in her hand and nut all over her face. Then she got the nerve to jump up and try to lie to her moms. Shorty moms flipped, talking about where her machete at and how she gonna cut my dick off and shit. I said fuck this and boated. I walked ten blocks down to the train station and not one cab passed me."

Wyte Yak calmed down knowing Rahtiek wouldn't lie to him.

"It sounds like you had one hell of a night," Wyte Yak said.

"Did I? Shit. It was definitely one for the books."

"Alright, you didn't have a choice, but from now on, you don't ride the train."

"Fuck the train!"

Rahtiek raised up out of bed and started to put on his pants. Wyte Yak said, "You can go back to sleep, nigga. I'm about to be out."

"Where you going?"

"I'm taking Trap to bag this Jew making a drop at the check cashing place on Flushing."

"Hold up. I'm coming."

"Nah, we gotta lay for him, and we don't wan't to bring too much attention to ourselves. Besides, I need you to get a hold of J-Bigg and Web. We gotta meet Pooh Berry at the strip club tonight. One of his bitches got something set up for us."

"Alright, cool. I got something to take care of in a

few anyway."

"What you gotta do?"

"I have to go talk to these people over at child services to see about getting my daughter in my custody."

"Alright, good luck."

Wyte Yak grabbed the newspaper, opened the bedroom door, and walked out. He handed Yiddo the newspaper so he could read up on his roommate's latest adventure, and he and Trap exited the apartment.

CHAPTER 18

It was 10:00 a.m. and Wyte Yak and Trap were on Vanderbilt Ave., near the corner of Flushing. They were sitting in Wyte Yak's Expedition waiting for a white van to pass with a Jewish man driving. Trap lit a cigarette, inhaled and said, "So that was Rah that layed them niggas out on the train?"

"Yeah, he ain't have no choice. Them shitheads tried to rob him."

"They tried to rob Rahtiek? They must of been listening to too much Mob Deep. They shoulda known, ain't no such thing as sticking up the stick-up kids."

"Word up! Any real stick-up kid always got the rachet on him. You might get lucky and body a stick-up kid if you catch him sleeping. But ain't too many stick-up kids getting robbed. Not none I know."

"It's unheard of."

The van they were awaiting passed, U-turned, and pulled up in front of the check cashing place.

"That's him, Dun," Wyte Yak said looking over at Trap. "Handle your business."

Trap tossed the cigarette he was smoking out of the window and leaped from the truck with his hand on the 9mm tucked in his waist. He peeped around the corner then rushed towards the Jewish man getting out of the van. The man stepped out of the van carrying a large manila envelope. Trap snatched him and placed his gun beneath the man's chin and took the envelope, saying, "If you don't want to die, don't do nothing stupid!"

Trap then smacked the man with the gun and blood gushed from his head as he slowly fell down the side of the van. Trap ran back around the corner and jumped back in the Expedition. Wyte Yak put the vehicle in reverse and sped up Vanderbilt Ave driving backwards until he reached Park Avenue. He then put the car in drive and jetted down Park Avenue. Trap opened the enevlope and pulled out stacks of hundred dollar bills.

Trap's adrenalin was pumping, and he was breathing hard. "That was easy as hell, Yak. How you know about that spot back there?"

"I been was supposed to hit that spot. The Jews been making drops off at that check cashing place back there for years."

"That spot is on the low," Trap said. "I woulda never thought to try and catch a vic back there."

They headed back to the Projects and went back up to Yiddo's crib to count the money and found out that they had just caught sixty-two thousand dollars.

Over at child services, Rahtiek was in an office talking with Mrs. Jenkins, the counselor who placed his daughter with foster parents.

Speaking as pleasantly as possible, Mrs. Jenkins said, "I'm sorry, Mr. Davis, but under the circumstances we feel that it would be best if Quanesia stayed with the family she's been with for the last three years."

Trying not to sound too aggressive Rahtiek said, "I want my daughter. I'm her father. It's time she got to know me."

Feeling compassion for Rahtiek Mrs. Jenkins said, "I agree, Mr. Davis, but you will need a permanent address and a steady income before we would even consider placing her in your care. We have to do what we believe would be best for the child. You are a convicted felon, and it's hard for a man of your background to maintain steady employment."

"I understand you have my daughter's best interest at heart, but so do I. I'm not starving. I can provide her with whatever she needs. I love my daughter, and you couldn't begin to understand how much I miss her."

"I'm sorry, but my hands are tied. There isn't much I can do. It's up to the courts.

"I understand, Mrs. Jenkins, but can I at least see her? I know I have some kind of visitation rights."

"Not at this time. The courts feel that it would be best for the child if you didn't contact her until you're in the proper position to take care of her."

"I'm prepared to take care of her right now. She's my daughter, she belongs with me."

"I'm sure she does belong with you and I pray that you do regain custody of her, but right now you're not ready. You don't have a job and you're living with a friend. That's no way to raise a little girl."

"Come on, lady. I have to see my daughter. Her mother passed, my mother passed. She's all I got."

Rahtiek pleaded with the counselor hoping she'd be sympathetic, and she was.

"The court refuses any visitation, but I feel for you. So this is what I'm going to do."

The counselor wrote down an address on a piece of paper and handed it to Rahtiek. She looked into Rahtiek's pleading eyes and said, "I can get in serious trouble for this, but this is the school she attends. She usually goes to lunch in about a half hour from now. You can watch her in the playground to see that she's well taken care of, but any contact will only make it harder for you to regain custody."

"Thanks, Mrs. Jenkins," Rahtiek said. "I really

appreciate this."

Rahtiek shook Mrs. Jenkins hand and left the office. Mrs. Jenkins looked at Rahtiek's behind as he exited, thinking to herself, "if I was only twenty years younger I'd give him the thrill of his life."

Rahtiek left the building and took a cab to Quanesia's school. Children were just starting to enter the playground after eating lunch in the cafeteria. Close to a hundred little girls Quanesia's age ran out into the playground and started playing. He stood by the gate and searched around for ten minutes until he finally saw Quanesia. He smiled because she looked so much like her mother and was amazed by how much she had grown since he'd last seen her. He wished he could just run over pick her up and give her big hug and kiss but since he couldn't contact her he became sad and a tear rolled down his cheek.

DY, Yiddo, and Nite were all in Yiddo's apartment. Nite and Yiddo were in the living room sitting on the couch smoking a blunt and watching CNN. DY was sitting at the kitchen table talking to his mother on the telephone. He slammed the telephone down and said, "Damn! I can't stand that bitch," then walked into the living room.

Yiddo passed him the blunt and asked.

"Who was that, DY?"That was my moms. She just told me my baby moms taking me to court for child support."

Yiddo shook his head and said, "That's fucked up."

"This bitch know I just got fired two weeks ago."

"That's how they do. My baby moms did the same thing."

Nite interrupted, saying, "Nigga, what you talking

about? You ain't never had no job.

"I know," Yiddo said, "but, if I was ever to get one, they'd probably take all my money. She done fucked me all up."

"Go ahead with that bullshit, Yiddo," Nite said laughing.

"Nite, I never hear you say nothing bad about your baby moms. You must got her in check," DY said.

"Don't I wish. My baby moms more trifling than both of y'all's put together."

"I don't know about that, Sun. My son moms be on some other shit. She got a few screws missing or something," said Yiddo.

"Man, your baby moms is a angel compared to mine," Nite said shaking his head, "trust me. I went to check her the other day. Y'all know I got the key, right."

"Nah, Nite, I ain't know you had the key," DY said.

"Yeah, she gave me them one day when I was over there. I told her I was going to the store and I went and got a copy made. Then I went over there another day calling myself sneaking up on her. It was late so I knew my daughter was asleep. So I walked past my daughter's room and crept over to my baby moms room thinking I'm gonna catch her fucking, right. Man, I underestimated this bitch."

"Don't tell me she was fucking," said DY.

Nite cut him off and said, "Yep, two niggas, one had his dick in her mouth, while the other was hitting her from the back."

DY and Yiddo burst out laughing. Yiddo said, "Get the fuck outta here!"

Nite raised his right hand and said, "Word to my daughter."

"Damn city. I thought you was gone say she was

with a chick or something, but your baby moms of the hook," DY said.

"I'm laughing, but it aint funny," Nite said as they all continued laughing.

They sat around watching TV and smoking blunts. Then they got the munchies and sent DY to the store for a pizza pie. Before DY could return Sugar and Trap walked in with a bag filled with money they had taken from the Dominican number runner after he had made a pickup on Myrtle Avenue.

Later around 7:00 that evening Rahtiek, J-Bigg, Web, and Wyte Yak were sitting at a booth in Pooh Berry's strip joint, "Club Captivity." A sexy stripper with small perky breasts, a slim waist, and a fat ass and wearing nothing but a G-string walked over to them and asked, "Would any of you gentlemen like a lap dance?"

"Nah, baby," J-Bigg said, "but I got a dollar for some head."

The stripper rolled her eyes, put up her middle finger, and said, "Fuck you. Give it to your mama. I'm sure she can use it," and walked away.

"That Mud dissed you, Sun," Web said. "You going for that?"

Wyte Yak watched the stripper's ass as she walked away and said, "Leave that bitch alone. I'd fuck her. She don't look like no Muddy Waters to me."

"Every bitch in here is 'Sucio Aguas.' If they wasn't they wouldn't be in here shaking their ass for money," said J-Bigg.

"Word! Right, Rah?" Web said, agreeing with J-Bigg.

Rahtiek didn't answer so Wyte Yak asked, "What's

wrong with you? You ain't fucking with the 'ho's and you haven't said a word all night.

"Ain't nothing."

Pooh Berry walked over with a stripper, a light-skinned hottie with a banging body. She had a round fat bottom and huge triple D titties. She was wearing four-inch stilettos and a leopard body suit. Pooh slapped everybody five and introduced the stripper to his friends. "This is Web, this is J-Bigg, that's Rahtiek, and that's my brother, Wyte Yak. Everybody, this is Sinsation."

"She sure is sensational," said Web.

"How's everybody doing?" Sinsation asked.

They all say, "Hello."

She sat next to Wyte Yak, and Pooh Berry sat next to Web.

"So what's the deal, Sinsation?" Wyte Yak asked.

Sinsation didn't waste anytime and got right to the point, "Well, I got these two tricks. There's this white boy from Sheepshead Bay named Fred. He runs a chop shop, and this motherfucker is handling. He drives a Porsche and wears a platinum watch with enough ice to build an igloo."

"Is it a Roley?" Web asked, raising his eyebrows.

"Nah, some other shit. Frank Muller or Frank some fucking body, I don't know. But, trust me, the shit is fly. He said it cost close to two hundred thousand. Plus, he keep tons of cash in his bottom dresser drawer."

"He let you see that?" J-Bigg asked.

"Let me see it," Sinsation said. "Shiitt, he spreads it across the bed every time we fuck. He said all he live for is money and pussy. He always bless me with a nice tip and I get turned on rolling around in all that cash. He trust me. We been fucking going on two years now."

"Alright, what's the deal with this other cat?" asked

Wyte Yak.

Sinsation paused then said, "This other guy is black. His name is Andrew. He sell weight over in Bed Stuy but he live in Canarsie. He's a funny motherfucker, always trying to impress me. Every time I come over he's counting money, which he puts in his safe behind the picture of the dogs playing pool in his living room. He also keep jewelry and drugs in the safe. He a cheap-ass nigga. All he ever give me is what I charge. He don't never tip. I can't stand his ass, but he do know how to eat some pussy."

Web asked, "You ain't worried that these dudes might think you set them up?"

"Hell no!" Sinsation said, pulling a small six-shot .380 automatic from her purse and placing it on the table. "I take my gun with me wherever I go. Besides, both of these niggas are soft as a baby's ass."

"Alright then, Sinsation," Wyte Yak said. "Write down their addresses, and these fools are as good as got. Of course, you get twenty percent of whatever we take."

"That's what's up," Sinsation said, writing down the addresses.

They took the addresses from her, and Wyte Yak let her know that he'd get back at her in a couple of days.

Two days later around 10:00 in the evening, Wyte Yak and Rahtiek were sitting across the street from Fred's house in Yak's Expedition waiting for him to come home. For the last couple of days, Rahtiek had been pretty quiet, and Wyte Yak wanted to know what was troubling him.

Wyte Yak looked over at Rahtiek and with true concern asked, "Sun, what's wrong? We family. If you got a problem, I got a problem. I can see something's eating you up. So, tell me, what's going on?"

"Man, I saw my daughter the other day, and it fucked me up," Rahtiek said. "I couldn't hold her, I couldn't talk to her or nothing. All I could do was watch her running around playing."

"Why?"

"Her counselor said the courts don't want me having any contact with her until I'm in a position to take care of her."

"Man, fuck the courts!" Wyte Yak got upset and yelled. "Once we take enough money, we gonna open up a legit business, and you gone get your daughter--even if we gotta take her and hide out in the Florida keys."

"Be real."

"I am real. Nigga, you know my word is my bond. Have I ever lied to you?"

Rahtiek looked over at his partner and said, "No, you've always kept it funky."

"Alright, then. If I said y'all gone be together then y'all gone be together. So don't wet that. Let's concentrate on getting this money and, trust me, everything's gone be alright. That's my word."

The two men tapped fists, and Fred pulled up in his Porsche and parked in his driveway.

Rahtiek saw Fred and said, "There he go. They put on ski masks and black leather gloves and waited until he was on the way up the steps of his house. They stepped out of their vehicle and crept up the stairs behind him. As they reached the top of the stairs, Fred had his door open and was about to enter. They rushed in behind him with their guns drawn.

Rahtiek pinned Fred to the wall while Wyte Yak closed the door. Rahtiek held his gun on Fred, walked him to into the living room, and tossed him to the floor. Wyte Yak headed towards the back room. Fred was scared shitless and looked up at Rahtiek, who said, "Face the fucking floor!"

Fred, fearing for his life, said, "Take anything you want, man, but please don't kill me."

"Shut the fuck up! If you don't resist, you won't be hurt."

Rahtiek took a fat platinum Italian link chain from Fred's neck and a platinum diamond pinky ring off his left pinky. As he took his iced-out platinum Frank Muller watch off his wrist, he smiled as he admired it and said, "This shit is pretty as hell."

Wyte Yak returned from the back room carrying a drawer filled with cash, placed it on the coffee table, and said, "Damn, Dunn! I gotta find a bag to put all this cheddar in."

Rahtiek looked at the drawer filled with cash and said, "Check in the kitchen."

Wyte Yak walked into the kitchen, and Rahtiek said to Fred, "You's a stupid motherfucker keeping all that cash in the drawer. What the fuck is wrong with you?"

"You think that's something?" Fred thought to himself. "You should see what I got in the basement."

Wyte Yak returned carrying a big black garbage bag and some duct tape, which he tossed to Rahtiek. While Rahtiek taped Fred's mouth hands and feet, Wyte Yak emptied the money in the drawer into the bag. Wyte Yak then ran to the back of the house and searched every drawer and closet he came across.

He came from the back with a box of jewelry, which

he stuffed into the bag and said, "We out."

"Thanks for the generous donation," Rahtiek said to Fred.

The two men exited the house, calmly walking back down the steps and smoothly stepping into the Expedition before slowly pulling off.

That same night, Web and J-Bigg were in Andrew's apartment quietly sitting in the dark and patiently awaiting his arrival. After about an hour Web heard Andrew at the door fumbling with his keys. He tapped J-Bigg, who had fallen asleep, and he immediately woke up. They put on their ski masks and drew their guns as they awaited his entrance. Andrew entered the apartment and closed the door behind him. He clicked the light on and found a Desert Eagle and a Glock .40 a foot away from his face.

"What the fuck is this?" he asked.

"You know what time it is," J-Bigg said. "You ain't stupid."

Hoping the men only wanted what they saw Andrew said, "Alright, fuck it."

Andrew took a platinum link chain with a four-inch long platinum Jesus piece flooded with diamonds from around his neck and a platinum Rolex watch from off his wrist and handed the jewels to Web.

"Thanks," Web said. "Now open the safe."

Andrew pretended he didn't know what they were talking about and asked, "What safe?"

J-Bigg looked over at the picture on the wall in the living room and said, "The one over there behind the picture of the dogs playing pool."

Andrew shook his head and said. "Damn!" Andrew

moaned. "Somebody done set me the fuck up."

Web grabbed him by the arm and pulled him over to the picture. J-Bigg snatched down the picture, and the safe was revealed.

Web placed the Glock to the back of his head and said, "Open it.'

Fearing for his life, Andrew pleaded, "Before I open the safe, please promise me y'all not going to kill me."

"If we had intended on killing you, what the hell would we need the mask for?" J-Bigg asked.

Andrew looked at Web, who nodded in agreement. Then Andrew opened the safe. As soon as the safe was opened, J-Bigg hit Andrew in the back of the head with the butt of his Desert Eagle, knocking him unconscious. They both put their guns on their waist. Web pulled a black bag from his jacket pocket, and they begin filling the bag with the contents in the safe. The safe contained two ki's of cocaine, three pounds of marijuana, some jewelry, and over a hundred thousand in cash.

The next evening the entire Career Criminal clique was in Yiddo's crib, gathered around the kitchen table. Sitting in the middle of the table was close to four hundred thousand dollars, two ki's of cocaine, two and a half pounds of weed, and a small mountain of gold and platinum jewelry. Wyte Yak was sitting at the head of the table with Bryan and DY standing behind him. Rahtiek was sitting on the left side of the table with J-Bigg and Web standing behind him. Pooh Berry was sitting on the right side of the table with Trap and Little standing behind him. Pillsbury was sitting across from Yak at the bottom of the table with Dikki Jah in his wheelchair to the left of him, while Yiddo and Nite stood behind them.

Wyte Yak looked around making sure he had everyone's attention then said, "I asked everybody to come here today so that y'all could see the progress we've made in just two weeks."

"Damn! Niggas took all that already? I didn't even know niggas started sticking shit yet," said Pillsbury.

"That's how it's supposed to be," Rahtiek said. "Nobody supposed to know how we eating."

"And from now on, we gone be eating well," said Web.

"The only thing I need for everybody to do is hold your heads. We about to put in a lot of work these next few months. I don't want anyone who isn't here with us right now to know about nothing we got going on." Wyte Yak looked around to make sure everyone was paying attention. "Not your girls, not your moms, not your cousins, nobody. From here on out, everything we do is on the low. Does everybody understand that?"

Everyone agreed, and Wyte Yak continued talking. "Now we all know we can't do this shit forever. So I say we go all out for the next six months taking as much money as possible. During those six months I'm going to be setting up legitimate businesses for us to run. So from now on, eighty percent of anything any of us takes goes to the "fam." Does everybody understand that?"

Everybody agreed.

"Alright, then. This meeting is adjourned. Pooh Berry got some strippers coming through in a few minutes so put on some music, crack the Hennessy, pop the Crystals, and let's celebrate." As the rest of the family started to celebrate, Wyte Yak and Rahtiek gathered the money, drugs, and jewelry and took it to the back room.

CHAPTER 19

It was 4:00 in the morning. Sinsation had just got off from work and was sitting in the back of a cab fantasizing about what she was going to do with the forty grand Wyte Yak promised her. She said to herself, "Hmm, I kinda like Pooh Berry's brother, Wyte Yak. He's about his business. I wonder if I can throw this pussy on him and have him strung. Nah, he ain't trying to fuck with my stripping ass. Damn! Why I had to be a stripper? Well, I won't be stripping for long. With forty G's I can open up a beauty salon. Shitt, I already be lacing everybody hair that works at the club. I think that'll be a wise investment. I'm sure all those heifers will come through to support me, me with my own salon. Who woulda ever thought it? I think I'll name it Sinsational Hairstyles."

The cab pulled up in front of her building, and the cab driver said, "That'll be eleven dollars." Sinsation was still fantasizing and didn't hear him. So he knocked on the bulletproof glass partition separating the driver from the passenger to gain her attention.

Sinsation snapped out of her trance and asked, "What?"

"That'll be eleven dollars," the cab driver repeated.

"Oh, I'm sorry," she said, realizing she was in front of her apartment building. Then she put a ten and a five in the money slot and said, "Keep the change," as she hopped out of the cab.

She entered her building and walked up one flight to her second floor apartment. She put the key in the door and started to open it. She sensed that something wasn't right and started to reach in her purse for her .380 automatic, but before she could get it out, Andrew rushed her from behind, knocking her into the apartment and onto the floor. Her purse fell from her hand and slid across the floor. Andrew slammed the door behind him as she scrambled along the floor trying to get to her purse. She was only inches away when Andrew grabbed the back of her neck, snatched her to her feet, and placed his .357 Magnum under her chin, saying, "You set me up, you fucking bitch, didn't you?"

Noticing the fire in Andrew's eyes, Sinsation was scared shitless but still managed to say, "I don't know what you talking about."

He slapped her across the face with his pistol.
"Bitch, you know what the fuck I'm talking about."

"I don't know nothing. Why are you doing this to me?"

"I don't know nothing," he mocked. "Why are you doing this to me?" He slapped her with his pistol again and blood started leaking from her right eye.
"You think I'm fucking playing with you, huh, bitch?"

He grabbed her by her hair and dragged her into the bedroom, tossing her onto the bed. She was crying, and her head was bleeding as she pleaded for her life.

"Please don't kill me, Andrew. I swear to God it wasn't me.

He pointed his gun at her as he reached in her closet and pulled out a pair of pink stiletto Timberland boots and took the laces out. Then he placed his gun on the dresser and hopped on top of Sinsation and continuosly slapped her across the face until she was dizzy and dazed. "You gone tell me who got my shit, bitch," he said, using the shoe strings to tie her hands to the headboard of her brass bed. He pulled a pocket knife from his back pocket and held the point just under her right eye and said, "Now tell me who took my shit before I start fucking this pretty little face of yours up."

"I swear I don't know, Andrew. Please stop. It wasn't me.

He sliced her across the face, and she started kicking and going wild, knocking Andrew onto the floor. He jumped up in rage and lost all control, stabbing her in the stomach at least fifteen times and shooting her in the head.

The sound of the gunshot brought him back to his senses, and his anger quickly turned into terror as he realized what he had just done. He was shaking. He rushed into the bathroom and returned with a towel to wipe his finger prints off of everything in the apartment he thought he may have touched. When he was through cleaning up, he walked to the front door and looked through the peep hole to see if any of Sinsation's neighbors was awaken by the gunshot and was in the hallway trying to find out what was going on. He didn't see or here a soul so he used the towel to open the door and left the apartment.

The next morning Wyte Yak was in bed sleeping when Jeremy walked into his room carrying a gym bag, wearing a Black velour Sean John sweatsuit and a pair black Michael Jordans. He pushed Wyte Yak on the shoulder to awaken him as he said, "Daddy, wake up."

"What you want?" asked Wyte Yak, keeping his eyes closed.

"I need twenty dollars. I'm on my way to the Boys' Club to practice."

Wyte Yak pointed to his pants lying on the floor and said, "Look in my pants pocket."

Jeremy kneeled down and picked up Wyte Yak's blue Ralph Lauren jeans from off the floor next to the bed and reached in the right front pocket, pulling out a mitt of money. He took a twenty-dollar bill and placed the rest back in the pocket and asked.

"You coming to my game at the Boys' Club later, right?" he asked.

"What time?" Wyte Yak asked, squinting his eyes.

"It's supposed to start at 4:30."

"Yeah, I'll be there."

"You sure?" he asked, hoping his father was being sincere. "It's the championship."

"Yeah, I'm sure. You know I'm not trying to miss your championship game. In fact if y'all win I'm gone take your hold team downtown and buy them the new Jordans that just came out."

"Alright, bet."

Jeremy started to head out of the room, but Yak called him. "Hold up, Jerm. Who taking you to practice?"

Jeremy turned around to face his father and said, "My coach. He outside waiting on me right now."

"Alright, see you later."

Jeremy walked out the door, and Wyte Yak got out of bed and went to the bathroom. After he brushed his teeth he walked back into the bedroom and noticed that the red light on his phone was blinking, indicating that someone left him a phone message. He pressed the play button and the voice said, "Hello, Mr. Whitehead. This is Rob Miller, general contractor of the construction crew you hired. I was hoping you could stop by the club some time today. I have some blueprints I need to go over with you. If you won't be able to make it, give me a call at 347-996-7366. Thank you."

Wyte Yak then walked back to the bathroom and hopped in the shower. A few hours later Wyte Yak, Pillsbury, Rahtiek, and J-Bigg were walking through the

Projects. As they were about to reach the bridge leading to the other side, Pillsbury whispered to Rahtiek, "Yo, Rah, watch me get Wyte Yak hype."

He then tapped Wyte Yak and said, "Sun, kick a little something for Rahtiek. He didn't hear you flow in a while."

"Word, Yak!" J-Bigg said. "Hit him in the head. Let him know you still got it."

"Yeah, Yak, let me hear some new shit. I used to be kicking your rhymes up north. Niggas used to think I could rap."

Just as they stepped foot on the bridge, Wyte Yak started flowing:

Alright, check thisHow's it going down
It's going down like this
I'm gone cock the heat
And shoot the rounds like this
Because my brains the gun
It's cocked and aimed
So when the impact lays you flat on your back
I'm the blame
Because I don't have sixteen shots
Like you Glock
Or fifty to a hundred
Like you're AK and Oow-wop
Nah my gat's gone bust
From now until infinity
Leaving the soles empty
Of those who try to injure me
It's the real mobster
Don't eat shrimp or lobster
So real I don't need steel
To rearrange your posture
Man you know the verbal
Is enough to curve you
Have that ass bent
When you ain't touch the herbals
Now your internals
All bloody and crippled
By this black gorilla
Whose words literally ripped you
Don't vomit because I promise
To give you a breather
But before it's all over
Bet I make you a believer
Rahtiek slapped Wyte Yak five and said, "Damn,

Yak! You still got it. How come you aint never put nothing out?"

"I was too busy being a gangsta'."

"I can understand that."

The four men exited the bridge on the middle side of the Project, walked around the corner, and entered 188 Monument Walk. They walked up to the second floor and knocked on 2A, where Pillsbury's uncle, Ron-B, lived.

Meanwhile back on their side of the Project Pooh Berry was searching for his brother, Wyte Yak. He walked down the basketball court and bumped into Chess Piece, one of Wyte Yak's homeboys. He was a hustler, too.

Chess Piece was sitting on the bleachers and adjusted the gun on his waist as he slapped Pooh Berry five and said, "What up, Pooh Berry?"

"What up, Chess Piece? You seen my brother?"

"Who? Yak? Nah, I ain't seen him all day."

Chess Piece then yelled over to Mo, better known as "the godfather," who was sitting over at the chess table playing dominoes with Chico, Fat David, and Floyd.

"Yo, Mo, you seen Wyte Yak?"

"Nah, he hasn't been down here all day."

Turning back to Pooh Berry, Chess Piece said, "He ain't come down here. Maybe he at the Center on the Avenue with Web and them niggas."

"Alright, Chess Piece," said Pooh Berry.

They slapped five, and Pooh walked to the Community Center on Myrtle Avenue.

Pooh Berry walked into the Community Center, and the man sitting at the front desk asked him to sign in. The front of the community center was filled with kids sitting at the table doing their homework, reading books, and playing board games. A few were gathered around the TV playing video games. There were five girls jumping rope and a group of boys playing basketball.

Pooh grabbed the pen to sign in and asked the man at the front desk, "Is Wyte Yak in here?"

"I didn't see Wyte Yak, but the rest of his home boys are in the back."

In the back of the center a few guys were sitting around waiting to play pool, ping pong, or air hockey, but the Career Criminals were the only ones playing. Web and Bryan were shooting pool on one table while DY and Nite were using the other pool table. Little and Sugar were playing ping pong while Trap and Yiddo played air hockey. Dikki Jah was in his wheelchair, sitting in the middle of all the tables, and Yobie was complaining, "Man, I don't give a fuck about the rest of these dudes, but I ain't gone stand around and watch y'all play the best three out of five. Nah, fuck that, I got next!"

He then walked over to Sugar and Little over at the ping pong table and asked, "What's the score, Little?"

"I got seventy and Shoogs got eighty."

"Damn! What the fuck is game?"

Little smiled as he said, "A hundred."

"What y'all counting by, fives?"

"No, twos," Little said.

"Get the fuck out of here. Y'all niggas bugging."

Pooh walked into the back room. Everybody froze and looked at him. They knew something had to be wrong because Pooh Berry never came in the Community Center. Pooh Berry had a disturbed look on his face.

"Where's Wyte Yak?" he asked.

"Last time I seen him," said Sugar, "he was headed to

the other side to check Ron-B with Pillsbury and them."

Pooh motioned the crew to come to him and said, "Alright, then. Y'all come in here for a minute. I need to talk to y'all."

"Me, too?" asked Yobie, following the Clique.

Pooh Berry held his hand up to Yobie and said, "Nah, you stay there."

Pooh walked into the conference room behind him. With the exception of Dikki Jah, the Career Criminals paused their games and followed Pooh Berry into the room. The guys sitting around started to get up to play on the tables, until Web turned around and said, "We still playing. We'll be right back. Dikki, hold it down until we get back."

"I got you," Dikki Jah said.

Dikki screwed his face at the guys waiting to play, to let them know they better not touch anything. In the conference room the "fam" gathered around Pooh as he delivered the bad news.

"They found Sinsation in her apartment earlier today. Somebody tied her to the bed stabbed her fifteen times and blew her brains out with a .357 Magnum," he told them.

"Damn! That's fucked up," Web said. "Anybody seen who did it?"

"Nah, one of the neighbors said they heard a gunshot around four in the morning but when they looked out of their peep hole and didn't see anybody they just went back to sleep."

J-Bigg looked at Web and asked, "You think it was that nigga, Andrew? He did know it was a setup."

Web said, "I don't know. It coulda been."

They all just stood there with their heads down for a few minutes. Then Pooh Berry left, and the rest of the crew continued playing their games.

Later that day, Wyte Yak was driving his Expedition with Rahtiek in the passenger seat. They were on the highway riding down the Belt Parkway, listening to the new Jay Z CD. They were bopping their heads to the beat and caught in the trance of Jigga's lyrics. Wyte Yak exited the highway at Atlantic Avenue. The exit merged into the left lane, but Wyte Yak, not paying attention to the oncoming traffic, crossed over into the right lane and almost slammed into a grey minivan driven by a heavy-set, white lady in her late fifties. The lady slammed on her brakes, mashed the horn, stuck her head out the window and cursed at Wyte Yak.

Wyte Yak saw a Mexican walking the divider selling roses and motioned him to come. As the Mexican approached the vehicle Wyte Yak asked, "How much are the roses?"

"Three for five dollars," said the Mexican.

Wyte Yak handed him a ten dollar bill and said, "I need six."

The Mexican took the ten dollar bill from Wyte Yak's hand and was about to hand him the roses, but Wyte Yak held his hand, saying, "Give them to that lady behind me."

As the Mexican walked over to the lady in the van, Rahtiek gave Yak a strange look and asked, "What the fuck you do that for? That bitch was just cursing you out."

"She was, but look at her now," Wyte Yak said.

Rahtiek looked back and saw the lady smiling holding up the flowers yelling, "Thank you."

He looked at Wyte Yak and said, "Damn, Yak, you just made her day. She went from wanting to kill you to wanting to kiss you in less than thirty seconds."

"That's Don status," Wyte Yak said. "You'll get it

someday."

The light changed and Wyte Yak drove off.

"There's one thing you gotta always remember, Rah," Wyte Yak said. "Always respect your elders and children and, no matter what else you do, you'll always be alright."

"I feel you," Rahtiek said.

Wyte Yak looked over at his partner and said, "Don't say nothing to nobody else yet, Sun, but I took some money and bought that club on Prince Street by the precinct that used to be the strip joint."

"Get the fuck outta here! Say word, the mother," Rahtiek said, getting excited.

"Word, the mother. That shit is ours. I got a construction crew in there right now hooking it up. It should be ready to open in a few weeks."

Rahtiek slapped Wyte Yak Five and said, "That's what's up!"

"I was thinking about hiring what's his name. You know dude who be singing them jazzy, hip hop, gangsta' blues?"

"Who you talking about, Fat Daddy Capone?"

"Yeah, that's him. Dude get busy."

"That's my nigga."

"Mines, too." Wyte Yak said. "And that's not all the good news I got, my nigga."

Wyte Yak reached in his shirt pocket and pulled out a set of keys and handed them to Rahtiek.

"What's this?" Rahtiek asked curiously.

"Those are the keys to your new crib."

"What crib?" Rahtiek asked, still confused.

"You know Little Man from Cooper Projects moms,

right?"

"Who, Mrs. Miriam?"

"Yeah, she be helping people get apartments. So I hit her off with some dough and she laced you with the butter, two bedroom over in Sunset Park."

"Word up, Sun. Two bedrooms?"

"Yep."

"Hold up. Why would I need two bedrooms?" Rahtiek asked.

"Because I had my lawyer pull a few strings for you and, come Monday morning, your baby girl will be moving in with you."

"Say, word!"

"You know I wouldn't play like that," Wyte Yak said seriously.

Wyte Yak's actions touched Rahtiek heart and he became sentimental. "That's why I love you, Yak. I know I can always count on you, no matter what."

"No doubt."

Rahtiek was smiling from ear to ear, happy that he was finally going to regain custody of his daughter.

Wyte Yak cut through downtown and headed to the PJs. He made a right on Bond Street and rode pass Fulton Street, making another right on Willoughby Avenue, which he took to Flatbush Avenue. He then made a left, cut over to Prince Street down to Johnson, and made a right into the Project parking lot, stopping in the parking lot.

Rahtiek jumped out and said, "I'll be right back."

Wyte Yak parked the Expedition and as he got out he noticed Abdul, a childhood friend who turned Muslim and moved to Africa. He was standing near the rear of the vehicle. "What up, Wyte Yak?" he asked.

"Mac Daddy...I mean Abdul Rahiff, what's good, my

brother?"

Wyte Yak walked over to Abdul, and they hugged.

"How you been, Abdul? I haven't seen you in a minute."

"I'm good. How you?"

"I'm doing alright. What brings you to America?"

"You know I still gotta come check the fam and see how my peeps doing."

"No doubt."

Abdul cut his eyes at Wyte Yak and said, "I know you not still out here messing with these 'Cathers.' You know it's about time you took your 'Shahatta.' "

"Yeah, I know but I'm still not quite ready."

"You better get ready before it's too late. You know Allah is the true God. He need good men like you on his team."

Just then they were interrupted by Drizz, who walked up carrying a forty ounce of Olde English malt liquor. "What up, Wyte Yak?" Drizz said.

Wyte Yak slapped Drizz five and said, "What up, Drizz?"

"Oh shit. What up, Mac Daddy?" Drizz said, surprised to see Abdul.

Drizz and Abdul shook hands. Abdul held onto his hand and said, "My name's not Mac Daddy, it's Abdul Rahiff."

"My bad, Sun, I didn't know," Drizz apologized.

"I'm not your son. We the same age, how can I be your son?

"I didn't call you son, like you mine. I called you Sun because you shine. You know that."

"Yeah, alright. Just checking. You know a lot of

these dudes don't know the difference."

Drizz smiled and said, "Yeah, I know. But what's up with you? I heard you moved to Africa."

"Yeah, I bought a house in Morocco."

"Word! What's up with the honeys out there? You married you one of them big-butt African shorties yet?"

"Yeah, I'm married. How about you?"

"I just got married six months ago. Me and my wife stay in the Stuy."

"That's good."

Drizz looked over at Wyte Yak and said, "Jerm Dogg and them just won the championship. They on their way home with their trophies right now."

"Damn! I missed Jeremy's game. I know he pissed. Did Jerm get busy?"

"Did he? Jeremy was busting ass. He was the MVP. I didn't know Jerm had skills like that. He damn for sure didn't get it from you because you was a scrub."

"Yeah, alright," Wyte Yak laughed.

Drizz and Abdul laughed then Drizz slapped both men five and said, "I'm out on that note.

Rahtiek crept up from behind and tapped Abdul on his shoulder. Abdul turned around and was surprised to see Rahtiek.

As the two men hugged Abdul said, "What up, my brother?"

"Ain't nothing. Just chillin', maintaining."

"That's good."

"Wyte Yak told me you turned Muslim after the accident."

"No doubt. I had to show gratitude to Allah. He wouldn't let me die. He must need me here on earth."

"I'm glad to see you alright. I was bugging when I

heard you jumped off the promenade and landed on a passing truck. Then the next day you jumped out of the hospital
window. What was up with that?"

"Yeah, they said I jumped out of the fifth floor window and landed in a tree. I hit my head when I landed in the
tree and got a little brain damage. Which was why I really
don't remember what went down."

"You's one lucky dude. But damn! You don't even
know why you jumped."

"Not at all. I didn't even believe I jumped."

Just then, Jeremy and his team came up carrying
their trophies. Jeremy spotted Wyte Yak and ran over to his
father.

Wyte Yak hugged him, and Jeremy said, "We did it,
Daddy, we did it!"

"I knew y'all could do it."

"Man, we blew them dudes out by twenty-two
points," said Tony, one of Jeremy's friends.

"Y'all did them dirty like that?"

"No doubt!" Tony said, nodding his head.

Jeremy and Tony slapped five, and Jeremy asked his
father, "So what up? You know what you said you was
going to do."

"I didn't forget."

"You know you missed my game so I think you
should buy me a sweatsuit, too."

"Yeah, alright. I got you," Wyte Yak said laughing.
Wyte Yak walked off with the peewee ball players in tow.

"What up, Yak?" Rahtiek asked.

"I'll be right back. I'm going downtown. I promised
Jerm Dogg I'd buy his team Jordans if they won the champi-

onship."

"Alright, big baller, toss me the keys to the truck. I wanna go get something to eat."

Wyte Yak tossed the keys to Rahtiek, and he and Abdul hopped in the Expedition. Once they entered the truck Rahtiek cut the vehicle on.

"I don't have nothing but love for that dude," Abdul said. "When I was in the hospital, he came to check me on the reg."

"Yak's a good dude. I'm definitely glad he's on my team," Rahtiek said.

Rahtiek put the vehicle in reverse and backed out of the parking space. While Wyte Yak was downtown buying sneakers for the peewee basketball team, Rahtiek and Abdul headed over to the Halal soul food restaurant on Fulton Street and Franklin Ave and sat down to eat a kosher meal.

Sugar and Trap were on the basketball court playing a two-on-two against Quacko and Trocko. Game was twenty one. The score was seventeen to eighteen. Sugar took Trocko to the hole and scored nineteen. Rahtiek walked over and took a seat on the bleachers to watch the game. Sugar saw Rahtiek and said, "What up, Sun? I'm gone kick it with you in a minute. We only need two more points."

"So let me see some of that Ted "Sugar" Richards shit I been hearing about."

Trap took the ball out and passed it to Sugar. Quacko and Trocko double-teamed Sugar trying to steal the ball. He threw the ball through Trocko's legs and, as Quacko reached for it, Sugar tossed it through Quacko's legs. Then he grabbed it and tossed it behind his back to Trap, who was waiting down low and scored the easy bucket. Sugar looked over at Rahtiek.

"Alright, that was cool," Rahtiek smiled. "Now let me see you score."

Trap took the ball out again and passed it to Sugar, who tossed it through Brocko's legs then grabbed it, brought it in front of Brocko, then wrapped it around Brocko's back, and shot the ball from behind his head making the winning basket. He laughed, slapped Trap five, and told him, "Good game!"

They went over to Rahtiek, slapped him five, and sat down on the bleachers.

"What up, stupid face?" Sugar said.

"What's the deal, Sun? Where you been? I haven't seen you all week."

"I was with Kayshon. He got me hooked up in this league up in Canada."

"What, the Canadian NBA?"

"Something like that. Only, we don't get paid like the NBA."

"Y'all don't get paid?" Rahtiek asked, giving Sugar a curious look.

"Yeah, we get paid, but not like the NBA. We make anywhere between fifty and two hundred thousand. NBA scouts be coming to the games, though."

"That's good, Sun. Make it happen."

"No doubt!"

Rahtiek looked at Sugar and said, "You can still come eat with us. You don't gotta do nothing. You fam."

"That's what I been telling him," Trap said.

"I know. I'm just doing what I gotta do to stay focused."

"Just as long as you know, pro or no pro, you always

got 'fam.' "

"I hear you."

"So what's up with a little one-on-one?" asked Rahtiek.

"Nigga, I'll beat you with one hand."

"You sound stupid."

Sugar jumped up and said, "Let's do it then."

"I was just fucking with you," Rahtiek sat back down and said.

"I thought so," Sugar said laughing.

Sugar called for the ball, and Drip tossed it to him. He dribbled over to the three-point line and shot. The ball went straight through the hoop without touching the rim.

"I see you finally getting a little jumper," Rahtiek teased.

"It's coming."

Rahtiek and Trap stood, and the three men walked up to the avenue to the store. A few members of the crew were sitting at the chess table at the side of Yiddo's building. DY, J-Bigg, and Pillsbury were sitting around watching Yiddo and Web play a game of chess. J-Bigg saw Cody coming and said, "Ah man, here comes horse head Cody."

Cody was a little tipsy, carrying a pint-sized bottle of E&J.

"How you gone try to play chess, Yiddo?" Cody asked. "Nigga, you failed the block test. He gone try to put a triangle through a square hole."

"Who the hell let this horse out its stable?" Yiddo asked.

"You got jokes, teen wolf?" Cody asked.

"Oh there go my mule. Now all I need is my forty acres," said Yiddo.

"Get out of here, Mr. Ed, before I start charging kids

to ride your ass," said J-Bigg.

"Word! Let my son get a ride," said DY.

"Oh, y'all jumping me? I'm out," Cody said laughing.

"Break out! We don't need no glue!" Yiddo said.

Cody put his hands up indicating that he'd had enough and walked off with the crew still insulting him. Nite walked up to the chess table slapped everybody five.

"Web, I need to talk to you it's important," Nite said.

"Alright, I coming, right after this move."

Nite walked over to the other chess table and sat down. Web made his move then said, "Hold up a minute, Yiddo. Let me see what Nite want."

Web walked away from the chess game and walked over to the other chess table and took a seat across from Nite. "What's good, Nite?" he asked.

"I got something set up for us if you with it," Nite said.

"What is it? Where is it? And who is it?"

"It's a gambling spot in Manhattan on 28th Street and Fifth Ave. It's run by this kid from the lower east side who calls himself Frank White."

"What type of paper be in the joint?"

"My cousin told me bank be reaching over a hundred thousand. Nothing but big boys be in the spot-iced-out Rolexes and all that good shit."

"If it's money in there like that, somebody got to be holding heat."

"Nobody's not packing up in the spot. They got raided a few times so Frank won't allow it. He got shit sewed in manhattan. Niggas know not to fuck with his spot."

"Them Manhattan niggas might know. But us

Brooklyn niggas don't know shit."

"That's what I'm saying."

"When you trying to hit it?"

"Tonight."

"It's a done deal."

"Say no more."

They slapped five, and Web walked back over to the chess table sat down and finished his chess game with Yiddo.

Later that night Pillsbury and Yiddo were in Yiddo's apartment playing a game of NBA live. Yiddo yelled, "It's Pauly, baby," as he hit a three-pointer with Paul Pierce of the Boston Celtics.

"That's alright. Watch what McGrady do to you," said Pillsbury.

Wyte Yak and Rahtiek walked into the apartment.

"What up, my niggas? Where's everybody else at?" asked Rahtiek.

"Niggas went to stick up this gambling spot in the city," said Pillsbury.

"I didn't hear nothing about no gambling spot," said Wyte Yak.

"Nite put Web on to it earlier. They was waiting for you to come through, but you took too long," said Yiddo.

Rahtiek frowned and said, "Niggas ain't call our cells or nothing. I hope them dudes know what they doing."

"You not the only nigga that know how to do a Jux," Pillsbury shot back.

"I didn't say I was. But everybody know I get busy."

"Everybody get busy. What you saying?" Pillsbury said, becoming more agitated.

"Everybody don't get busy. Some niggas scared to

take money. They eat but they don't put in no work."

Wyte Yak, knowing that Rahtiek just said the wrong thing, said, "Chill, Sun."

"Hold up. You talking about me?"Pillsbury said, clearly offended.

"I aint say no names. What, you got a guilty conscience or something?"

Pillsbury got heated and said, "Fuck that, Wyte Yak. The next time niggas hit anything I'm rolling."

Wyte Yak said, "I don't have a problem with that. In fact I got some ice you and Yiddo can take tomorrow."

"That's what's up," Pillsbury said, looking over at Yiddo. "You with it, Yiddo?

"No doubt."

Pillsbury and Yiddo continued playing their game, while Wyte Yak and Rahtiek sat down at the kitchen table and waited for the rest of the crew to return.

CHAPTER 20

Frank White's gambling spot was packed with about thirty-five to forty big ballers from throughout the city. There were also twelve waitresses wearing nothing but bras and G-strings. You would've thought it was a Rolex convention because damn-near everybody in the joint seemed to wearing one. Most of them were also wearing platinum chains and rings flooded with ice. It was plain to see that these were some of New York's biggest drug dealers, not your petty nickel and dime hustlers, but the big boys.

They were all gathered around two dice tables. At one table you had to be betting a thousand and better, and at the other you had to be betting five thousand and better. Money didn't seem to be a problem for these guys because every man in the room was placing bets at one of the two tables.

The Career Criminals were riding in two PT Cruisers. They turned off of Fifth Avenue onto 28th Street and they all smiled when they saw the exotic cars parked along the block. There were at least ten different 600 Benz--nine sedans and one coupe-a couple of convertible Bentleys, a Lamborghini, five 4.6 Range Rovers, three 500 Benz--two sedans and one coupe--one 745SI BMW, seven Cadillac Escalades, two convertible Lexus, a Prowler, and a Ferrari, all sitting on twenty or more inches of chrome.

Web, who was driving one of the PT Cruisers, looked over at Nite who was on the passenger side and said, "Damn, Nite! You wasn't bullshitting."

Web double-parked in front of the spot, and Bryan, who was driving the other Cruiser, pulled up right behind him. They turned off the lights on the Cruisers but left the cars running. Everybody checked their weapons to make sure that they were loaded. They pulled ski masks over their faces, stepped out of the vehicles, and rushed into 220 28th Street. They ran up a flight of stairs then paused by the door. They listened for a second and, once they heard the gamblers behind the door, Web nodded his head and J-Bigg kicked the door in. They rushed in, and J-Bigg let off a slug into the ceiling with the pistol grip pump shotgun he was carrying. The gamblers froze, and they had everybody's attention.

Nite, who was holding a huge .44 Magnum in his hand, said, "Y'all know what this is. Any sudden moves and we blasting. I want everybody to strip butt-ass naked and place your clothes money and jewels in these bags."

DY tossed three large black garbage bags to the gamblers, and they did as they were instructed. The women also took off what little they were wearing and put it into the bags. Little snatched the telephone cord out of the phone and pocketed it. Frank White approached the masked men, and J-Bigg stopped him in his tracks, pressing his shot gun on Frank's stomach.

"What the fuck is wrong with y'all niggas?" Frank said. "Do y'all know who house y'all just entered?"

Web and Nite placed their pistols on either side of his head.

"Nigga, you better start stripping like everybody else before we send you to meet your maker," J-Bigg said.

As Frank White started to undress, he said, "Alright, y'all got it. As long as y'all know I'm the real Frank White and I'm gone find out whose up under those masks and when I do..."

Nite smacked him with his .44 Magnum knocking him to the floor then grabbed Frank by the collar and placed his gun beneath his chin. Nite stared directly into Frank White's eyes and said, "Nigga, you ain't gone do shit. I'll splatter your brains right now if you say another fucking word."

Frank remained quiet and took off his clothes and jewelry and placed them in the bag. Once they had everyone's possessions, Nite said, "Thanks for contributing to the poor and unfortunate."

As the Career Criminals were backing out of the door J-Bigg said, "Just look at us as the IRS. You know it was about time you dudes paid your taxes."

They then rushed out of the spot, down the steps and into their cars, speeding away in their PT Cruisers, with their guns in their laps and feeling like mobsters from the 30's who just did a heist for Al Capone. They safely made it back to the PJs in less than twenty minutes. They headed into 340 Hudson Walk and didn't even bother waiting for the elevator, running up the five flights of stairs and rushing into Yiddo's apartment. Wyte Yak and Rahtiek were relieved when their homeys entered the apartment.

They poured the merchandise from the bags onto the kitchen table. There was close to two hundred thousand in cash and twenty-seven Rolex watches, nothing but iced-out platinum jewelry. There were thirty-nine cell phones, twenty-four two-way pagers, and thirty-two different sets of car keys.

Wyte Yak proudly smiled, picked up a mitt of cash in one hand, and grabbed a handful of iced-out jewelry in the other, saying, "It looks like y'all hit the jackpot on this Jux. This looks like close to four hundred thou in cash and merchandise."

"Yak, you shoulda seen it," J-Bigg said. "When we pulled up outside the spot, I knew we was about to come off big. There wasn't nothing but fly-ass shit parked along the front of the spot." J-Bigg held up three sets of keys. "Keys to a Bentley, a Ferrari, and a Lamborghini."

"What? Y'all took the keys and y'all ain't take none of the cars?"

"For what, to joy ride in? Web asked. "We don't know where no chop shop is."

"I do. I'm Wyte Yak. I know a couple of them. We coulda gotten over fifty G's for late-model Bentleys, Lamborghinis, and shit like that."

"We still can," said Nite. "We left them niggas butt-ass naked and we got all of their cell phones. And Little got the in-house phone cord." Little held up the phone cord, smiling.

"The nearest pay phone is a block away and them niggas probably in there right now trying to figure out who gone walk to the phone butt-ass naked," Nite added.

J-Bigg nodded, saying, "Word!"

"So what y'all saying? Y'all wanna go back out there?"

Everybody yelled, "Hell, yeah!"

"Fuck it, then. Let's roll."

They all grabbed a different set of keys and rushed out of the door, back down stairs and into the parking lot. Bryan jumped in his S500 Mercedes Benz, along with J-Bigg, who sat in the passenger seat, while DY and Web jumped in the back. Wyte Yak jumped in his Ford Expedition with Pillsbury in the passenger seat, and Rahtiek, Trap, and Little all hopped in the back. They sped off rushing back to the city.

After the robbery Frank and the gamblers were trying to figure out who robbed them. They argued about who should run up the block to make the call for help. After about a half hour of debating, Frank forced Shanaya, a pretty, well-built, caramel-complexioned waitress with long, brown hair, to go to the phone. She ran up the block butt-ass naked, holding her breast. Her nipples hardened as the cool night air breezed between her legs. She reached the pay phone and made four collect calls to different numbers that Frank gave her to call for help. Nobody answered the first three times, but on the fourth try she reached J-Boo, one of Frank's workers. He told her he'd be there in fifteen minutes, and she hung up and ran back down the street.

As she ran back down the street and across Fifth Avenue she noticed a group of men walking down the block. At first she was going to ask them for help but then realized that something wasn't right about them. So she hid in-between two cars and watched the men to see what they were up to. She had a feeling they were the same men that robbed the gambling spot so she stayed low to make sure they didn't see her. She knew she was right when she saw them cutting off alarms and hopping into different vehicles which she knew belonged to the men upstairs in the spot.

Wyte Yak drove down the block in his Expedition followed by Little, who was now driving Bryan's Benz. They stopped at the corner, and the rest of the crew pulled out behind them in the stolen vehicles. Bryan pulled out in a red Lamborghini, followed by J-Bigg in a red Ferarri. Web pulled out behind him in a blue convertible Bentley, DY in a black 600 Mercedes Benz, Rahtiek in a silver Range Rover, Pillsbury in a green Range Rover, and Trap in a burgundy Prowler.

Wyte Yak made a right on Lexington Avenue, and the rest of the cars followed.

Shanaya ran back into the spot to let Frank and the

gamblers know that J-Boo was on his way and that some of their cars had just been stolen. Frank was really heated when he realized not only that he had just been robbed of over thirty thousand in cash, but the robbers had the balls to come back forty minutes later and steal his brand-new Ferarri. He slammed his fist on the bar and cussed like a sailor.

To nobody in particular, he said, "I'm know I'm gone find out who these motherfuckers are before the week is out. They gotta be from Manhattan, or else they wouldn't have been able to come back so fast. When I find out who they are, you can bet your last dollar that they gone regret the day they were born.

As the fleet of luxury cars followed Wyte Yak to the chop shop. Wyte Yak picked up his cell phone and called Rick, a cool white boy he knew that ran a chop shop out in Brooklyn. The phone rang three times then Rick answered, "Rick speaking."

"Slick Rick, what's good?"

Not recognizing Wyte Yak's voice, Rick asked, "Who's this?

"Wyte Yak."

"Hey, Yak, how's it hanging?"

"I got a fleet of luxurious shit for you. I'm on my way out to your spot on the docks right now."

Surprised, Rick asked, "No bullshit?"

"You know it's always about business with me."

"How much we talking?"

"I'm gone need about two and a half large."

"That much?"

Wyte Yak smiled as he said, "Trust me, you gonna want to kiss me when you see what I'm working with. I'll be there in about twenty-five minutes."

"Cool. I'll be there."

"Alright, I'm out."

Wyte Yak hung up the phone, and he and the fleet of luxurious cars hopped on the Williamsburg Bridge to North Brooklyn and headed to the Cooper Docks. They arrived at the chop shop, and Wyte Yak parked his Expedition out front and jumped in the Lamborghini with Bryan. Little parked Bryan's Benz and hopped in the Bentley with Web. The gate opened, and the Career Criminals drove the vehicles into the garage.

Rick was waiting for Wyte Yak inside the shop with two of his Italian bodyguards and four of his Puerto Rican workers. Rick was amazed by what he saw and hugged Wyte Yak as he stepped out of the Lamborghini.

Rick handed Wyte Yak a black briefcase with two hundred thousand cash and said, "You really came through for me, Wyte Yak. There's only two hundred grand in the briefcase, but come see me in two days and I'll have the rest."

"Alright, cool. Handle your business. We out."

The Career Criminals exited the shop and hopped back into Wyte Yak's Expedition and Bryan's Benz.

Pillsbury looked over at Wyte Yak and said, "Damn, Yak! You know a little bit of everybody, don't you?"

"I have to. You know that saying, 'it's not what you know, it's who you know,' is true."

They left the docks and headed back downtown Brooklyn. They went back to Yiddo's crib. They put the money in the briefcase and the merchandise they left on the table in their safe in Yiddo's closet. They popped a couple bottles of champagne and called Pooh Berry and told him to send some strippers over. They took turns fucking the five strippers Pooh sent over until early the next morning.

The following afternoon out in Bay Ridge, Brooklyn, Pillsbury was driving one of the PT Cruisers down a one-way street with Yiddo in the passenger seat. They were in front of a short, fat German driving a black 420S Mercedes Benz. Carrying five hundred thousand in diamonds in his jacket pocket he was to be their next victim. Pillsbury slammed on the brakes, and the Benz ran into the back of the PT Cruiser. Pillsbury grabbed the bag of his neck, pretending to be hurt from the accident. The German man looked in the sideview mirror of the Cruiser and noticed Pillsbury holding the back of his neck. He stepped out of his Benz and rushed over to the Cruiser to see if Pillsbury was alright. Pillsbury saw the man coming through the rearview mirror and stepped out of the Cruiser with his head down still holding the back of his neck. The man walked over to Pillsbury and asked, "Sir, are you alright?"

Pillsbury threw an uppercut, striking the man directly beneath the chin and knocking him unconscious, saying, "I am now."

He then searched the man's jacket pockets and found a black velour pouch. He opened the pouch, saw the diamonds, and said to the still unconscious man, "Good looking out, duke." He then jumped back into the PT Cruiser, handed the pouch to Yiddo, smiled, and drove off.

"If you was going to do everything yourself, what the hell did you need me for?" Yiddo asked.

"Company. You know you my nigga, Yiddo."

Yiddo reached into the pouch, pulled out one of the huge rocks, and held it up admiring it. They reached the highway, jumped on the Belt Parkway, and rushed back downtown to the 'hood.

CHAPTER 21

It had been a month and a half since the Career Criminals started doing strictly robberies. Half of the crew was riding in two Navigators they purchased. They were with their girlfriends, headed to the movie theater on Church Avenue and Flatbush. They parked the SUVs on Flatbush Avenue and walked around the corner to the theater. The line to get in the movie was down the block. They didn't have to worry about the line because Little had picked their tickets up earlier for the eight o'clock show.

The Career Criminals and their girls were wearing matching Rockawear sweat-suits and Air Force Ones, with the exception of Rahtiek and Nikki. Rahtiek had on an old school black Guess jean suit with a black T-shirt and a pair of black timberland chuckers. Nikki had on a yellow Sean John sweatsuit with a yellow pair of female classic Reebok. Yiddo and his girl Adina both had on all red. J-Bigg and his girl Latasha were wearing dark blue. Web and his girl Joy were sporting beige. Little and his girl Pam were rocking light blue. DY and his girl Carol had on white, and Pillsbury and his girl Debra were wearing green Rockawear sweat-suits. The guys were all wearing iced-out Rolex watches and platinum chains with iced-out pieces. The girls were all wearing white gold chains with iced-out pieces. Everybody who was wearing a sweatsuit, with the exception of Nikki, had a belt strapping their pistols around their waist and holding it in place. And, of course, Rahtiek had his "American Express cards."

As the Career Criminals entered the theater they were the center of attention. Two guys standing on line at the concession stand weren't impressed and immediately started hating. They were Phooquan and Tahmel, a couple of thugs from Vanderbilt Houses.

Phooquan said, "Look at these characters. They all dressed up and pick this raggedy-ass theater to come to."

"Word! They stunting. We should call the clique and stick these shitheads," said Tahmel.

"Yeah, I'm gone call Rock right now and tell him to bring the boys through with some heat," Phooquan said.

Phooquan pulled out his cell phone and started to dial. The Career Criminals walked upstairs and entered Theater 4, which was showing Shattas, a gangsta' Jamaican flick. The girls immediately started to complain as they entered and took their seats. The theater was smoky, the seats were in poor condition, and there was graffiti all along the walls and even on the twenty-foot-high ceiling.

"What the fuck is this?" asked Adina, looking at the surroundings.

"For real! This look like some shit straight out of Watts or some motherfucking where," Latasha said.

"Word! Look at the seats," Joy said.

"This is the most ghetto movie theater I ever seen in my life," Nikki said. "Why the hell did we come here?"

"Two reasons: this is the only theater we can blow trees in; and it's the only theater in the city that's showing Shatta," said Yiddo.

The guys tried to calm their women, who didn't stop complaining until the movie started. Ten minutes into the movie the women had completely forgotten about the shape the theater was in, intrigued by the action of the movie.

When the movie was over they exited Theater 4 and headed back downstairs. Phooquan and Tahmel were waiting for them along with Rock and four other thugs downstairs in the lobby. Once Phooquan saw them walking down the steps he tapped Rock and said, "There they go right there, Rock."

Rock looked over at the steps and saw the Career Criminals. He looked over all of the faces and got stuck on Rahtiek. His face tightened as he realized he knew Rahtiek and had it out with him once before.   Rock thought back to the time he and Rahtiek crossed paths in prison. They had a beef and, although Rahtiek had a small army of soldiers following him, he shot a fair one with Rock. He beat the shit out of Rock, which embarrassed him, and he stayed in his cell for two weeks after that, only coming out to eat meals. Rock said to himself, "He's in my 'hood now. Time for a little payback."

As the Career Criminals walked down the steps Rahtiek noticed Rock screwfacing him and he thought to himself, "Not this clown again."

He said, "Yak Yak," to alert the rest of the crew that there was trouble up ahead. Rahtiek then pulled his weapons and held them behind his back, and the rest of the crew and their girlfriends all just held their hands on their pistols ready to pull and fire if necessary.

Rock signaled for his crew to follow him, and they stepped to the Career Criminals, who met face to face with Rock's crew. Other people were walking past them in each direction.

"Remember me, player?" Rock said to Rahtiek.

"Yeah, I remember your bitch-ass," Rahtiek said, screwing his face.

Surprised by Rahtiek's reaction, Rock said, "What?"

Rock was offended and reached for the gun on his waist. He wasn't quick enough because, by the time he lifted his shirt to retrieve his pistol from his waist, Rahtiek revealed the two guns which he was holding behind his back. He placed his 9mm on top of the hand Rock was reaching with and placed the .38 auto on the side of Rock's neck. Rock realized he had been beaten to the draw and paused. His crew noticed that their leader was in trouble and started to reach for their guns, but the rest of the Career Criminals and their girls drew their weapons, cocked the hammers, and threw their pistols in Rock's crew faces. Rock's crew froze, realizing that they too had been beaten to the draw, and put their hands in the air.

Rahtiek told Nikki to take Rock's gun as the rest of the Career Criminals disarmed the rest of his crew.

When Rock and his crew were completely disarmed, Rahtiek looked into Rock's eyes and said, "Didn't I tell you the last time we met that if you stayed ready, you don't never have to get ready?"

Then he took the butt of his guns and slammed them on both sides of Rock's temples, knocking him unconscious. Rahtiek looked into the eyes of each of the men that were with Rock as he placed his guns back on his waist and walked through them followed by the rest of the Career Criminals--with the exception of Web.

Web pointed his gun at the unconscious Rock laid on the floor and said, "Fuck that, Rah. I'm smoking this nigga."

"Leave that nigga alone. He's not a threat."

"Fuck that, Sun. You can't sleep on nobody."

"Trust me, these niggas realize we're out of their league. They not coming looking for us after this unless they wondering how can they get down with us. Ain't that right, fellas?"

He looked at Rock's crew, and they all agreed.

Web put his gun back on his waist, kicked Rock, then

looked at his crew and said, "Y'all bitch-ass niggas better recognize the real." Then he followed Rahtiek and the rest of the "fam" out of the doors. They exited the movie theater, walked back around the corner, and entered their vehicles. Nikki was staring at Rahtiek, amazed by the way he had just handled the situation. They made a U-turn and took Flatbush Avenue back downtown to the 'hood.

Wyte Yak and Jeremy were in their living room sitting on the couch eating home made Pop Secret Popcorn and watching a movie. Out of the blue Jeremy asked, "Dad, do you think you'll ever get back together with my mother?"

Wyte Yak was surprised by the question. He gave his son an awkward look and said, "I don't know, Jeremy."

"I think y'all should."

"Why would you say that?" asked Wyte Yak, curiously.

"Because I feel sorry for my mother. She's down South in that big ol' house by herself. I know she wants us to be a family more than anything."

"How you know? Did she she tell you that?"

"Nah, she never said nothing, but I can see it in her eyes."

"You can, huh?"

"Yep. I can see it in your eyes, too."

"Shut up and eat your popcorn."

Wyte Yak tossed a handful of popcorn at Jeremy, who said, "You know you miss her."

Wyte Yak returned his focus to the television, saying, "I'm alright."

Wyte Yak would have loved for them all to be a family. But Jeremy's mother betrayed him in the past and he wasn't sure he could ever forgive her. He stared at the television, and Jeremy dropped the conversation.

A few days later the Career Criminals were in the parking lot. Rahtiek and Wyte Yak hopped in a rented blue Jaguar sedan. The rest of the crew hopped in their PT Cruisers. They were about to head uptown to rob some Dominican drug dealers. Wyte Yak looked to his left and saw Pillsbury seated on the passenger side of one of the PT Cruisers.

Wyte Yak yelled, "Pillak, Geeatha!"

Pillsbury looked at J-Bigg, who was in the driver's seat and asked, "What did he say?"

"You heard him. He said 'Geeatha.' "

"What that mean?" Pillsbury asked.

"You know what that mean. Geeatha fuck outta here!"

"Tell him I'm rolling. As a matter fact I'll tell him myself."

Pillsbury stepped out of the Cruiser and walked over to Wyte Yak sitting in the Jaguar and said, "I'm rolling."

"Chill, Pillak. I need you to stay here."

"Fuck that! I'm rolling. I'm tired of niggas acting like I don't get busy."

"Cut it out, Sun," Rahtiek said. "Niggas know you get busy. You just took half a mill in diamonds a couple of days ago without even having to pull your gat."

"Why I can't go on this mission?"

"You stand out too much, Pillak. I would hate for somebody we stuck to recognize you and some ol' bullshit go down. As a matter of fact, take that chain off before somebody recognizes their shit."

"If I take the chain off, can I roll?"

Wyte Yak shook his head and said, "No."

"Then fuck it."

Pillsbury started to walk away, and Rahtiek moved the Jaguar up so Wyte Yak could finish talking to him.

"Sun, take the chain off."

"I am. I'm just going to walk over to Joe Johnson's and get me some hot wings. Then I'm going up to Yiddo crib and put this chain with the others. How long you think y'all gone be?"

"We'll be back in a couple of hours. I'll kick it with you when we get back."

"Yeah, alright," Pillsbury said.

The Jaguar pulled out of the parking lot, followed by the two PT Cruisers. They made the right on Prince and headed for uptown Manhattan. Pillsbury walked across Prince Street to Joe Johnson's and ordered twelve hot wings and some cheese fries. He paid for the order received his food and exited the store.

Pillsbury stopped near the pay phone on the corner, dug in his bag, and pulled out a hot wing. As he put the hot wing in his mouth, Jeremy rolled up on a dirt bike.

"What up, Pillsbury? Did you see my father?" Jeremy asked.

Pillsbury pulled the bare chicken bone from his mouth, tossed it to the ground, and said, "What up, Jerm Dogg? He just left a few minutes ago. He'll be back in about couple of hours."

"I hope so. He supposed to take me to the movies."

Pillsbury smiled and said, "I heard y'all won the

championship. How many points did you score?"

"Twenty-one," Jeremy said proudly.

Pillsbury slapped Jeremy five and said, "You the man, Jerm Dogg."

As they conversed a Cadillac Escalade passed, and the driver, Andrew, noticed Pillsbury was wearing his chain. He stopped the vehicle, put it in reverse, and pulled over in front of Pillsbury and Jeremy. Andrew hopped out of the Jeep, approached Pillsbury, and asked, "Yo, Money, where did you get that chain from?"

"Why?"

Andrew's face tightened as he said, "That's my motherfucking chain!"

"I don't know what the fuck you talking about. This is my chain."

"Oh, you wanna act stupid?"

Andrew reached on his waist and pulled his .357 Magnum. Pillsbury attempted to rush Andrew but wasn't swift enough, and Andrew let off four shots. Two slugs struck Pillsbury in the chest, and the other two struck him in the belly. As Pillsbury fell to the ground, Andrew let off the remaining two slugs at Jeremy, who was riding off on his bike. The first slug just missed his head, and the other one struck him high on the left side of his back making him tumble over the bike and fall to the ground. Andrew then looked at Pillsbury on the ground gagging, blood coming out of his mouth. He snatched his chain from off Pillsbury's neck, jumped back in the Escalade, and peeled off.

Pillsbury's lungs collapsed, and Jeremy went into shock, unable to move. A crowd formed around the two bodies, and Police rushed onto the scene. A few minutes later two ambulances arrived. One took Pillsbury's to

Brooklyn Hospital, and the other rushed Jeremy to Saint Vincent's Hospital in lower Manhattan. Jeremy pulled through, but Pillsbury died.

The rest of the Career Criminals were uptown Manhattan. J-Bigg, Web, DY, Trap, Little, Bryan, Yiddo, and Nite were on 146th Street and Amsterdam Avenue lying low in the PT Cruisers awaiting a signal from Wyte Yak, sitting in a Jaguar with Rahtiek one block away and waiting for a drug dealer who could supply the amount of weight they were asking for.

A green Range Rover parked in front of the Jaguar and Pablo, a Dominican drug dealer hopped out. He approached the passenger side of the Jaguar, leaned over so that he was face to face with Wyte Yak, and spoke in a Dominican accent, "What's up, Bee? I'm Pablo. My man tells me choo trying to make a big score. How big we talking?"

Wyte Yak stared in Pablo's eyes and said, "I need five ki's of pure, uncut, powder cocaine and three ki's of pure heroin. I want the good shit--the China white, not that bullshit you sell these nickel and dime motherfuckers. I'm spending top dollar so I want top choice product."

"Alright, Poppy," Pablo said. "Don't worry. I'll give choo the best. Choo know we talking around two hundred and seventy thousand. Choo got that kind of money with you?"

"I got two fifty."

"Two fifty? I can work with that. Let me see the money."

Rahtiek pulled a briefcase from behind his chair. He opened it so Pablo could see the money. They could see the excitement in Pablo's eyes as he said, "Alright, Poppy, follow me up to the spot."

"Nah, Poppy, it's not going down like that," Wyte Yak said. "I trust you about as much as you trust me."

"So how choo wan to do this, Bee?"

Everybody know you Dominicans got shit sewed up here. So you don't have to worry about me trying to get slick. So you send one of your soldiers upstairs to get the product while you jump in the back and count this money."

"Alright, Poppy, if that's the way choo want to do business, it's cool with me. Hold up a minute. I'll be right back."

Pablo walked over to one of his men and told him in Spanish what he needed him to do. As Pablo walked away from the car Rahtiek said to Wyte Yak, "What's wrong with this dude? He don't even know if we the Feds."

"He know we not no Feds. I don't even think the Feds fuck with these dudes. They must be hitting them off or something."

"Word! It looks like these same dudes been pumping on this block since the 80's. I guess the Feds rather run up in our cribs and knock us with our little couple of ounces to try and make it look like it's a real war on drugs."

Pablo walked back over and jumped in the back seat. Rahtiek handed him the briefcase, and he started counting the money.

Wyte Yak's cell phone rang, and he answered it, "What's good?"

Pooh Berry was on the other line. He said, "Somebody just killed Pillsbury, and they shot Jeremy, too."

"What?"

Wyte Yak dropped the cell phone, cursing, and started banging on the dashboard. Rahtiek picked up the phone, and Wyte Yak reached in the back and grabbed the briefcase from Pablo.

Wyte Yak closed the briefcase, slid it beneath his chair, and said, "The deal's off, Poppy."

With a confused expression on his face Pablo asked, "What do choo mean the deal's off?"

"Exactly what I said."

"Hey listen. I don't know what just happen, Bee, but my man will be back in five minutes with the stuff. Choo can wait five minutes?"

"I said the deal's off," Wyte Yak said rudely. "Now get out!"

Pablo started to get upset and said, "You can't renege half-way into a deal with me. Just hold up a minute."

Wyte Yak became furious. He pulled his pistol from his back, reached in the back of the car, and grabbed Pablo by the collar. Wyte Yak placed his gun underneath Pablo's chin and said, "Get the fuck out of the car before I blow your fucking head off!"

Rahtiek hung up the phone and turned around to calm the situation. "Chill, Yak. Don't shoot him. Poppy, get out of the car. We got some major shit we need to handle. We'll get at you some other time."

Wyte Yak released Pablo, and he stepped out of the vehicle. Rahtiek turned on the car and started to pull off. Wyte Yak stuck his hand out of the window to signal the rest of the crew who were waiting up the block to move with them.

As they drove off, Pablo lost his cool, saying, "Fuck that! You niggas don't know who you're fucking with."

He pulled a 9mm from his waist and ran into the street shooting at Wyte Yak and Rahtiek in the Jaguar. J-Bigg sped up the Cruiser he was driving and slammed into the back of Pablo, knocking him onto the hood of a parked car. A group of Dominicans came running out of the building shooting at the PT Cruisers. The back door of the second cruiser, which Bryan was driving, flew open, and the Career Criminals returned fire. Rahtiek called Bryan and J-Bigg on their cell phones and let them know what had happened. He told them he and Wyte Yak were headed to Saint Vincent's Hospital and told them to go back to the 'hood to find out what happened.

Wyte Yak and Rahtiek arrived at the hospital and rushed into the lobby of the hospital, where they met up with Pooh Berry.

Breathing hard, Wyte Yak asked, "Where's my son?"

"Calm down, Yak. Jeremy's alright. He just got a little flesh wound. The slug went straight through without hitting anything vital."

"That's good," said Rahtiek.

Still very anxious, Wyte Yak said, "I still need to see him. Where is he?"

"He's in room 306."

Wyte Yak started to walk off, and Pooh Berry grabbed his arm and told him, "Coretta's in there with him."

"Coretta?" Wyte Yak asked with a surprised expression. "What is she doing in New York? Who told her what happened?"

Pooh Berry lowered his head and said, "Rosie. You know she got a big mouth."

"Damn, man. This is all I need."

As Wyte Yak walked down the hall, Rahtiek said to Pooh, "What happen? Who shot them?"

"The way I see it, it had to be Andrew. Jeremy and Pillsbury were shot with a .357 Magnum, and Sinsation was also."

"Damn! Pillsbury was wearing his chain. Yak told him to take that chain off." Rahtiek held his head down shaking it then said, "Fuck it, man! Tell Wyte Yak I'm out."

They slapped five, and Pooh Berry asked, "Where you going?"

"To handle business. Where else?"

"Be careful," Pooh Berry warned.

Rahtiek nodded his head and walked out of the hospital.

Jeremy was lying in bed with an IV in his left arm and a tube in his nose to help him breathe, his mother and Aunt Rosie at his side. As Coretta rubbed the side of Jeremy's face she said, "Since you gonna have to be on bed rest for a few days after you're released I'm going to buy you some more games for your Play Station 2. Is there anything else you want?"

"I want my father," Jeremy said sadly.

"Uncle Pooh called him. He'll be here soon," said Rosie.

Wyte Yak entered the room, and a smile appeared on Jeremy's face.

"Who shot my nephew?" Rosie approached Wyte Yak and asked.

"I don't know yet."

Rosie screwed her face and said, "I'll find out and, when I do, I'll kill the bastard myself."

Coretta walked over to Wyte Yak, hugged him, and started crying, saying, "They tried to kill my baby. Why did they try to kill my baby?"

"I don't know, but I will find everything out before this day is over."

"What kind of idiot would shoot a twelve-year-old

kid?" asked Rosie.

Wyte Yak looked at his sister and said, "Rosie, please, you and Coretta leave the room for a few minutes. I need to talk to Jeremy."

"Alright. Come on, Coretta."

Rosie grabbed Coretta by the arm and led her out of the room. Wyte Yak walked over and sat on the bed next to his son.

He started rubbing Jeremy's head and asked, "How you feel, Jerm?"

"I'm alright, but the doctor said I won't be able to play basketball for a few weeks."

A tear ran down Wyte Yak's cheek as he said, "I'm sorry, Jeremy."

Wondering why his father was apologizing, Jeremy said, "It's not your fault, dad. This man was trying to rob Pillsbury. I tried to ride off to find help. But he started shooting and I got shot. I was scared."

Jeremy started crying, and Wyte Yak leaned over to comfort him saying, "I know you were scared, Jerm. But you know something, I don't never want you to be scared anymore. They want you to be scared. I used to be scared."

Jeremy looked up at his father and asked, "You, daddy? I didn't think you was afraid of anything."

"Yeah, well, sometimes when I'm driving my car and the police pull me over, I get nervous, and my body trembles."

"For what? Why would you be afraid of the police?"

Wyte Yak lowered his head and said, "Well, me being a black man in America, I know I didn't do anything wrong. So I ask myself why are they pulling me over? Are they going to drag me from my car, handcuff me, and beat me senseless, or are they going to take me to the precinct and give me the plunger treatment like Abner Louima?"

"Dag, daddy! They make you feel like that."

"They used to."

"Man, I hate cops."

"Never hate anyone, Jeremy. Just never be afraid. Just face every situation that approaches you head on. That way nine times out of ten you'll come out on top."

"Alright, dad, from now on I'll try not to be afraid of anything."

"That's my boy."

Wyte Yak rubbed Jeremy's head, got off the bed, and started to walk away.

"Where you going?" Jeremy asked.

"I'll be back. I have to have a talk with your mother. I'll send Aunt Rosie back in here with you."

"Are you spending the night?"

"Of course. What kind of question is that?" He winked at his son, and Jeremy smiled as his father walked out of the room. Wyte Yak walked down the hall and entered the waiting room. Coretta, Rosie, and Pooh Berry were sitting conversing.

"Rosie, Jeremy want you," Wyte Yak interrupted.

Rosie stood and started to walk off then turned and said, "Y'all make sure y'all tell him what I said."

"Alright, Rosie," said Pooh Berry.

"What's she hollering about?" Wyte Yak asked.

"Nothing. She was over here bugging, talking about it probably was the Bloods."

Wyte Yak looked around then asked Pooh Berry, "Where's Rahtiek?"

"He left. I told him what I think happened, and he

jetted."

"He just left without me?" Wyte Yak asked, upset.

Wyte Yak turned and started to leave. Pooh ran behind him, saying, "Hold up a minute, Yak. I told him I think it was Andrew, the guy Sinsation set up for us, because Jeremy and Pillsbury both got shot with a .357 Magnum. Sinsation also was shot with a .357 Magnum."

"Oh yeah. Then I'm going to kill that bastard."

"Rahtiek can handle that coward by himself. You need to stay here and talk to your baby mother."

Wyte Yak looked at his brother and said, "You right, fuck it." He then walked back into the waiting room and said to Coretta, "We need to talk. Come on. Let's go get something to eat."

"I'll go hang out in the room with Rosie and Jeremy until y'all get back."

"Alright, Pooh. Thanks."

Coretta and Wyte Yak walked over to the elevator. On the way downstairs Wyte Yak stared at Coretta and thought to himself that she was even more beautiful than he remembered and that if he could only put his pride aside, the three of them could be the family they were meant to be.

The elevator opened on the main floor, and the couple walked through the lobby and out of the hospital, making a left and going down the block. They crossed the street and found a restaurant in the middle of the next block, where they entered and waited to be seated.

CHAPTER 22

Meanwhile back at Yiddo's apartment, Web, Night, Yiddo, Trap, DY, Bryan, and J-Bigg were all sitting around the apartment upset, trying to figure out what happened.

"It was the Blood's man. I know it," said DY.

"Word! They probably tried to rob him, but Pillsbury wasn't going for it," said Trap.

"Get the fuck outta here!" Little said.

"Word! Don't let the media hype y'all up. When have you ever heard of the Bloods in our 'hood trying to rob a real nigga like Pillsbury? Them cowards only fuck with weak niggas. Besides, every Blood in this motherfucking Project know better than to fuck with anybody in our crew," said J-Bigg.

"True. They know they'd have a better chance at getting away with shooting a cop than fucking with one of us," said Little.

"That's what I'm saying," said J-Bigg.

"Then who was it, Milk and them niggas from the other side?" DY asked. "Them faggot-ass niggas think they gangsta'."

Sounding extremely upset, Bryan said, "Fuck all this guessing game shit! Pillsbury was all of our man, but my family also got shot. I'm killing who ever did it. I don't give a fuck who he is. So if you don't know who did it don't guess, you might get the wrong nigga killed. All we gotta do is hit the streets and find out. Somebody had to see something."

They all were about to exit the apartment when Web stopped them. "Hold up a minute," Web said. "I think I know what happened. Y'all remember the other day when

Pooh Berry told us Sinsation was murdered, but we didn't know who did it?"

"Yeah," everybody answered.

"Well, now I know who did it."

"Who?" asked DY.

"It was Andrew, the guy me and J-Bigg bagged in Canarsie."

"What makes you think it was him?" Little asked.

"When I talked to Pooh Berry a little while ago he said Pillsbury and Jeremy were both shot with a .357 Magnum, and so was Sinsation."

"Pillsbury was wearing Andrew's chain. It had to be him," said J-Bigg.

"Damn! Wyte Yak told him to take that chain off," said Nite.

"That's all I needed to hear. Where this character live?" asked Bryan.

"1251 East 83rd Street," said J-Bigg.

"Alright, I'm out."

"I'm coming with you," said J-Bigg.

"Me too," said Web.

"We all going," said DY.

They all were about to follow Bryan out of the apartment, but he turned around and stopped them, saying, "Everybody don't need to go. Trust me, I got this."

"What you mean you got this? We all want a piece of this pussy-ass nigga," said Web.

"Word, Web. We should have smoked his ass when we robbed him," said J-Bigg.

Reasoning with the crew, Bryan said, "If we all go, we're going to be sloppy. We are all way too upset. We're liable to make a mistake and wind up locked down for the rest of our lives. Let me handle this. I'm trained to kill."

"Alright, then bring back a finger or something so we can be sure it's a done deal," Little said.

"Alright, I'll bring back a souvenir."

"Make sure it's something good-- like a ear or his eyes or something."

"Yeah, alright."

"Are you sure you got this?" J-Bigg asked Bryan, looking him in the eye. "You don't need nobody to come with you?"

"Not at all. I work best by myself."

Web slapped Bryan five and said, "We going to let you handle this, but make sure that nigga suffers."

"Trust me, he will."

As Bryan opened the door to leave DY grabbed his arm and said, "Make sure you bring back a souvenir."

"I got you, DY."

Bryan rushed down the five flights of stairs and hopped into his Benz, screeching his tires as he sped out of the parking lot. He made the right at the bottom of Prince Street and sped up Park Avenue. He made another right on Washington Avenue, which he took to Ocean Avenue and stopped off at his apartment.

Bryan entered the apartment and walked straight to the bedroom. He reached on the top shelf and pulled down a suitcase filled with guns, a crossbow, and a few hunting knives. There were two pistol-grip pump shotguns, a sniper rifle, a Smith & Wesson 9mm, a Luger 9mm, a .44 Bull Dog, and .44 automatic with a home-made silencer. There was also an AK47 and a Browning 9mm with silencer. He checked the .44 automatic to see if it was loaded and put it on his waist. Then he checked the clip of the Browning with the silencer and put it on his waist. Then he grabbed a huge, double-edged hunting knife.

He closed the suitcase, placed it back in the closet, and exited the apartment. Bryan drove out to Canarsie and looked at the windows of the house located at 1251 East 83rd Street. He parked around the corner on Avenue K, cut through the back alley, and walked to the back of 1251 East 83rd. All the lights were out, so he knew nobody was home. He climbed up to the window and tapped the glass with the butt of his gun until it broke and entered the house.

Over at the restaurant Wyte Yak and Coretta were seated looking through their menus. A waitress approached their table and said, "Good evening. My name is Tamara. I'll be your waitress for the evening. Are you ready to order?"

"Yeah, I'll have the barbecue chicken dinner with macaroni and cheese and broccoli as the sides," Coretta said.

"What kind of beverage would you like?"

"I'll take a spring water."

"Okay, and you, sir?"

"I'll have the fish dinner with mashed potatoes and gravy and sweet peas as the sides."

"What would you like to drink with that?"

"I'll take a diet Pepsi."

"Anything else?"

"Oh yeah, could you bring us some rolls?" asked Wyte Yak.

"No problem. I'll return with your rolls shortly."

The waitress walked off, and Wyte Yak stared at Coretta, asking, "What's wrong?"

"Nothing. I'm alright."

"I expected you to be cursing me out, talking about

how you're taking my boy away from me. I guess you're still busy enjoying the money I gave you."

"You know, I actually tried to enjoy the two million you gave me for allowing you custody of our child. First I bought a house and some acres for two hundred and fifty thousand--which even back then was a steal because after I did what I wanted to with it.... Let's just say it is now worth one point five million. Then I bought myself a beauty salon. We both know that was always my dream. I now own twenty-three of them throughout the Tidewater area, and business is going great."

"I'm glad to hear that. I always knew you had a good head on your shoulders and a knack for business."

"Thank you. I try, but honestly I think I got my business savvy from watching you."

"So what brings you to New York?" Wyte Yak asked, smiling. "Are you on a shopping spree?"

"No, Franklin, I came to bring you your two million dollars back with interest."

The waitress walked over to the table and placed some butter, rolls, and two glasses of water on the table. Coretta placed her hand on top of Wyte Yak's and said, "Franklin, I know you are a good father. You love Jeremy more than life itself. How many other men would pay two million dollars just to have custody of their child? I only did it because I felt guilty for betraying you. I know what happened to Jeremy wasn't your fault. So I'm not here to try and lay blame."

"Then why are you here? You know I'm not taking the money back. Just live up to our agreement. I stay in New York, and you stay in Virginia. Jeremy stays with me and visits you on his and your birthdays."

"That's not enough. I need to play a bigger role in

my son's life. The last twelve years have been hell on me. All the money and success in the world don't mean nothing if you don't have anyone to share it with."

"That's true."

"Yeah, and from what I heard you're not married, you don't have a girlfriend. So you must be just as miserable as I am."

"I'm not miserable. I have Jeremy, and you not taking him."

"I don't want to take him from you; I want to share him with you."

Wyte Yak nonchalantly said, "Yeah I know. But what you want me to do?"

"I want you to forgive me and except me back into your life. I still love you and I believe you still love me. So forget the past. I know I made a huge mistake, but I strongly feel we should get back together for the sake of our and our child's future."

"Sorry, but I can't do that."

"Why not? Because your pride won't let you?"

"My pride has nothing to do with it. You know what you did. I don't think I could ever trust you again."

Coretta got upset and a tear ran down her cheek as she said, "I made one mistake. Now I gotta pay for it for the rest of my life. I've suffered enough. You've suffered enough. Don't you think it's time we put all that behind us?"

They sat quietly staring into each other's eyes until the waitress brought their food. Andrew drove up to his house in Canarsie and parked his car in the driveway. He hopped out and walked up the stairs and started to open his door. Rahtiek placed a gun to the back of his head. Andrew was about to reach for the gun on his waist until Rahtiek said, "Go ahead. Be stupid."

Andrew stopped reaching, raised his hands above his head, and said, "You got it."

Rahtiek then reached on Andrew's waist to take his weapon, saying, "That's what I thought."

Rahtiek removed his gun from the back of Andrew's head and placed it in the middle of his back while he removed Andrew's weapon. Rahtiek noticed that it was a .357 Magnum and said, "I know this ain't the same Trey Pound that you killed my nigga, Pillsbury, and shot my little man, Jerm Dogg, with."

Andrew tried to explain, "Nah, it wasn't like that, bro."

"Shut the fuck up and get in the house!"

Rahtiek pushed Andrew into the house and walked in behind him, closing the door and locking it. He clicked the light on and was surprised by Bryan, who was standing in front of Andrew, holding a .44 automatic with silencer to his head in one hand and drinking a Heineken with the other.

"What the fuck you doing here?" Rahtiek asked.

"Chill, baby. I got this one."

"Nah, I got him."

Rahtiek then pushed Andrew past Bryan into the living room.

Bryan said, "Your gun's too loud, Sun. You'd have to kill him too fast."

"I don't care how he dies, as long as he's dead."

Andrew looked at the two men and said, "You're making a mistake. It wasn't..."

"Shut the fuck up, bitch!" Rahtiek cut him off. "Your mother made a mistake when she gave birth to you, pussy ass."

"This mother fucker played his self so he's got to suffer. We gone kill his ass real slow." Bryan then placed his gun on the counter, tossed Rahtiek some rope, and said, "Tie that nigga up while I grab us a couple of Heinekens out of the refrigerator. You know I brought a six-pack."

As Rahtiek tied Andrew to a kitchen chair, Bryan walked in the kitchen and came back with two Heinekens. Rahtiek tied Andrew's hands behind his back and his ankles to the legs of the chair. Bryan handed Rahtiek a Heineken and took off his scarf and tied it around Andrew's mouth. He then handed Rahtiek, who was sitting two feet away from Andrew on the couch, the 9mm Browning with the silencer and sat about six feet away from Andrew in a lounge chair facing him holding his .44 in his lap. He opened his fresh Heineken, held it to his mouth, started to guzzle, and shot Andrew in his left shin. You could here the bone split as the slug pierced through Andrew's leg. Andrew's eyes widened and his mouth opened as he let out a silent scream. Bryan grabbed the remote control and cut on the TV, flicking to the sports channel, as he said to Rahtiek, "Your turn."

Rahtiek pointed the Browning at Andrew and shot him in the right side of his stomach. Tears started flowing down Andrew's face. Rahtiek drank some of his Heineken, and Bryan let off another two shots, striking Andrew in the right thigh and right shoulder. As he guzzled down the rest of his beer, Rahtiek shot Andrew in both of his knees. The pain was excruciating, and Andrew's tearing eyes cryed out for mercy.

Bryan walked back into the kitchen and grabbed two more beers and returned to the living room. He tossed Rahtiek one and stood behind Andrew, placing his .44 on the back of Andrew's right hand, which he had clenched together with his left hand. Bryan shot threw the back of his hand,

and the slug went through both hands, leaving a huge hole in his hands. Andrew jumped from the pain and tumbled over in the chair. Bryan raised Andrew and the chair back to an upright position, opened his beer, and sat back in the lounge chair, saying, "Your turn."

Rahtiek took a sip of beer, and shot Andrew in both of his feet. Andrew's body was filled with blood, but he wasn't dead yet.

"I see why you wanted to kill him slow," Rahtiek said.

"Ain't nothing like watching a motherfucker die slow, but right about now I'm tired of looking at this shit-head's face."

Bryan stood and placed his Heineken on the coffee table. He walked back over to Andrew, pulled the scarf from around his mouth, and placed his gun in Andrew's mouth, pulling the trigger six times and using the five remaining slugs from his gun. The first one killed Andrew, blowing a hole through the back of his head. The last four only made the hole bigger. He then pulled the huge, double-edged hunting knife from his waist and began cutting Andrew's head off.

"What the fuck are you doing?"Rahtiek asked.

"DY and them asked me to bring them a souvenir."

"Shit, man. They were talking about his gun or a fin-ger--maybe even his ear--but not his motherfucking head."

Just then Bryan faced Rahtiek with Andrew's head in one hand and his bloody knife in the other. Rahtiek shook his head and said, "You's a sick motherfucker!"

"Don't tell me killer Rahtiek has never decapitated none of his victims. What kind of killer are you?"

"Yeah, I have, but not like that. You got the nigga blood all running down your wrist and shit. Fuck that. Let's get the fuck out of here."

Rahtiek gathered all of the beer bottles and wiped the fingerprints off everything. Bryan searched in the kitchen for a plastic bag and a box. He placed Andrew's head in the bag, put the bag in the box, washed his hands, and they left.

Back at Yiddo's apartment Yiddo, Web, DY, Little, J-Bigg, Trap, Nite, and Dikki Jah were sitting around waiting for Bryan to return. Dikki Jah was upset. "Man, I don't believe y'all let Bryan go handle this shit by himself."

"Bryan is a professional. He didn't want nobody to roll with him," said DY.

"That's what he said, but y'all ain't never see him get busy."

"Wyte Yak been told us that Sun get busy. So we not even worried about that," J-Bigg said.

Little nodded his head and said, "Word! Sun keep two or three guns on him."

"Plus he know how to make silencers and shit," said Trap.

"Word! He showed me a silencer he made for his .44 auto," said Nite.

"That don't mean nothing," Dikki Jah said.

"You right. That don't mean nothing. So we gone just wait until he gets back to find out just how busy he get," said J-Bigg.

Somebody knocked on the door. Yiddo walked over to the door and opened it. Pooh Berry entered the apartment.

"What up, Pooh Berry?" Yiddo asked. "How's Jerm Dogg?"

"He's alright. He just got a little flesh wound. He'll

be home in a couple of days."

"That's good," said Little.

"Is Wyte Yak still at the hospital?" J-Bigg asked.

"Yeah, he's going to spend the night with Jeremy. Where's Bryan?"

"He slid to Canarsie to handle that business. We figured it had to be that nigga, Andrew," said Web.

"Word? Rahtiek went out there, too."

J-Bigg held his mouth open for a second then said, "Say no more."

"Word! Both them niggas went out there. Duke fucked up," said Little.

Somebody knocked at the door again. Pooh Berry opened the door, and Rahtiek walked in, followed by Bryan carrying a box.

"What happen? Did y'all find him?" Dikki Jah asked.

"Yeah, we found him," Rahtiek said. "Bryan's got a present for y'all."

"What you got for us Bryan?" Yiddo asked.

"I know you brought back something good, like a hand or ear," DY said.

As Bryan reached in the box, Rahtiek pulled Pooh Berry to the back and said, "Come to the back, Pooh. You don't want to see what he got in the box."

"Why not?"

"Just trust me on this one."

Rahtiek and Pooh walked into the back room. Everyone else stayed out front waiting to see what was in the box. Bryan reached into the box and pulled out Andrew's head. They all started gagging and running towards the bathroom, with the exception of Dikki Jah and Trap, who just sat there smiling as they looked at each other and said,

"Off with the head."

Jeremy had his eyes closed and was smiling as he lay down in the hospital bed. He was happy that both of his parents were lying in the bed next to him watching television.

Coretta said, "Franklin."

"Yeah."

"Do you remember the first time we made love?" she asked.

"What's wrong with you?"

"What, I can't reminisce about old times?"

"You can do whatever you want to. Just don't include me."

"Why it gotta be like that?"

"Why you had to be working with the Feds?"

Coretta stared into Wyte Yak's eyes and said, "Come on, baby. Give me a break. That was almost twelve years ago. You can't live in the past. Do me a favor. Forget about the past and ask yourself what's going to make you happy right now."

"I trusted you once before and you let me down. I gave you my heart, and you crushed it. What makes you think I'd be silly enough to do it again?"

"You could never say that I let you down, because if I really would have let you down you wouldn't be here. You'd be somewhere locked down in a federal penitentiary, but you're not. So truthfully you really don't have anything to be mad about."

"I don't have anything to be mad about? You crazy! What about my money, my minimansion, the spot with the roller rink, bowling alley, club, and all that good shit in it, huh? What about that?"

"That stuff's material," Coretta said, rolling her eyes.

"You can get it all back, but this time try going about getting it the right way."

"So what you saying? I should just say fuck it. Fuck the fact that you caused me to lose my millions?"

"I got millions. You can have half--fuck half. You can have it all. It don't mean shit to me, without you and Jeremy."

Curious, Wyte Yak asked, "You saying if we get back together I would have control of all your money?"

"If that's what it takes, you can have it all. I trust you, Franklin. I know who you are. Your heart's always been in the right place. You just choose the wrong paths. You're a very intelligent man, but your impatience is your only downfall. You know how to make your dirty money legal, but don't you think you'd get a lot further if you started out with legal money from jump?"

"Where am I supposed to get enough legal money to do anything other than eat?"

"You simply do not give yourself enough credit."

Coretta rested her head on Wyte Yak's shoulder and fell asleep, and Wyte Yak stared at the ceiling in deep thought.

CHAPTER 23

Rahtiek and Nikki were lying in bed watching television in Rahtiek's apartment.

"Baby, when y'all coming to get the bank?" Nikki asked Rahtiek.

Trying to focus on the television program Rahtiek said, "When the time is right. We're not ready yet."

"Y'all better hurry up and get ready because I put in for a transfer. I'm leaving in another two months."

"Why you leaving?"

"I'm tired of Poughkeepsie. It's too boring. I'm trying to move closer to the city, if not in the city."

"What if we're not ready by then?" Rahtiek asked.

"Y'all should have been ready. I gave you the layout almost two months ago."

"Yeah, I know, but we didn't have a chance to come check the set yet."

"Well, what you waiting on?"

"I'm waiting on Wyte Yak."

"You can come check it out yourself."

Focusing back on the television, Rahtiek said, "That's not my job. It's Yak's."

"Oh, so you need Wyte Yak in order to make a move."

"Stop acting stupid."

Attempting to make Rahtiek feel low, Nikki said, "I'm not acting stupid. I thought you was the man. Now I see you just the man behind the man."

"What, bitch? Nobody's not the man in my crew. We a team. Everybody plays their position, and we all eat together. That's the rule we live by and, other than Pillsbury and little Jeremy getting shot, we haven't had any problems. It's Yak's job to check out the scenery. And when he's ready to do so, that's when we'll do it."

"I'm just saying what if he takes too long and I get transferred."

"You just get transferred."

"And we'll lose out on all of that money."

"Never that. If it's as easy as you say, we're going to hit it regardless."

A scream was heard coming from Quanesia's bedroom. They rushed out of bed and ran into her room.

Quanesia was having a nightmare. She was dreaming that her foster father was over her and swinging his belt. She was crying and screaming, "Stop. Stop. I'm sorry. Please stop."

Rahtiek rushed into her room followed by Nikki. He cut on the light and picked Quanesia up to comfort her. He held her in his arms and rubbed her back, saying, "It's alright, Qua. Daddy's here. It's alright."

Quanesia opened her eyes and saw her father. She wrapped her arms around him and held him tightly.

"It's alright, baby," Rahtiek said. "I got you."

"What's wrong with her?" Nikki asked.

"I don't know. Her mother never told me she be having nightmares when she was alive. This is the third time this week she's had one."

Over at Yiddo's crib, Yiddo was sitting at the kitchen table with his head resting on the table with a Guinness Stout in front of him. DY was at the other end of the table smoking a blunt and playing cards with J-Bigg and Little. Trap, Web, and Nite were sitting in the living room watching television.

Web tapped Nite and said, "Nite, you chillin' here? I'm about to roll out. Wifey waiting on me at the crib."

"Nah, I'm about to break out, too."

"Come on," Web said, motioning his head.

The two stood, and Web said, "I'm out."

"Me, too," Nite said.

Trap said, "Y'all niggas, chill."

They both slapped Trap five then walked into the kitchen and gave the three men playing cards five. As Nite opened the door, Web shook Yiddo's shoulder to wake him.

"Yiddo, wake up."

Yiddo raised his head and said, "I'm not asleep. I'm just resting my eyes."

"Me and Nite out. We'll be back over here in the morning."

Yiddo yawned and said, "Alright, chill."

"Get up and go to bed, Yiddo. You're out of it."

"Alright."

Yiddo stretched as he raised from the chair, and Nite and Web walked out of the door.

Yiddo locked the door behind them, saying, "I'm going to bed."

"Chill," said DY.

"Alright, Yiddo, see you in the morning," said Little.

As Yiddo walked in between the kitchen table and living room couch, Trap raised up from the couch and in a playful girly voice said, "Good night, Yiddo."

"Stop acting stupid, dummy."

Yiddo walked into the bedroom, and Trap walked over and sat where Yiddo was sitting. "What y'all playing, pitty pat?" Trap asked.

DY plucked a deuce, put it in his hand, then slammed his hand on the table yelling, "It's over!"

As DY reached out and grabbed his winnings from the pot. J-Bigg answered Trap, "What else we gone be playing? These niggas don't know how to play poker."

"I know how to play poker. You must be talking about this nigga."

As Trap gathered the cards DY said, "No. we're not playing poker."

"You heard him," said Little. "We're not playing poker."

"I don't want to play poker. I wanna show y'all something."

"Show us nothing," said J-Bigg, attempting to snatch the cards from Trap. Trap pulled the cards out of Bigg's reach and J-Bigg said, "Chill, Trap. Let us finish playing pitty pat."

Trap shuffled the cards and said, "Hold up a minute. Let me show y'all this card game I invented."

"You ain't invent nothing. It's probably some shit you learned in jail," said J-Bigg.

"Word! Trying to come home and act like he made it up," DY said.

"I did make it up."

"Alright then. Let's check it out," said Little.

"Alright, everybody throw five dollars in the pot," said Trap.

Everybody threw five dollars into the pot, and Trap dealt each player two cards face up.

"This better not be no stupid shit," warned J-Bigg.

"Look who made it up," said D.Y.

"Trust me, y'all gone be addicted to this shit," Trap

promised.

"Just tell us how to play," said Little.

"Alright, it's easy. Now that everybody got two cards, the object of the game is to bet that the next card the dealer turns up will be in-between the two cards in front of you. It's on Bigg First, he has a jack and a three. He could bet any amount that's in the pot, or he could fold his hand and it would be on the next player."

"I want to bet ten dollars."

"Come on, J-Bigg. You got a jack and a three. There's a lot of cards in between that.

"I'd bet it all," prompted DY.

"Word, Sun," said Little.

"You want it all?"

"No, I'm betting ten dollars."

"Alright then."

Trap turned up the next card. It was a deuce. Everybody had a surprised look on their face.

Trap said, "You lost J-Bigg. Put ten dollars into the pot."

J-Bigg added ten dollars to the pot, wondering how the hell he lost with a three and a jack.

"It's on you now, DY. You want to bet or fold?"

"I got a four and a nine. I'll fold."

"Alright then, it's on you, Little."

"I'll bet five dollars."

Little had an ace, the lowest card in the game, and a nine. Trap turned up a five.

"You won, Little."

"Yeah," said Little as he took his winnings from the pot.

"Now it's on me. I can't lose with numbers like these.

Give me the whole pot," said Trap, holding a deuce and a queen.

Trap turned up the next card, and it was a deuce.

"Deuce. Pay that note. Pot fifty dollars now," said J-Bigg.

"Damn!" said Trap, reaching in his pocket for twenty-five dollars.

Everybody laughed as Trap added twenty-five dollars to the pot. He then gathered the cards that were already played and placed them face up on the bottom of the deck. Then he tossed each player two more cards face up, and DY asked, "How come you still dealing?"

"Word, Trap! Let J-Bigg deal now," said Little.

"Not yet. The dealer doesn't change until the pot is gone."

"Alright, then. I want the whole pot."

"Chill, Bigg. If you lose you're gonna have to put up fifty dollars."

"Chill nothing. I got an ace and a king. I can't lose."

"Word! He can't lose," said DY.

"Yes, he can. He can get an ace or a king," said Little.

"And there's three more of each of them. Are you sure you want it all?" asked Trap.

"Yeah, I'm sure. Hit me."

Trap slammed the card on the table. It was another ace. DY started laughing hysterically.

J-Bigg said, "Damn!"

"See what I'm saying," said Little.

J-Bigg threw fifty dollars into the pot, and DY said, "Damn J-Bigg! You should have chilled."

The group took a liking to the game and continued playing all night. They switched up dealers, and the pot reached close to a thousand dollars more than once. They got caught up and wound up playing until the sun came up. Little asked, "What time is it, DY?"

DY looked at his watch and said, "It's 5:30. It don't even feel like it."

"Word! I'm not even tired," said J-Bigg.

"Me, neither, but I am hungry," said Little.

"Look out the window and see if you see Flam out there," said DY.

"He probably out there trying to catch the early morning rush," said J-Bigg.

Trap walked over to the window and stuck his head out looking for Flam. He saw Flam right in front of the building talking to a fiend and yelled, "Yo, Flam, what up? Come upstairs."

"Sun outside?" asked J-Bigg.

"Yeah, he coming upstairs now."

DY then pulled a pen from his back pocket and said, "I need something to write on."

"Grab that bag on the coffee table," said J-Bigg.

"Where y'all sending him?" asked DY.

"Joe Johnson's. Ain't nothing else open," said Little.

DY walked in the living room and grabbed the bag that had a 22-oz. of Bud in it to write a list for Flam.

"What y'all want?" asked DY.

"I want grits, eggs, and turkey bacon," said J-Bigg.

"I want the same thing," said Trap.

"Me, too, but I don't want bacon. Give me beef sausages," said Little.

Just then Flam knocked on the door. J-Bigg let him in and sat back down, asking, "What up, Flam? We need you to go get us some breakfast from Joe Johnson's."

"I'll go, as long as y'all hook me up."

"Of course, you can get whatever you want," said J-Bigg.

"Alright, cool."

DY handed Flam the list, and J-Bigg took thirty dollars from the pile of money in front of him and said, "Here's thirty dollars. That should be more than enough."

Flam turned around and started to leave the apartment. Little then asked, "You wrote down orange juice, DY?"

"Yeah, I wrote down two half-gallons."

Flam opened the door and exited the apartment.

"Whose deal is it?" Trap asked.

"Little's," said DY.

Little started to shuffle the cards, and the phone rang.

"Hello," DY answered.

"What up, DY?" It was Sugar calling from Canada. "I'm getting ready to go to the airport right now. I should be there around twelve."

"Alright, Dun."

"Everybody alright? How's J-Bigg? Did he calm down?"

"He alright. We sitting here playing cards. We've been playing since last night."

"Word? Y'all playing cards? Who's there?"

"Me, J-Bigg, Little, Trap. Yiddo in the back asleep."

"Alright, then. Tell Wyte Yak when he find out who did it let me take care of him."

"Too late. Dude is a done deal already. He's been well taken care of."

"Alright, Sun, let me finish getting ready I'll be there

in a few."

"Alright, chill."

DY hung up the phone, and J-Bigg asked, "What up with Sugar?"

"He'll be here around twelve."

Little dealt the cards, and they continued their card game.

Flam was in Joe Johnson's at the counter. The man behind the counter bagged the meals and handed them to him. Flam asked, "How much?"

The man behind the counter looked at Flam and said, "You hang with Pillsbury, right?"

"Yeah."

"So this breakfast is for Pillsbury's crew, right?"

"Yeah."

He put a few Dutch Master cigars in the bag and said, "Just take it. Tell Pillsbury crew they don't have to pay for nothing in my store today."

Flam smiled and said, "Alright, Ak, good looking out."

Flam exited the deli carrying a bag in each hand. He walked over to where Pillsbury was shot and stopped. Pillsbury's blood was still on the ground with two candles burning and an eight by ten framed picture of him behind the candles. One of the candles went out so Flam kneeled down, placed his bags beside him, and pulled out a lighter. As he lit the candle a tear ran down his cheek. He crossed his heart then stood and walked across the street.

Jeremy woke up in the hospital bed and cut on the television. That woke his parents cuddled together in the next bed. The curtain was pulled, and Jeremy couldn't see them. So he called out to his father, "Daddy, you woke?"

From behind the curtain Wyte Yak said, "Yeah, I'm woke, Jeremy. What's wrong?"

"Nothing. Is my mother still here?"

"Yeah, I'm here, Jeremy. Why?"

"Are y'all back together?"

Wyte Yak and Coretta looked at each other, and Wyte Yak said, "Not quite, Jeremy."

"But we're working on it," said Coretta, kissing Wyte Yak on the lips. Wyte Yak smiled, and Jeremy just laid there with a big smile on his face.

Rahtiek and Quanesia were sitting at the kitchen table while Nikki was hovering over the stove cooking eggs. There were two bowls of food on the table, one filled with biscuits and the other, turkey bacon. Rahtiek picked up the bowl with the biscuits and put three biscuits on his plate and one on Quanesia's plate. He then put six pieces of turkey bacon on his plate and two on Quanesia's plate. Nikki finished cooking the eggs and walked over to the table with the frying pan. She scraped some eggs into her plate, Rahtiek's plate, and Quanesia's. As Nikki returned the frying pan to the stove, Quanesia made a face.

Rahtiek asked, "What's wrong, Qua?"

Quanesia shook her head and said, "I don't like eggs."

Rahtiek laughed and said, "You don't have to eat the eggs if you don't want to."

"I'm not going to get a beating if I don't eat my eggs?"

Feeling compassion for his daughter, Rahtiek began stroking Quanesia's head, saying, "You know I'd never hit you. You're my sweetheart, my life. I could never lay a hand on you. You're too precious."

Nikki looked down at Quanesia and asked, "Why did you ask that, Quanesia? Did your foster parents beat you?"

Quanesia put her head down and remained silent. Rahtiek and Nikki looked at each other then back at Qua. The thought of anyone putting their hands on his daughter made Rahtiek furious. He removed himself from the table and stormed into the bedroom. Nikki followed him and, by the time she reached him, he was tucking his guns onto the back of his waist.

"Calm down a minute, Rahtiek. Don't do nothing foolish," Nikki said.

"These bastards put their hands on my daughter, and you're telling me 'don't do nothing foolish.' I'm not going to do nothing foolish. I'm going to give those bastards just what they deserve."

"No, wait. Let's investigate a little more."

"All the investigating I need is written all over my little girl's face."

Rahtiek pushed Nikki to the side and stormed out of the apartment. Nikki picked up the telephone and dialed Jeremy's room at the hospital.

"Hello," Coretta said.

"Hello, is Wyte Yak still there?"

"Yes, hold on."

Coretta held the phone out towards Wyte Yak, who asked, "Who is it?"

"Some woman. She sounds ecstatic."

"Hello."

"Wyte Yak, this is Nikki. You have to try and stop Rahtiek. He just stormed out of here. I think he's going to kill Qua's foster parents."

With a puzzled look on his face Wyte Yak asked, "Why would he want to do that?"

"Because Qua's been having these nightmares and when we asked her if her foster parents were abusing her she wouldn't say anything."

"Alright, I'll try to get to him before he does something stupid."

Wyte Yak hung up the phone and started putting on his clothes in a hurry. Once fully dressed and about to leave, Coretta asked him, "Where are you going?"

"I gotta go. It's Rahtiek. He's about to flip out. I have to stop him. Jerm, I'll be back in a few hours. Don't worry. Your mother will be here with you."

He kissed Coretta on the lips and rushed out of the room. Jeremy smiled at his mother thinking to himself that they just might become a happy family after all.

Coretta asked Jeremy, "What are you smiling about?"

"My father kissed you."

"Yeah, he did. So?"

"So that means he's not mad at you anymore."

"I wouldn't say that. Your father sure can hold a grudge, but he has good reason."

"What is he so mad at you about?"

"It's a long story, Jeremy. Something that took place before you were born."

"I'm not going anywhere. Tell me about it I want to know."

"If it was only that simple, I would have told you already."

Jeremy gave his mother a puzzled look, and she lowered her head, feeling guilty.

Over at Quanesia's foster parents' house, Rahtiek had both of them at gunpoint as they sat on the couch pleading for their lives.

"Please, man, we never touched Quanesia other than to show her love," said Qua's foster father, trembling with fear for his and his wife's life.

"You're lying!" said Rahtiek, his anger growing.

"We're not lying. We loved Quanesia as if she was our very own," said Qua's foster mother.

"Every other night she's been having nightmares about you bastards abusing her," said Rahtiek.

"That can't be true. We never abused her," Qua's foster father said.

"Stop lying and just die you bastards."

Rahtiek shot the mother in the chest then the father in the head, killing them instantly. Wyte Yak rushed into the house. He was too late. All he could say was, "Damn, Rah!"

Rahtiek looked at Wyte Yak and said, "Fuck that, Yak. These motherfuckers was abusing my daughter." He then looked back at the dead couple and emptied his gun into their corpse, saying, "You fucking bastards!"

"Alright, Rah, that's enough. Let's get out of here."

Rahtiek spit on the couple, and Wyte Yak grabbed him by the arm and led him out of the house.

J-Bigg, DY, Little, and Trap were still sitting at Yiddo's kitchen table playing cards. Yiddo had just woke up and walked into the kitchen. He walked to the refrigerator and took out a half gallon of Tropicana orange juice.

"Little, could you rinse me out a glass, please?"

Yiddo asked.

Little grabbed a glass from the sink, rinsed it out and handed it to Yiddo. Yiddo looked at the four men playing cards at his kitchen table and said, "Thanks. It looks like y'all was up all night."

"We was," said Little. "Trap showed us this card game he made up, and we been playing since you went to sleep."

"What's the name of the card game, Trap?" asked Yiddo.

"In-between."

Yiddo said, "Nigga, you ain't make that shit up. We used to play that up north for cigarettes."

The busted Trap said, "I know I didn't make it up."

"So why you lie then? asked J-Bigg.

"Word! You said you made it up," said Little.

Trap smiled and said, "I just said that to get y'all to play."

"Fuck who made it up," said DY. "This shit is alright. We was up playing all night, and I'm still not tired."

"Word. Me, neither," said Little.

Yiddo drank the last of the orange juice then put down his glass and asked, "Anybody hear from Sugar?"

"Yeah, he called earlier. His flight left at 9:30 this morning he should be here by 12, 12:30 the latest," said DY.

"Did Yak call yet?" asked Yiddo.

"He called late last night, but we didn't hear from him yet this morning," said J-Bigg.

Yiddo scratched his armpit and said, "Alright, then. I'm about to jump in the shower."

Yiddo headed for the shower while the rest of the crew continued playing cards.

CHAPTER 24

Rahtiek and Wyte Yak were in Fort Greene Park talking as they walked up the mountain of wide white steps. Wyte Yak looked over at Rahtiek and said, "You have to calm down, Rah. You're not using your head."

The still angry Rahtiek said, "Fuck that, Yak. You know I wouldn't even hit my daughter."

"How do you know for sure they were abusing her?"

They paused on the steps and Rahtiek looked at his partner and said, "She's only been with me a few weeks and seems like every other night she's been having nightmares about them motherfuckers. Kids don't have nightmares damn-near every night for nothing. Sandra never told me about her having any nightmares when she was living."

"I understand that but..."

Rahtiek interrupted, "But nothing. I did what I had to do. What would you have done if it was Jerm Dogg?"

Wyte Yak dropped his head and said, "I don't know, probably the same thing."

Raising his voice Rahtiek said, "I know you would have. So how you gone get mad at me?"

"I'm not mad at you. I just feel you shoulda looked further into the situation.

Rahtiek face tightened as he said, "Man, I looked into my daughter's eyes and all I saw was pain and fear. For all I know she could be having these nightmares for the rest of her life. So the way I see it, fuck them bastards! Anybody that would hurt a child to the point that they can't even sleep peacefully deserves to die. Bottom line, I have no regrets."

They continued to climb the steps as Wyte Yak said,

"I agree with you one hundred percent. But do you remember pretty-ass Angie from the other side who had a daughter by little Jahmel from the middle side?"

"Yeah, James and Rahliek sister."

Wyte Yak looked over at Rahtiek to make sure he was paying attention and said, "Well, she had some foster kids, two little girls who were abused by their parents. Now one day one of the girls fell down the steps and died. The police arrested Angie and the court system, feeling bad for the actual mother, gave the other daughter back to her."

Looking puzzled, Rahtiek asked, "Back to the mother who was abusing them from jump?"

"Yeah, and when Angie went to trial the mother told the other little girl to say that Angie pushed her sister down the steps."

"Damn! That's fucked up!"

"Damn sure is because now Angie's in jail for the rest of her life just for trying to take care of someone else's kids."

Feeling sorry for Angie, Rahtiek said, "But everybody know Angie wouldn't do nothing like that."

"You're right. Even the judge knew she didn't do it. But it just so happened that at the time a few other people were on trial for abusing children. So he used Angie as an example. That's why I said you should have done a little more investigating. But if you're sure you did the right thing, I'm with you."

Rahtiek stood there in a daze for a few seconds until Wyte Yak said, "Let's get out of here."

They walked back down the steps and exited the park. Rahtiek hopped in a red Navigator, and Wyte Yak hopped into his Expedition. They headed down Myrtle Avenue, made a right on Prince Street, another right on Johnson, and rode into the Project parking lot. They parked side by side and exited their vehicles. They exited the parking lot and stopped once they saw Robbito writing Pillsbury's name on the ground in graffitti while Dexter drew Pillsbury's picture beneath his name. Wyte Yak reached in his pocket and tried to pay the men for the art work, but they refused.

"Pillsbury was our man, too," said Robbito.

"Word. You don't have to pay us. This is from the heart," said Dexter.

"Everybody did love Pillsbury," Wyte Yak said.

"No doubt! You know it's always the good that die young," said Robbito.

"No doubt!" said Wyte Yak.

"Robbito, you saw J-Biggs and them?" asked Rahtiek.

"I think they up Yiddo's crib. Sugar just went up there."

"Good looking out," said Rahtiek, as he and Wyte Yak headed towards Yiddo's building. When they reached the front of the building they bumped into Flam and Phil-Boy, who were sitting on the bench. They all slapped five, and Wyte Yak said, "Phil, I need you to do me a favor."

"What's that, Yak?" asked Phil-Boy

Wyte Yak reached in his pocket and pulled out a mitt of money. He handed Phil four twenties and put the rest back in his pocket, saying, "I want you to go cop a half ounce of chocolate from Ron B on the other side and give it to Robbito and Dexter over there."

"Alright, Yak. Flam, walk me to Ron B crib."

As Phil-Boy and Flam walked to Ron B's crib, Wyte Yak and Rahtiek entered Yiddo's building. As Wyte Yak and Rahtiek entered Yiddo's crib, the whole crew was in the house, including Sugar. Everybody was either sitting or standing around the kitchen table playing cards. Rahtiek asked, "What y'all playing, In-between?"

"Yeah," said DY.

Wyte Yak said, "Hold up a minute. I need to talk to y'all."

Everybody quieted down and faced Wyte Yak.

"I know we just lost a part of us," Wyte Yak said, "but I need everybody to hold their head. I know how each and everyone of y'all feel because I feel the same way, if not worse. But this is America, and we all know that in America shit happens. So we have to learn from our mistakes and make sure it never happens again. Now, J-Bigg, did you go see Pillsbury's mother?"

"Yeah, I told her we was gone pay for the funeral and give her Pillsbury's share of the business."

"What did she say?" asked Wyte Yak.

"She said we could pay for the funeral, but she didn't want nothing else."

"Alright, then. On the morning of his funeral we'll have the hearse drive around the basketball courts a few times so that everybody can pay their respect. Then we'll toss Pillsbury's share off the roofs and let the hood have it."

"You do realize that Pillsbury's share would be a couple hundred thousand?" asked Trap.

"Yeah, and what's your point?" asked Yak.

"That's a lot of money to be giving away," said Trap.

"We're supposed to put back in the community. If we don't, nobody else will. Now, while some of you are tossing money off the roofs, Rahtiek, Web, and J-Bigg will be robbing the check cashing place on the Avenue.

"You're always business, Wyte Yak."

"That's the only way we gone make it. Everbody's

got to stay on point and handle their business," said Wyte Yak.

"You want to tell us anything else, Yak?" asked Sugar.

Yak smiled as he said, "Oh yeah, I almost forgot. We are the new owners of that club across the street from the precinct."

"The old strip joint?" Web asked, as everybody got excited.

"Yeah."

"We them dudes," said J-Bigg.

"The name of the club is going to be Pillano's, in honor of Pillsbury. We're having the grand opening on the third Friday in August. I'll finish on that note. So y'all can continue y'all card game."

The crew continued their card game, which Rahtiek joined.

Later that day the crew was gathered around the mural of Pillsbury, drawn on the ground. Everybody was holding an open bottle of Heineken. Wyte Yak said a few words out of respect for Pillsbury: "Hey, Pillsbury, I hope you can hear me. This is your boy, Wyte Yak. I want to say, on behalf of the crew, that we will miss you and will never forget you. You were a good dude and you touched a lot of people with your warm spirit. I guess it's true when they say the good die young but I guess that's just because God has to have a strong army with him up in heaven. Although you're gone in the physical sense, you'll always be alive in our hearts. We lost a lot of people throughout the years. So if you're with them, I ask that y'all watch over the rest of us that are still here in the struggle. Say hi to your brother and all the others and let them know we still have them in our hearts as well. Even though we're hurt over losing you we know that you're in a better place. A place where you don't need money to be happy because you're at peace and happiness is all around you. A place where the sun always shines, and the grass is always green. We'll try to hold down the fort without you, but we truly wish you were still here with us. Take care, Pillsbury. We'll try to stay strong without you, but it won't be easy because you were a valuable part of our team. We'll see you at the crossroads. Until then, Peace, my brother."

The Career Criminals then poured the Heinekens they were holding onto Pillsbury's mural.

Later that evening the Career Criminals were all in Yiddo's apartment sitting and standing around around the kitchen table having a meeting.

Wyte Yak said, "I wanna take it back to the old school. I got some jewelry store's set up for us to hit, but I wanna hit them the way we used to back in the days, if y'all know what I mean."

"I know what you mean," said Yiddo, putting his hands together and making like he was swinging a baseball bat, the rest of the crew nodding like they understood.

The next day the Career Criminals walked up to a jewelry store in the diamond district. J-Bigg and Web picked up Little, who was wearing a motorcycle helmet and a leather motorcycle suit. They tossed him through the jewelry store window head first. As the glass shattered the crew rushed the window, snatching up all of the platinum, gold, and diamond they could carry and ran off.

While the rest of the crew were in Manhattan hitting the jewelry store Wyte Yak and Rahtiek were upstate checking out the bank Nikki worked for. They saw the old, useless security guard and noticed where the cameras were located and the type of traffic flowing through the bank. With Nikki on the inside they figured it should be pretty easy to knock off. The next time the Colombians would be dropping off a large sum of money was the last Thursday in August. So they went home and started to plan for the robbery.

The morning of Pillsbury's funeral, the hearse circled a large crowd standing on the basketball court in the Projects. The wake had started half an hour earlier to allow those who couldn't make it to the church an opportunity to pay their last respects. As the hearse exited the Projects, Trap, Little, DY, Nite, and Bryan were all on different roofs of buildings surrounding the basketball courts and tossing money down to the crowd. The crowd went wild as everybody and their mother started running outside to the courts to grab some of the cash.

Meanwhile on Myrtle Avenue, Web, wearing glasses and dressed like a UPS worker, pushed a huge cardboard box into the Check Cashing Place and said to the female cashiers, "I have the new safe that your boss ordered."

There weren't any customers in the Check Cashing Place. The two women, not knowing any better, opened the gate to the back room and let Web in. He then handed one of the women a clipboard to sign for the delivery, and Rahtiek and J-Bigg busted out of the box wearing ski masks and brandishing firearms. The women, taken by complete surprise, were tied up and gagged. The three men then cleaned out the contents of the safe, taking in over five hundred thousand in cash. They rushed out of the Check Cashing Place and ran to Yiddo's apartment, where they switched clothes and hurried over to Pillsbury's funeral.

A couple of days later the crew was in City Park on the basketball courts. Yiddo and Rahtiek were playing a game of basketball against Nite and Trap. Yiddo passed the ball to Rahtiek who faked out Trap and drove to the hole to make the winning basket. Trap grabbed the basketball, and the four men started to walk off of the court and over to the benches where Wyte Yak, Web, Sugar, and Little were sitting.

Yiddo slapped Rahtiek five and said, "Yeah, Rah, we busted they ass."

"They know they can't fuck with us, Yiddo," said Rahtiek.

"Look who I had on my team," said Trap.

"Don't blame me because Rahtiek was busting your ass," said Nite.

"He wasn't busting my ass. Yiddo was busting your ass."

They reached the bench where the rest of the crew was sitting and Rahtiek said, "Hit us off, Little."

"Y'all won?"

"No doubt," said Yiddo.

Little handed Rahtiek two hundred dollars. Rahtiek handed Yiddo a hundred, and Sugar asked, "How much did y'all win by Yiddo?"

"The score was 21 to 12. We blew their asses out."

"Damn! Y'all let them blow y'all like that for fifty dollars a man?" asked Sugar.

"Nite aint shit," said Trap.

"That nigga is garbo," said Nite.

Wyte Yak looked over at Sugar and said, "Why don't you play me for fifty dollars, Sugar?"

Sugar started laughing and said, "Wyte Yak, I'll spot

you nine points and game is eleven, and I'll still bust your ass.

Wyet Yak stood and said, "Alright, come on."

"Give me the ball, Trap."

Trap passed Sugar the ball, and he and Wyte Yak walked over to the courts to play a one on one. Sugar let Wyte Yak take the ball out, and he shot a jump shot and missed. That was the last time he touched the ball on offense because once Sugar got the ball he scored continuously until the game was over, leaving Wyte Yak with the 9 points he spotted him from the start. They walked back over to the benches, where the rest of the crew was laughing. Wyte Yak sat down, out of breath, and tried to make an excuse.

"Man, I can't keep up with that dribbling mother-fucker."

"What, you too old?" asked Rahtiek.

"Yeah, I'm too old. Plus y'all know I got asthma."

Everbody started laughing, and Yiddo said, "Go ahead, nigga. You just a bum."

"I'll bust your ass," said Wyte Yak.

"Whenever you ready," said Yiddo.

There was silence for a few minutes then Rahtiek asked, "What's up with you and Coretta, Yak? Y'all been spending a lot of time together lately. Y'all back together?"

"Something like that. Truthfully, I've been thinking about taking it to the next level."

"What you talking about, getting married?" asked Rahtiek.

"I don't know. I was thinking about it."

Rahtiek smiled and said, "Do you, gangsta' rapper. You can't dwell on the past. We survived. It's time to move on. We both know she's the only woman you ever really cared for."

"True," Wyte Yak said, nodding his head.

Sugar stood and said, "I'm thirsty. Let's go to the store to get something to drink." And they all stood and walked out of the park and back to the Projects.

CHAPTER 25

Since Jeremy was released from the hospital, Coretta had been staying at Wyte Yak's apartment and taking care of Jeremy. Wyte Yak managed to start putting in a lot of valuable time with the two of them. The three of them started to do a lot of things as a family. They went to the movies together. They had a few barbecues in the park. They went to the museum and Aquarium together. And when they took a trip down to Disneyland, Wyte Yak got down on one knee and proposed to Coretta. She accepted, and the wedding was set for Labor Day, the 8th of September.

Although Coretta had a little over twenty million in the bank and gave Wyte Yak full rights over the loot, Wyte Yak was still loyal to his crew and continued to set up missions for them.

The Career Criminals had over 3 million dollars stashed in their safe. After they pulled off the bank job they would all be set for life. Wyte Yak was planning on buying out all the stores surrounding the Projects so they could look out for their own.

The night of the grand opening of club Pillano's, the line snaked around the corner filled with anxious partygoers waiting to get in. Trap and Web were out front checking the guest list when Jahmel and his brother, Dream, approached the ropes. Trap and Web slapped Jahmel and Dream five and Web said, "What up, Jahmel? What's good?"

"Aint nothing. I'm just chillin', sitting on a half a million. I heard y'all bought this joint. So you know I came through to show my support."

"No doubt," Web said. "When you get in, let the bartender know who you are. We got a complimentary bottle of Crystals waiting for you."

"That's love," said Jahmel.

Jahmel and Dream entered the club, and Dana Dane, Fort Greene's legendary rap artist, walked up with Pillsbury's uncle, Ron B. They slapped Web and Trap five, and Dane asked, "Where's Wyte Yak?"

"He's inside," said Trap."

"Wyte Yak told me a year ago he wanted to buy this joint. I guess y'all put y'all minds to it and made it happen," said Ron B.

"No doubt," Trap said. "We got complimentary bottles of Dom Perignon for y'all at the bar."

"Say no more," said Ron B as they entered the club.

The inside of the club was packed. The Career Criminals had a V.I.P. section roped off where the crew was seated at different tables with their girlfriends. Wyte Yak, Coretta, Rahtiek, and Nikki were all sitting at the same table sipping on some champagne. J-Bigg and Sugar were sitting at the table to the right of Wyte Yak and Rahtiek with their girlfriends, while to the left in between Wyte Yak and Rahtiek's table and the table DY and Nite were sitting at with four women surrounding them, Dikki Jah had his shorty sitting on his lap.

Fudd Dee Cash, the club's MC walked out on stage, and the music stopped. Fudd asked, "Is everybody having a good time?" The crowd cheered, giving a good response. "I want to thank each and everyone of you for coming to the grand opening of Pillano's. The club was named after one of our people who recently passed. We have a wonderful show set up for you tonight that I'm sure you're going to enjoy. So, first up, I'd like to introduce you to none other than the legendary Fat Daddy Capone. The crowd clapped as Fat Daddy

Capone, a huge, pot-bellied, blues singer, in his early fifties, walked onto the stage carrying his guitar. Fudd handed him the microphone and headed backstage.

Fat Daddy took control of the crowd. "Tell me, are you youngsters ready for some gangsta' blues?"

The crowd went wild, and Fat Daddy started to stroke his guitar.

"Alright, then. Repeat after me. I'm getting paid by the day."

The crowd said, "I'm getting paid by the day."

"I'm getting paid by the day."

The crowd repeated, "I'm getting paid by the day."

"I'm getting paid by the day."

Don't really care what nobody say. Now check it.

I ran in the bank. Told everybody to freeze.

Geatha fuck down on your motherfucking knees. I grab the manager, took his ass to the voltslapped in the head with my .45 Colt. He tried to swing and I shot. But I didn't shoot him in the head, nah, I shot him in his ass, had him shitting out led. Then I grabbed his assistant, slapped that bitch in the face, told her to open up the motherfucking safe. The manager got scared and tried to get up and jet so I let off another slug in his motherfucking neck. Well the volt opened and I grabbed the cash, heard the police coming so I jetted out fast. They let off shots as I ran down the block, they screamed out 'Freeze!'but I still didn't stop.

I got glazed in the leg which put me in suspense, as I thought should I stop or jump the barb wire fence. I jumped the fence thinking nothing could save me luckily I stumbled upon a pregnant lady. The police surrounded me and sai 'Throw your hands in the air!' Meanwhile I'm thinking, how the fuck I'm gone get outta here. I knew I had to proceed with extreme caution.

So I said 'Back up' before I give this bitch an abortion! The police backed up and I thanked my lucky stars cause just then my boy pulled up in the getaway car. I pushed the bitch in the car and at the police I sprayed rode off laughing because, man, I got paid. I getting paid by the day"

The crowd said, "I'm getting paid by the day."

"I'm getting paid by the day I don't give a rooting, tooting, shooting, looting care what nobody say."

Fat Daddy bowed, and the crowd burst into applause. Rahtiek slapped Wyte Yak five and said, "That nigga freaked that shit, Yak."

"You know Fat Daddy's the man."

"No doubt!"

Wyte Yak raised from his chair and walked over to the bar to get another bottle of champagne. The bartender handed it to him, and as he turned to walk away he was approached by Lisa--the girl he always tried to kick it to from the Projects.

"How you doing, Wyte Yak?" Lisa asked. "I'm feeling your club. This joint is popping."

"You know I had to represent for the 'hood."

Lisa bit her bottom lip and gave Wyte Yak a seductive look, saying, "You looking good enough to eat tonight."

Wyte Yak's dick hardened immediately as he looked over the curves of Lisa's body in the tight Coogi dress she was wearing. He said, "I'll be right back." He walked back over to the table, handed Rahtiek the bottle of champagne and said to Coretta, "I'll be right back. I have to check on Web and Trap."

He walked back over to the bar and motioned his head for Lisa to follow him into his office in the back of the club. He closed the door behind them.

"So you finally ready to get with the Don?" Wyte Yak asked.

"I been ready."

"How ready?"

Lisa looked into Wyte Yak's eyes, walked up to him, dropped to her knees, and unzipped his pants. She pulled out his third leg and started sucking him off. He was open off of the head he was receiving and he closed his eyes, thinking to himself, "I'm gone fuck the shit out of this bitch." Then he regained his composure, looked down at Lisa, and became disgusted. He had been trying to get with her for months and now she see that he's got it going on, she wanna fuck with him. "Nah, it's not going down like that," he thought. He grabbed the back of her head and pumped in and out of her mouth until he felt himself about to nut. He held her head, pulled his dick out of her mouth, and busted all in her face. Then he backed up, looked at her, and said, "Get the fuck out!" Lisa was shocked by his actions as she reached in her purse for some napkins to wipe her face.

"What's wrong?" Lisa asked. "Why you acting like that?"

"Fuck you, bitch! I'm not fucking with you."

"Why? What I do?"

"I just don't like your style. Beat it!"

Lisa rushed out of the office, with her head down, upset, and with a sticky face. Wyte Yak walked out of the office and back over to his table. Coretta and Nikki weren't there so he asked Rahtiek, "Where's Coretta?" concerned that she saw Lisa follow him into his office.

"Her and Nikki went to the ladies' room," said

Rahtiek.

Relieved that Coretta had no idea about his little episode with Lisa he said, "Oh, I thought something happened."

"Why you say that?"

"No reason."

Rahtiek smiled and asked, "Where the fuck you was at, Sun?"

Wyte Yak sat down and explained to Rahtiek what had happened.

Coretta and Nikki were in the ladies' room in the mirror putting on make up and making sure their clothes and hair was intact. Nikki looked over at Coretta through the mirror and said, "Girl, you know it's on."

Not knowing what Nikki was talking about, Coretta asked, "What's on?"

"Rahtiek brought Wyte Yak upstate the other day so they could check out the

bank I work for," explained Nikki.

Still curious, Coretta asked, "Why were they checking out the bank?"

Nikki, looking at Coretta as if she was slow, said, "Girl, you know why? They're planning to rob it."

Coretta was stunned at the information and couldn't hide her shock.

"Damn, girl!" Nikki added. "Your man don't tell you nothing."

Coretta shook her head in disgust as they exited the ladies' room. The women returned to their table, and Coretta gave Wyte Yak a disappointed look as she sat down.

"What's wrong?" Wyte Yak asked.

"Nothing. We'll talk about it later."

Wyte Yak knew she had no idea about the episode

he'd just had or else she would've acted a fool right then and there. So he decided to just be cool and wait till later to find out what was troubling her.

The party ended at 5:00 a.m., and Wyte Yak and Coretta got home at 5:30 a.m. As soon as Wyte Yak closed the door behind them Coretta turned to him and said, "I just don't understand you, Franklin."

Yak walked up to Coretta and grabbed her, pulling her close to him and said, "What don't you understand? I know the 'ho's was clocking me tonight, but you don't have anything to worry about. You're all the woman I need."

"Please. That's not even what I'm talking about. I'm talking about the fact that you're so smart, you stupid. Wyte Yak pushed off of Coretta, stepping back a little.

"What's that all about?" he asked.

"You got everything you need in life to make you happy. If you don't have enough money to satisfy you, you know what we have together is more than enough. So why would you want to rob a bank?"

Finally understanding what Coretta was talking about, he said, "So Nikki told you about the bank?"

Coretta placed her hands on her hips and asked, "So you're really planning on robbing a bank?"

Wyte Yak walked up to Coretta pleading, "Baby, I have to rob this bank. Not for me, but for the team. We've been planning this for the last few months. I can't let the crew down now. This is a chance for all of us to get paid."

"There you go again, always worrying about every-body else. What about me? What about Jeremy? Don't we count? When are you going to start putting your family first? We're the ones who really love you."

"You know I love both of you more than anything,

but I got love for my peeps, too."

Coretta raised her voice as she said, "Later for your peeps! They don't care about you. All they care about is what you can do for them."

Wyte Yak held his hand up to stop her and said, "You don't know what you talking about. Don't go there. My peeps been holding me down for the last twelve years."

"I don't know what I'm talking about. Alright, then tell them you're not down and see how they react. If they really care for you, they gone want you to do what's best for you, not what's best for the crew."

Coretta stormed into the bedroom leaving Wyte Yak standing there thinking. Later that afternoon Jeremy noticed that Wyte Yak and Coretta weren't getting along. He woke up and to find his father sleeping on the couch and his mother in his father's bed. When they woke up Jeremy saw the distance between them. When one entered a room, the other left. When Wyte Yak came into the kitchen and sat down at the table to make a sandwich, Coretta grabbed her plate and got up to leave.

"Don't tell me y'all fighting already," Jeremy said. "Come on now. We just became a family. Whatever y'all fighting about, forget it. It can't be more important than us being together. Can it?"

Coretta looked at Wyte Yak, who stared back at her then dropped his head. A few days later Wyte Yak and Rahtiek went up on the roof of 340 Hudson Walk to have a talk.

"So what's on your mind, Wyte Yak?" Rahtiek asked.

"The bank."

"What about the bank? I know you didn't change your mind. It's a simple job. You said so yourself."

"I know, Rah, but…. Wyte Yak paused for a few seconds then continued, "…it's Coretta. I don't think she trust Nikki."

"You don't think she trust Nikki? Man, I don't trust Nikki. After we hit the bank, fuck Nikki! That bitch is crazy. She think I'm her man when, to tell you the truth, I don't even like that bitch."

"You don't like her, you don't trust her. When was you gonna tell me this? After we rob the bank, you diss her, then she tell on us."

"How the hell she gone tell on us when she the one setting it up? She the one talked us into it, not the other way around."

"You really don't get it, Sun. This is a big job. If you don't trust her we're not fucking with it, bottom line."

"You're not fucking with it? We talking too much money. I'm going to get that, no matter what!"

"You'd literally disobey me like that?"

"Disobey you? I'm not your motherfucking son. You my man and all, but, nigga, you just the OG of the crew, with a good head on your shoulders. So we let you guide us, but you ain't nobody's father, but Jerm Dogg. You and your girl already got cheddar. The rest of us got whatever we took, but this bank job is going to make us millionaires."

Surprised by Rahtieks reaction, Wyte Yak said, "Look at how you talking to me? Can't you see something's not right. Anything that turn you against your people has to be wrong."

Rahtiek walked back into the building, saying, "I said what I had to say. I'm sorry I can't let you call the shot on this one."

Wyte Yak followed Rahtiek into the building and said, "I guess you can give a fool knowledge, but you can't knowledge the fool. Alright, Sun, do you, but just make sure you let everybodyelse know what time it is with that bitch."

They walked in the building and down two flights of stairs. Rahtiek opened Yiddo's door and walked in with Wyte Yak. The rest of the crew was lounging around the apartment.

"You gone tell them, or you want me to tell them?" Wyte Yak asked Rahtiek.

"Tell us what?" asked Yiddo.

"This nigga bugging. He don't want to rob the bank now because I told him I don't trust Nikki..like that makes a difference."

"That makes a hell of a difference," Web chimed in. "If you don't trust her why the hell would we even fuck with her?"

"Twenty five million dollars! That's why."

"That's reason enough for me," said Trap. "She can't snitch on us. She down."

"That's what I'm saying," said Rahtiek.

"Y'all missing the whole point. She can't snitch, but you don't know what she gone do once Rah diss her."

Rahtiek looked around the room at all his homeboys and said, "She can't do nothing, but fuck it. Anybody that don't want to roll doesn't have to."

"I ain't fucking with it," said DY.

"I'm with it," said Trap.

"Me, too," said Little.

J-Bigg nodded his head and said, "Word! That would be taking a bit more than usual. Sorry, Yak. I can't resist the chance of being a millionaire."

"We gone get our millions when the time is right," Wyte Yak said, trying to reason with the crew.

"The time is right now," Rahtiek said. "That shit is

just sitting there waiting for us. So what up, Yiddo? You with it?"

"Yeah, I'm down."

"How about you, Web?"

Web looked at Rahtiek then over at Wyte Yak and said, "I'm going with these dudes, Yak. Somebody's gotta look after them."

"Alright, y'all on y'all own, then. Good luck."

Wyte Yak opened the door and left the apartment, letting the door slam shut behind him.

"That nigga girl got him tripping," Rahtiek said. "He'll be alright. We gone still give him a piece of the pie."

CHAPTER 26

It was the last Thursday in August. Wyte Yak, Coretta, and Jeremy were loading their luggage in the back of Wyte Yak's truck. "We got everything, Jerm?" Wyte Yak asked when they were seated inside the vehicle.

"Yeah," Jeremy said, nodding eagerly.

Coretta placed her hand on Wyte Yak's thigh and said, "I got my two men. That's all I need. I'm so glad you decided to come with me to Virginia, Franklin. I know you're doing the right thing."

"I'm sure I am," said Wyte Yak. Then he leaned over and gave Coretta a kiss, adding, "We're a family now. That's what we're going to be from now on. Nothing will ever separate us again."

Coretta and Jeremy smiled as Wyte Yak put the key in the ignition, turned the car on, and drove off.

The rest of the Career Criminals were upstate in Poughkeepsie, sitting in the bank parking lot in their two PT Cruisers. A green Ford Caravan pulled up in front of the bank, and four Colombian men got out, carrying four large duffle bags filled with money. Twenty minutes later, the men exited the bank, hopped in the van, and drove off.

Right away the Career Criminals stepped out of their cars, wearing ski masks and carrying guns. As soon as they entered the bank, J-Bigg held a shotgun to the security guard's head while Little took his weapon. J-Bigg then hit the security guard under the chin with the butt of his shotgun, knocking him unconscious.

There were three bank tellers and seven customers as well as Nikki, who was the assistant manager, and the manager, a white man wearing a blue suit and in his early fifties.

Rahtiek fired a shot to gain everybody's attention. Everyone in the bank froze and turned their heads towards the masked men.

"Everybody, get on the fucking floor!" Rahtiek demanded. Then Web, Trap, Yiddo, and Nite jumped the counter and entered the open vault. In less than two minutes they all returned to the front with the same duffle bags that the Colombians had just brought in.

As they started to leave the bank, J-Biggs turned around and said, "Stay on the floor and count to one hundred before anybody gets up, or we'll come back in here letting off shots. Now start counting!"

The people on the floor started counting, and J-Bigg exited the bank. He jumped in one of the Cruisers, and they sped off.

Wyte Yak, Coretta, and Jeremy were driving south along I-95 on their way to Virginia like one big happy family.

Coretta looked in the backseat at Jeremy, who was sleeping, and said, "Look at our little man, sleeping like a baby."

"He always go to sleep on the road," Wyte Yak said.

"Franklin, why did you decide to leave today? Are your boys planning on robbing that bank today?" Yak didn't answer. "I hope they're alright," Coretta added.

The Career Criminals were in Nikki's apartment waiting for her to arrive. There was a large bag of money on the floor, and the crew was smoking weed and drinking beer, celebrating the bank heist.

The weed had J-Bigg paranoid so he approached

Rahtiek and said, "I'm ready to get the fuck out of here."

"Relax, Bigg," Rahtiek said. "We're out as soon as Nikki gets here."

"I won't be able to relax until we're back in Brooklyn."

Web walked over to Rahtiek and J-Bigg and said, "Something's not right, man. My stomach fucking with me."

"Everything's alright, Sun. Go upstairs and take a shit. That's probably that big-ass breakfast you had at that restaurant earlier."

"You're right. I probably just need to release some of them pancakes I had," Webb said.

Web walked upstairs to use the bathroom, and Nikki entered the apartment.

Rahtiek hugged her and said, "We did it, Nikki. We were in and out in less than two minutes."

"I told you it was easy, didn't I?" Nikki laughed and said.

"You sure did, baby girl. Now check this out," Rahtiek said, leading her to the bag of money on the floor. "This bag of money is yours. The boys are ready to be out so we bouncing. He then turned to the crew and said, "Alright, y'all, we out."

The crew started to exit the apartment, and Nikki said, "Hold up, boo. I'm coming with you. My boss said the bank was going to be closed for the rest of week while they investigate."

"Nah, Nikki, it all ends right here," Rahtiek said, grabbing Nikki's arms and looking into her eyes. "We got what we wanted, and you got what you wanted."

"Fuck that money. I want you."

"Sorry, baby, but I'm not feeling you like that. It's

over."

Surprised at what she was hearing, Nikki said, "Oh, you gone do me like that, after all I've done for you?"

"You didn't do nothing for me. We made each other rich. Now enjoy your money because I'm out."

Rahtiek released Nikki and walked out of the door. She was steamed. "Your punk ass ain't gone play me like this," she screamed, slamming the door behind Rahtiek. She pulled her phone book from her purse and searched for the phone number of the Colombian drug family.

Then she walked over to the telephone and started dialing. It rang a couple of times then was answered by one of the Colombians. "Mr. Domingo, please," she said. Just then Web came out of the bathroom and overheard Nikki.

"Yeah, Mr. Domingo, this is Nechemiah Jackson from the bank. The guys who robbed us earlier..."
Web drew his gun and started creeping down the steps.

"...I just saw them loading up in two PT Cruisers," she added. "It looks like they're on their way out of town right now. You know there's only one way out of town so you better hurry up and catch them if you want your money."

Nikki hung up the phone, turned around, and saw Web pointing a Glock 40 at her.

Web said, "You fucking bitch! You need a man that bad?"

"No, wait..." Nikki pleaded.

Web shot her in the heart, killing her instantly. She fell to the floor, and Web searched her purse for the keys to her car. He found them, picked up the bag of money, and looked down at Nikki. "You's a stupid bitch," he spat. "You shoulda took the money and been happy."

He exited the apartment, hopped in Nikki's car, and

sped off. He pulled his cell phone from his hip and dialed Rahtiek.

J-Bigg, Trap, and Little were in their PT Cruiser following Rahtiek, Yiddo, and Nite in the other when J-Bigg, suddenly remembering they left Web behind, picked up his cell and dialed Rahtiek. Rahtiek answered, "What up?"

"We forgot Web,"J-Bigg said.

"Damn! Fuck it. Let's turn around."

Rahtiek hung the cell phone up, and it rang again. He made a U-turn then answered the phone, "My bad, Web. We're coming back to get you right now."

"Sun, I killed that bitch. She set us up. Them Colombians are on their way after y'all right now."

The Colombians' van along with two other cars pulled out from a dirt road right behind the two Cruisers and started shooting. They shot out the tire of the second Cruiser with J-Bigg, Trap, and Little. J-Bigg lost control and ran into a tree. J-Bigg, Trap, and Little jumped out and started shooting out with them. Rahtiek stopped the vehicle he was driving, and he, Nite, and Yiddo jumped out and started shooting. Then the Colombians stopped their vehicles and jumped out shooting.

It was an all-out war as the guns blazed, claiming casualties. Little shot a Colombian in the chest with his automatic .357 Desert Eagle. Blood gushed from his chest as he tumbled to the ground. Less than two seconds later, Little himself, was fatally struck, once in the chest and once in the gut, by a slug from one of the Colombians' Glock Forty, sending him hurling to the ground and ending his short-lived life.

J-Bigg and Trap watched their partner go down and lost it. They charged the Colombians' van, guns blazing. J-Bigg was blasting his pistol-grip pump shotgun, taking out two of the Colombians, splattering their chests with slugs. J-Bigg was then dropped by a slug to the head from one of the Colombians in the first car behind the van.

Trap, busting off the two 9mm he clutched in his hands, took out two more of the Colombians in the van before taking two Glock Forty slugs to his chest and falling to the pavement.

Rahtiek, Yiddo, and Nite attempted to seek revenge for their friends, putting six holes in the Colombian who shot J-Bigg and two more in the chest of the one who shot Trap. But they were overmatched by the three remaining Colombians, who jumped out of the last car firing their automatic street-sweeper shotguns. The left side of Nite's face was torn by a hail of shotgun pellets, and Yiddo's chest was ripped open by another flurry of pellets. Rahtiek, realizing he was outgunned, attempted to duck behind the van but was hit in the leg, sweeping him off his feet. The three remaining Colombians ran up on him and emptied their street-sweepers on him, mauling him beyond recognition.

The Columbians entered the Cruisers and took out the three bags of money stashed in the Cruisers back to their car and sped away.

Web, rushing to arrive at the shootout, slowed his vehicle down when he heard the last weapons to be fired weren't the ones his crew was carrying. He realized that the Colombians had already won the war and had too much fire power for him to go up against alone. When they left he drove up to where the shootout had taken place and counted thirteen dead bodies on the ground, seven Colombians and six of his friends. He jumped out of his vehicle to check for survivors.

Trap was the only one still breathing. Web carried

him to Nikki's vehicle and fled the scene. Two miles down the road he picked up his cell phone and called Wyte Yak.

Wyte Yak and Coretta were relaxing in Coretta's Jacuzzi. Wyte Yak's cell phone started ringing. Jeremy walked over and picked it up.

"Hello," Jeremy said.

A sad sounding Web asked, "Jerm, where's your father?"

"What up, Web? He's in the Jacuzzi with my mom. Hold on."

Jeremy walked through the beautiful house to the Jacuzzi room, where Wyte Yak and Coretta were cuddling and relaxing.

Jeremy said, "Daddy, the phone. It's Web."

Jeremy handed his father the cell phone and walked off. Coretta leaned on Yak's shoulder and rubbed his chest while he talked on the phone.

Happy to hear from Web, Wyte Yak smiled as he asked, "What up, Web?"

"You was right, Yak. We shoulda listened to you."

Wyte Yak's smile quickly turned sour. "What happen?" he asked.

"Hitting the bank was simple. We did it just the way we planned, but when Rahtiek told Nikki it was over she flipped out and called the Colombians whose money we took. Man, everybody got murdered except me and Trap, and he's shot up pretty bad. I'm trying to wait till we get to the Bronx so I can take him to the hospital."

"Everybody else is dead?"

"Everybody. Rahtiek, J-Bigg, Yiddo, Nite, and Little. The only reason I'm alive is because they forgot me at Nikki's crib," Web said, looking at Trap moaning in the backseat. "Hold on, Trap baby. Be strong. We gotta make it to the Bronx. They gone arrest you if I bring you to the hospital anywhere up here."

"Damn! I told niggas to chill. Why the fuck they didn't listen?"

"Fuck that, Yak! Them our boys and the whole nine, but you the Don, we been listening to you and shit was going smooth. Niggas let the thought of all that money fuck with their heads. Nobody wanted to deal with reality. Now look what happened."

"Man, this shit is fucked up."

"Yeah, it is, but I got the bag of money Rahtiek left Nikki. This should be a few mill. You want a cut?"

"Nah, I'm good. Do you with that. I'ma tell Pooh Berry, Bryan, and DY to hold down the club and stash in Yiddo's crib."

"Alright, then. I'm gone rush Trap to the hospital then take this dough and get low. I'ma holla at you. Peace out."

"What happen, baby?" Coretta asked. "I know something went wrong."

"Everything went wrong. That bitch set my niggas up. The whole crew got murdered, except for Web and maybe Trap--if he survive."

"That's messed up. I new something wasn't right about that girl. I'm glad you decided not to go with them."

"Me, too, baby. Me, too."

Coretta wrapped her arms around Wyte Yak's waist, laid her head on his shoulder, and said, "I think we should go and get Quanesia."

"Yeah, let's bring her down here and try to give her a good life."

"Poor girl. She lost her mother, her grandmother,

and now her father."

"Man, this shit is fucked up.'

A tear dropped from Wyte Yak's eye as he and Coretta held each other.

THE END.